D0189871

By the time she hit her teens, SUSIE BOWER had lived in 8 houses and attended 7 schools. This theme continued in her working life: she's been a teacher, a tour-guide, a typist, a workshop facilitator, a PA and a painter. She formerly wrote and directed TV programmes for children at the BBC and Channel 4, for which she won a BAFTA Award, and she currently writes audio scripts. *School for Nobodies* is her debut novel. Susie lives in Bristol.

# SCHOOL FOR NOBODIES

SUSIE BOWER

PUSHKIN CHILDREN'S

Pushkin Press
71–75 Shelton Street
London WC2H 9JQ

*School for Nobodies* was first published in 2020 by Pushkin Press

1 3 5 7 9 8 6 4 2

ISBN 13: 978-1-78269-271-3

Designed and typeset by Tetragon, London
Printed and bound by CPI Group (UK) Ltd, Croydon, CRO 4YY

www.pushkinpress.com

*For Charlie and Dave*
*with love*

# THE GIRL WITH NO NAME

**I**'m going to tell you a secret.

Until the day of my tenth birthday, I had no name of my own.

Sonia and Claude, who adopted me when I was three, called me Claudia. It wasn't *my* name—it was *their* two names joined together.

Even worse, their last name was Finklebottom.

Only, they pronounced it FinkleBOME, because it sounded posher.

Sonia was tall and skinny, had pouty lips and wore long dangly earrings and overalls smeared with paint. She told everyone she was an artist. Claude was short, fat and bald, and made lots of money in the City. He talked in an old-fashioned way, and called Sonia vomity names, like *my little piggy wiggy* and *pootlekins*. His chins and belly shook when he laughed—*haw-haw-haw!*—and Sonia's mouth always crinkled up in disapproval like a cat's bottom until he stopped.

My birthday began like every other day, except that two envelopes were propped against my plate. A little bit of me hoped, every year, that inside one of the envelopes would be a ticket to the circus, but that never happened. I'd been crazy about circuses ever since I was small—I'd secretly read every single book about them in the school library. Each year, the circus came to town and everyone at school told me about the acrobats in their sparkly leotards, and the way the clowns squirted water at the crowd, and how daring the tightrope walkers and the trapeze artists were. But Sonia and Claude disapproved of circuses, so I'd never actually seen one in real life.

I opened the first envelope. Inside was a birthday card. It had a picture of a girl holding a basket of kittens. She had long, shiny hair and a perfect, pretty face. Inside, it said:

To Claudia,
         Wishing you a happy birthday.
                              Sonia and Claude

There was no 'with love', and not even one kiss.

The second envelope contained my present, which was a donation to a charity called Save the Andalusian Donkey. There was a badge which said: I SAVED A DONKEY TODAY!

Sonia and Claude didn't appear at breakfast. Sonia said I was too restless in the mornings, which gave her a migraine. She and Claude wanted a girl like the one on the card—a girl who smiled nicely and sat still. The trouble was, I *couldn't*. It was like I had an everlasting itch just out of reach for scratching. My feet needed to tap, my fingers to wiggle, my legs to jump and dance and kick. And my mouth needed to talk a LOT, and to say shocking and unusual things, and I had to press it closed so it wouldn't. Every time Sonia snapped, 'Be *quiet*, Claudia!' or Claude said, 'Turn that frown upside down—*haw-haw-haw!*', I got That Feeling. Have you ever had it? The feeling where your insides are about to erupt like a volcano, or crash like a giant wave, or fizzle and hiss like a bolt of lightning—so you have to wriggle about, or else explode.

I didn't tell anyone at school that it was my birthday. Afterwards, I cycled back to the Gables, which was the name of Claude and Sonia's house. I dumped my bike in the garage, hurried up to the front door and let myself in.

The Gables was painted grey on the outside, in a colour called Cool Pavement, and white on the inside, in a colour called Arctic Fox. There was a notice just inside the front door which said: REMOVE SHOES AND WASH HANDS!—because the furniture was white, and so were all the rugs and carpets, and Sonia had One Of Her Turns if she spotted a fingerprint or a footprint.

I took off my shoes and put them in the shoe rack, and raced upstairs before Claude or Sonia spotted me. My room (which was also painted white) was up in the attic, as far away as possible from Sonia and Claude's part of the house. It had:

- a television (*for educational and instructive programmes only*),

9

- a laptop (*for homework only*),
- a walk-in wardrobe, full of horrible, muesli-coloured cardigans and skirts with pleats and brown leather sandals,
- and a bathroom, which Sonia called the Wet Room. It had white towels and white quilted toilet paper. It used to have a mirror, only I took that down and hid it under my bed.

Sonia made sure the neighbours knew all about the television, the laptop, the Wet Room and the walk-in wardrobe.

'We've given her *everything* a child could want,' I once overheard her saying on the phone to Mrs Weebly next door. 'Of course, we adopted her out of *charity*. Who else would take her on, with *that problem*?'

*That problem* was the burn mark on my face. Shrivelled and pink and ugly, it ran from my left eye, down over my cheek to my chin. Ever since a boy shouted *Scab Face* in the street, I wouldn't look at myself.

I asked Sonia and Claude how I got it.

'An accident,' muttered Sonia.

'What sort of accident?'

Sonia frowned. 'A fire.'

'My... my face got burnt?'

Sonia's lips went all tight, the way they did when Claude told one of his jokes, and she picked at a dry patch of green paint on her overalls.

'You're upsetting Sonia,' said Claude, putting his arm

round her shoulders and murmuring in her ear. 'It's all right, pootlekins.'

Sonia shrugged his arm away. 'I'm *not* upset,' she snapped. 'I just don't see the point in raking up her background. And *don't* call me pootlekins!'

'Quite right, poot—er, precious poppet,' said Claude. 'Let sleeping dogs lie. Water under the bridge.'

'What background?' I said.

'The subject is *closed*, Claudia,' Sonia said. 'I forbid you to speak of it again.'

'Least said, soonest mended,' said Claude, and that was that.

Or it *was*, until today.

# THE FIRST MESSAGE

**F**our thirty until five thirty was timetabled as Outdoor Activity and it was My Best Thing, the one hour I looked forward to all day. The garden was long and thin and boring, like Sonia. She'd made Claude build a posh shed halfway down it, where she painted enormous pictures of naked people with triangular faces and eyes in the wrong places. The shed had a sign above the door which said, THE STUDIO—and I was strictly forbidden to enter it.

But if you walked past the Studio and down the manicured lawn, at the very bottom you'd find a high brick wall with a gate in it, and if you pushed the gate open you found yourself in an overgrown, secret place. In a corner was a collection of broken pots and garden furniture and a compost heap, where Claude emptied the grass from his ride-on mower. There was a rough circle of lawn in the middle. It was here that I practised my cartwheels and somersaults and walked on my hands and dreamt about being in a circus.

Best of all, there was Tree.

Tree was my friend: tall and ancient with huge twisted roots and helpful knots for footholds. There was a sitting place halfway up, like a nest, and when I wriggled in and settled into the curve of the branches, it felt like Tree was hugging me. Tree's leaves hung down around me like soft hair and when the breeze whispered through them, Tree sang to me. Sometimes I'd see how long I could balance on a branch with my arms stretched out. Sometimes I'd hang upside down like a monkey and pretend I was swinging on the flying trapeze. I'd chatter like a monkey too, telling Tree all the forbidden things.

Things I dreamt of, such as:

1. Having a real family, and *especially* a sister, who'd be my best friend. Who wouldn't roll her eyes when I spoke, like Amelia Peacock did. Or stare at my burn *all the time*, like Emma Crouch.
2. Running away to join the circus.

And things I wished would disappear, such as:

1. The burn on my face.
2. Sonia and Claude.

Today, the garden was full of birdsong and magic. Orange poppies bobbed in the wind and wildflowers buzzed with fat bumblebees and fluttered with butterflies. I stood and breathed in the smells of cut grass and warm, soft earth and rose petals until I couldn't stand still a second longer and I whirled in circles, faster-and-faster-until-I-was-dizzy and I had to lie on my back on the grass while the world spun.

Then I saw it. The balloon.

It was a red one, fat and full, and its string had caught high in Tree's branches. It bobbled about cheerfully as if Tree was holding it and wishing me a happy birthday.

I got to my feet, still dizzy, and stared up at it.

'Is that for me, Tree?' I asked.

A breath of wind blew Tree's leaves into a rustle, like a whispered *yeeeeeeeeesss* and I knew I had to get it.

I began to climb. Up past my sitting place, further than I'd ever been before. It was like climbing a ship's mast at sea—the higher I went, the more the wind gusted among Tree's branches, and the more Tree rocked. If only I could climb on, up and up till I got to the sky, till the world turned blue.

Now I could see right over the wall to the Studio and the house. Of course, climbing Tree was strictly forbidden. But at this time of day, Sonia liked to recline on the white chaise longue (a posh name for a sofa), reading magazines with titles like *Wallpaper* and *House Beautiful*, while Claude, home from work, chuntered around the neighbourhood in his most prized possession, an ancient car he called Mildred. He wore aviator's goggles and sounded the horn at unfortunate cats.

The balloon was just out of reach, its string wound around a twig. I wedged my foot in the fork between two branches... stretched up as far as I possibly could... and reached... and reached...

... until my fingers found the string.

I tugged. But the balloon stayed stuck. There was a label attached to it and it was this that had got tangled in the leaves. I tugged harder, and harder still, but it just...

... wouldn't...

... budge.

Suddenly—so suddenly that I almost lost my balance—there was a wild flapping of wings in the branches. A little blue-grey dove, its feathers dappled with soft patterns, landed on the branch beside the balloon. It gazed down at me with dark eyes, its head on one side.

*Turrrr... turrrr!* it called, and my tummy suddenly filled with a warm, huggy sensation—like when you drink hot chocolate.

Then the dove reached to the tangled string and, using its bill, gently pulled the label loose.

The balloon came free.

The dove watched as I wound the string safely round my wrist. Then it gave its strange, purring cry—*turrrr, turrrr*—and was off, spiralling up into the sky, higher and higher. My heart fluttered, like there were wings in my chest. I stared at the dove until it was nothing but a speck in the blue.

It was harder climbing down, because the balloon kept getting caught in the branches. I *so* wanted to read that label. But I made myself wait. It would be my reward for getting back in one piece. At last I jumped down from Tree into the circle of grass.

Then I read the label. There were just two words written on it: POP ME.

I sighed. I'd never had a birthday balloon, and this one was so big and red and yummy. I didn't want to jump on it, so I carried it over to the rose bush and looked for a long thorn. Squeezing my eyes tight shut, I pushed the balloon down on it.

*BANG!!!!!*

The sound echoed round the garden. I stood very still and listened, in case Sonia stalked out to see what was disturbing the peace, or Mrs Weebly peered over the fence, saying she could swear she'd heard a gunshot.

All was silent. The balloon was a shrunken sliver of red rubber lying in the grass. And there was something else: something which must have been hidden inside it.

It was a scroll of paper, tied with a gold satin ribbon. Not the sort of paper Claude used in his printer, but thick and heavy, like parchment. *What could it be?* My fingers trembled as I untied the ribbon and unrolled the paper. Written across it, in old-fashioned script, were the words:

*Look in the mirror, if you dare.*
*Your name is hidden under your hair.*

My name? A shivery feeling made my knees wobble, and I reached up to my hair and felt around.

Nothing.

It was probably Claude's idea of a joke. Maybe he'd tied the balloon to the top of Tree to send me on a wild goose chase on my birthday. I could just see his fat belly shaking with laughter—*haw-haw-haw!*

There again, Claude and his belly would never get up Tree.

Carefully, I pushed the message into my pocket. Then I threw my arms as far as I could around Tree's trunk.

'Thank you for my birthday present,' I whispered, as Tree's branches creaked in the breeze. 'And I *will* dare to look in the mirror. I'll do it right now!'

And I raced up the garden path, before I could change my mind.

# IN THE MIRROR

**B**ack in my bedroom, I groped around under the bed until my fingers found the mirror I'd hidden. I dragged it into the Wet Room—it was very heavy—and hung it back on its hook.

I pulled out the parchment scroll from my pocket and read the words again.

> *Look in the mirror, if you dare.*
> *Your name is hidden under your hair.*

I really, really didn't want to look at myself.

I wasn't a coward. It was just that my burn took up all the room. People's eyes got stuck to it, like it was a magnet. No one noticed the rest of me—my browny-gold eyes, the freckles on my nose, or the flurry of marmalade-coloured curls down my back—except when Sonia glared at the curls as if she was itching to brush them flat. But she refused to let me have them cut.

'*No*, Claudia!' she snapped. 'Short hair is not *appropriate*.'

Which was strange, considering her own hair was cut above her ears.

I made myself stop thinking about Sonia. The mirror was waiting for me. Dust lay like a mist over its surface and I could only just make out the shape of myself. Taking a deep breath, I wiped the glass with my sleeve, and looked.

There it was, my burn. Like a map of a strange country no one wanted to visit. I tore my eyes away from it, scooped up a handful of my curls and lifted them above one ear. There was nothing there. Then I did the same on the other side. Still nothing.

I turned sideways to the mirror, grabbed all my hair, twisted it high into a ponytail, then tied it in place with the gold satin ribbon.

What was that, on the very back of my neck, just below where my hair grew? I twisted my head and screwed up my eyes. Was it writing? Blue and faint, like...

A tattoo.

Tattoos, like curly hair, were among the many things that Sonia disapproved of.

'They're *common*, Claudia,' she sniffed. ('Common' was Sonia's worst word.) 'And they're so ugly.' Her eyes went straight to my burn, as if to say I was ugly enough without a tattoo.

It was no good. However much I twisted and turned, I couldn't make out the strange blue writing.

Back to my bed I went, scrabbling underneath it until I found the hand mirror—the one that used to be on my chest of drawers. I stood with my back to the full-length mirror and held the little mirror up to my face.

19

Then I saw it quite clearly. A name and a date, written high on the back of my neck:

*FLYNN*
*11 JUNE*

Today was 11th June. My birthday.

And Flynn? I reached up to my neck and ran my fingers over the word, as if it could speak. If only my real parents were here. If only I could ask them. On and on I stared, until my arm began to hurt and I had to put the mirror down.

Was Flynn my real name?

I whispered it to the mirror.

'*Flynn.*'

Short and true and real. Claudia made me think of claws, of Sonia's long painted nails. Flynn just felt... right. It felt like it belonged to me.

My own name. The name my real mum and dad gave me on the day I was born. This was My Best Birthday Present Ever. That same warm, huggy feeling filled my tummy again.

Then I had a shocking thought.

Sonia and Claude must have known about my name all along. Sonia would have seen it when I was little every time she washed my neck. No wonder she'd refused to let me have my hair cut. But why had she and Claude kept my name a secret from me for seven whole years?

'*Clau-dia!*'

Sonia was shouting from the kitchen. 'Hurry *up*! Supper's ready.'

20

I reached to unfasten the gold satin ribbon and let my curls down. Then I stopped.

Let Sonia and Claude see my name. Maybe then, at last, they'd tell me the truth.

Sonia and Claude were sitting at the dining table under the most horrible of Sonia's paintings—a bare man holding a dead fish while two bare women danced around him. Sonia was pouring water into three glasses and didn't look up. Claude did. He went pale and gave Sonia's elbow a sharp nudge, sending one of the glasses flying.

'You're so *clumsy*, Claude!' Sonia snapped, grabbing a tea towel and mopping at the spreading stain.

My name felt like it was burning, like it was shouting, *Flynn*! But Sonia was too busy fussing over the tablecloth, and Claude's mouth was hanging wide open like a fish's.

'Er, piggy wiggy...' he muttered.

Sonia finally looked up. She glared at my ponytail.

'*What* have you done to your hair?' she said. 'Untie it *immediately*.'

'No,' I said. 'I won't.'

My knees were shaking under the table. I'd never disobeyed Sonia, ever. Maybe my new name was making me brave.

'*Whaaaaaat?*' squawked Sonia, stretching her eyes and turning to Claude. 'Speak to her, Claude.'

'Do as you're told, Claudia,' he said.

'My name *isn't* Claudia.' My teeth were chattering, but I carried on. 'It's Flynn. And I... I want to know about my family.'

21

Sonia's eyes flashed. 'Family? *We* are your family.'

'No, you're not!' My fists were clenched and I felt hot all over. I took a deep breath. 'I've asked you and asked you, but you always refuse to tell me. Who are my real parents? Where are they? And why did they leave me here with you?'

There was a long, uncomfortable silence.

# THE TRUTH

'**W**hat's past is past,' said Claude. 'No point in raking all that up.'

'All what?' I said.

A burning smell meandered in from the kitchen.

'The coq au vin!' shrieked Sonia, and Claude leapt to his feet and hurried out.

Sonia was about to follow him, but I stood up and grabbed her sleeve.

'Stop pretending my parents don't exist,' I said.

Sonia shook my hand off. 'Has it never occurred to you,' she hissed, 'that we might be trying to protect you?'

'Protect me from what?' I said. My voice sounded shaky and scared.

Sonia's eyes narrowed into angry slits. '*Enough*, Claudia!'

Claude lumbered in with the coq au vin and began ladling it onto our plates.

'Sit down, Claudia,' he said. 'And please demonstrate that you can behave in a civilized fashion.'

We ate the coq au vin in silence, apart from Claude loudly slurping his gravy and Sonia tutting at him. I pushed most of mine to the side of my plate. I felt sick. Why wouldn't Sonia and Claude tell me about my parents? What could be so terrible that they refused to even mention them? I had to wriggle on my seat and clench my fists over my mouth to stop myself shouting.

At last, Claude clattered his knife and fork together. 'What's for dessert, my heavenly honeybee?'

Sonia frowned. 'Rice pudding. But we're not having it until Claudia finishes her coq au vin.'

'My name is *Flynn*,' I muttered, pushing my plate away. 'And I'm not hungry.'

Sonia pursed her lips. 'Then you can go to your room!'

'I want to know the truth,' I said. 'And I'm not going anywhere until you tell me.' And I folded my arms and stared at the horrible painting without blinking.

There was a long silence. Claude and Sonia looked at each other. Claude's belly gave an enormous gurgle.

'Tell her, Sonia-kins,' he said. 'Then we can have our rice pudd... I mean, then we need never speak of the matter again.'

Sonia sighed, picked up a napkin and dabbed at her lips.

'Very well,' she said, and turned to me. 'You are a very foolish child. You will regret hearing what I have to say. But, if you insist...'

I nodded. My heart was thudding and my mouth was dry. Under the table, my feet twitched and jumped, as if they wanted to kick Sonia.

'Your birth parents are dead,' Sonia said.

A cold, hard pebble seemed to drop into my tummy.

'H-how did they die?' I whispered.

'I'll tell her, sweetest snookums,' said Claude, patting Sonia's hand. 'They died in a fire.'

My fingers went up to my burn.

'Yes,' said Sonia coldly. 'The same fire that scarred your face.'

'You were fortunate to be rescued,' added Claude. 'Otherwise you would have died that night, along with your parents and your twin—'

He slapped a fat hand over his mouth and Sonia gave him a killer stare.

'My twin?' The words seemed to come from a long way away. *I had a twin.*

Sonia stood up. 'I hope you are satisfied now,' she said, and began to gather up the dishes. 'Perhaps you will learn, one day, that some things are better left unsaid.'

'Ignorance is bliss,' said Claude. He gave a sharp sniff and dashed into the kitchen, returning with a blackened casserole dish. 'And now, thanks to all this nonsense, the rice pudding is ruined.'

And they both looked at the smoking dish with more interest than they'd ever shown in me.

My insides were doing That Feeling again, boiling and curdling and wanting to erupt. But this time, the words wouldn't stay in.

'Why couldn't it have been *me* who died? I'd rather be dead like my parents and my... my twin than living here with you. You've never loved me. You don't even *like* me.

I hate you. I hate you both! And I'm *glad* your rotten old rice pudding is burnt. I hope it chokes you!'

Sonia looked like she'd swallowed a wasp. 'Impertinent child!'

'Go to your room, Claudia,' said Claude.

I stood up. 'My name is *Flynn*,' I shouted.

'Go to your room—*now*!' said Sonia.

'And stay there till morning!' added Claude.

In my bedroom, I wrapped the duvet round me as tightly as I could, and thought and thought. I thought about my parents, who I had never known, who I would never know, because they had died in the fire. And I thought about my dead twin.

This felt worst of all. What would it have been like to have a twin? The sister I'd always dreamt of, who looked just like me—only without my burn. A sister who would *always* be there, just the way Tree was, to talk to and play with and hug—who would *never* whisper about my messed-up face, or call me names like they did at school.

The empty hole in my heart felt twice as big. And my room seemed to get smaller and smaller, closing me in. I ran over to the window and opened it. Down in the garden, an owl called. The other windows were all dark. Sonia and Claude must have gone to bed. With my duvet still wrapped around my shoulders, I slipped down the stairs, through the back door and down the path.

In the secret part of the garden, Tree waited, a tall black shadow in the night. The owl hooted again, somewhere nearby. I found the soft place between two roots, made a little nest with my duvet and snuggled into it, my back against Tree's trunk.

'Oh, Tree,' I whispered. 'I'm so alone. What will I do?'

There was no reply. Tree's bark was warm against my back. I shuffled around and put my arms about Tree's trunk, hugging as if I was hugging my twin, who died.

And then I couldn't help it. I cried myself to sleep.

# THE SECOND MESSAGE

**S**omeone was gently brushing the burn from my face, back and forth, back and forth... or was it Tree's leaves, softly waving over my skin? I opened my eyes.

At first I thought I was dreaming.

Dangling from Tree's lowest branch, blowing back and forth in the wind, was something golden and feathery, sparkling and turning in the early-morning sunlight.

I scrambled to my feet, rubbing my eyes. *It must be a dream.*

But it was still there. It was a leotard—just like the ones the acrobats and trapeze artists wore at the circus. It was as fine as a cobweb, embroidered in golden thread. Running across it were strange patterns of pearls and sequins and crystals, like back-to-front words. Who could have left it here?

Then I heard a soft, haunting cry.

*Turrrr! Turrrr!*

There, on a branch just above my head, was a dove. Was it the same one that had helped me untangle the balloon? It sat very still, peering down at me with its dark eyes as if it wanted to tell me something important. It bobbed its grey head, as if pointing to the leotard.

I turned back to it. A word was embroidered inside the neckline: FLYNN.

That warm, hot-chocolatey feeling filled my tummy and spread through my whole body, just the way it had when I saw the dove for the first time. I began to tingle with excitement. Could this really be for *me*? Was it another birthday present? I reached out to touch my name, half expecting it to disappear under my fingertips like a mirage. But it didn't.

I slipped the leotard off the branch. Shards of golden sunlight bounced over my skin. I *had* to try it on. But not here—Mrs Weebly was always on the lookout. I spread open the crumpled duvet, which was damp with the dew and with my tears, and folded the leotard carefully inside it.

I looked up at Tree. The dove had disappeared.

I bundled the duvet under my arm and made for the house.

Claude's snores rumbled across the landing. He and Sonia stayed in bed until ten at weekends. I tiptoed up to my room, silently shut the door, lay the duvet down on my bed and unfolded it. Maybe the leotard would have disappeared, like a dream disappears when you wake up. But it was still there, shining soft and gold in the white duvet.

I slipped off my pyjamas and held the leotard up in front of me. It was so fine and cobwebby that my fingers felt like sausages. Hardly daring to breathe, I drew it up over my body.

It fitted me perfectly, without a wrinkle or a sag, as if whoever made it knew every inch of me. It made me want to cartwheel and handstand and jump. Then I remembered my burn. However beautiful the leotard was, I'd still look like me.

The mirror hung where I'd left it, in the Wet Room. I took a deep breath, and looked at myself.

A girl stood in front of me. She had my burnt face, but from the neck down she was golden and gleaming and glittering. She looked like a real circus performer.

I ran my fingers over the sequins and crystals. And then I read the back-to-front words embroidered in pearls, reflected the right way round in the mirror:

> *You aren't alone—it's not too late!*
> *Your twin's ALIVE, in Middlethwaite.*

In the mirror, my mouth made a big O. I'd never believed in magic. But three magic things had happened since yesterday: I'd discovered my real name; I'd been given a golden leotard; and now—could it possibly be true?—my twin was alive!

Did she know about me? Did she look like me? I knew I'd recognize her straight away when I found her, and she would recognize me. We would run into each other's arms and hug and hug and hug, and that empty space in my heart would be filled at last.

But what, or where, was Middlethwaite?

Shaking with excitement, I opened my laptop. I was

just about to type in *Middlethwaite* when Sonia shouted up the stairs.

'Claudia! Are you ready? We're leaving in two minutes!'

My heart sank as I remembered that we were going to the shops to buy me a new dress. Quickly, I slipped out of the leotard, pushed it carefully under my pillow and pulled on one of my muesli-coloured skirts. As soon as I got back, I'd find out about Middlethwaite. And then I'd make a plan to find my twin.

Sonia was tight-lipped and still cross after the row last night. I hardly noticed. My mind was fizzing with my discovery. Maybe my twin was living somewhere nearby! Maybe she too was out shopping with her adopted parents—just like me!

'A nice girl,' hissed Sonia, yanking my arm, 'doesn't *stare*.'

There were plenty of girls my age in the changing rooms, trying on skinny jeans and pink sparkly tops. Any one of them might have been my twin. Sonia and the shop assistant had gone to the most old-fashioned section of the store and picked out three dresses for me: a salmon-pink one with pleats; a shiny orange one with puffed sleeves; and a long dreary one, the colour of sicked-up porridge, which was of course the one Sonia chose for me. The assistant wrapped up the dress and Sonia and I went out into the street.

On the way to the car park, we passed a newspaper stand. Right across it, in big black letters, was a headline:

## *LION CAPTURED NEAR MIDDLETHWAITE!*

I stopped in my tracks. Middlethwaite! That was where the message had said my twin was!

'Get a move on, Claudia!' snapped Sonia.

'Can... can I buy a paper?' My eyes were stuck to the name in the headline.

'Whatever for?'

'It looks like an exciting story,' I said. 'A lion on the loose!'

Sonia glanced at the news stand. 'What nonsense. A made-up story probably.'

'I'd like to read it anyway.'

I counted out some change and handed it to the man at the news stand. Carefully, I tucked the newspaper into my rucksack.

'A ridiculous waste of time and money,' said Sonia. '*Really*, Claudia.' And she pressed her lips together, which meant the conversation was over.

'*Flynn*,' I muttered under my breath.

# TWO SCHOOLS

**A**s soon as I got back to my room, I shoved Porridge Dress to the very back of the walk-in wardrobe, shut the door firmly and opened the newspaper. There, on the front page, was a photograph of a lion, caught in a net. The article said:

A lion has been captured in a dense forest near the village of Middlethwaite. The animal was spotted by picnickers in the forest, who immediately called the police. Staff from a nearby safari park sedated the lion with a dart and took her away. She is said to be thin but otherwise healthy. How she came to be in the forest is a mystery.

'We were terrified when we heard about it,' said Mrs Petunia Pomfrey, a resident. 'A dangerous animal like that living so close to the village! We have two schools here, both backing on to the forest. Only think what could have happened!'

I opened my laptop and typed in *Middlethwaite*. It was only about fifteen miles away. Then I typed in *Middlethwaite schools*, and immediately two appeared. Both were boarding schools. My heart began beating very fast. Surely my twin must be at one of them! The odd thing was that the two schools were right next door to one another, in a row of grand old houses joined together, but they couldn't have been more different.

The school on the right was called the Academy. It was painted gleaming white, and surrounded by a high brick wall. Its windows shone and its roof had new, red tiles, with spikes to stop the birds nesting. The photographs showed an Olympic-sized swimming pool, a computer room and a cinema. It cost £10,000 a term.

The other school was called the Cruet Establishment for Lost and Wayward Children. It looked as if it had once been painted white too, only the paint was peeling off in lumps. There was no brick wall around it, just a rickety fence. A creeping vine grew up the walls, almost hiding the crumbling sash windows. Its roof was missing a few slates, and was green with moss and bird poo. No way would my twin be there: I was sure she'd been adopted by rich people, like Sonia and Claude—people who could afford to send her to a posh, expensive school like the Academy.

I *had* to get there and find her. I just needed to come up with a plan.

One rainy day, a week later, I cycled back from school with the clay head I'd made in pottery class hidden under my coat to keep it dry. I was quite proud of it. It was skinny and cross-looking, with dangly earrings and a cat's-bottom mouth. When Miss Merryweather told us to be sure to wash our hands, I'd stood at the sink with everyone else, but I didn't wash them.

Back at the Gables, I put my bike in the garage, opened the front door and stepped into the hall.

REMOVE SHOES AND WASH HANDS! said the notice by the door.

I didn't take off my muddy shoes and put them on the shoe rack. Instead I carefully placed the clay head on the hall table. Then I looked at the white walls and the clean white carpet.

I hesitated. Being this bad felt strange and guilty. All my life, I'd been polite and quiet and good—at least, until the row about my family. Now I planned to be so disobedient that Sonia and Claude would have no option but to send me away to the Academy in Middlethwaite, where I was sure I would find my twin.

I took a deep breath. Then I walked slowly down the hall, running my muddy, clay-covered fingers along the wall. My wet, brown footprints made an interesting pattern over the white carpet...

Sonia and Claude did not find the pattern interesting. Sonia screamed and retired to bed with a migraine, and Claude made me wash all the prints away with soapy water. Soon after this, I overheard them talking about me.

'I am approaching the end of my tether, Claude.'

'I know you are, my delectable duckling,' said Claude. 'She really is getting beyond the pale.'

'Something must be done, and quickly,' said Sonia.

'We will consider our options,' said Claude. 'There's always the boarding school in Middlethwaite.'

My ears pricked up. So they *were* thinking of sending me away! I wished they would hurry up. But I still hadn't done My Three Worst Things, and I was saving those up for the summer holidays.

# MY THREE
# WORST THINGS

**S**onia had taken to spending more and more time in the Studio during the school holidays, which was a good thing for me but a bad thing for the world of art.

One evening, when Mrs Weebly had called round (she often dropped by at supper time), Sonia sighed dramatically, and announced: 'I have completed The Painting.' And she sat back as if she expected us to burst into applause.

'How exciting!' gasped Mrs Weebly. 'What will you do to celebrate?'

'A party,' said Sonia.

Claude got up and embraced her.

'My artistic angel, I am so proud of you!' He gave her a sticky kiss (we were eating meringues) which she quickly wiped away with her serviette. 'And a party we shall have! A Grand Unveiling of the Masterpiece.'

Sonia simpered. 'We can invite all our friends.'

Claude's face dropped for a moment. They didn't actually have any friends. But he quickly nodded.

'Yes, my toothsome treasure,' he said. 'We can invite my colleagues from the office...'

'And Deirdre, of course,' said Sonia, smiling at Mrs Weebly.

'And all the neighbours,' said Claude. 'Let's do it next Saturday.'

'We can ask the mayor to make a speech,' said Sonia.

Claude looked annoyed. 'I think *I* should make a speech too, don't you, sweetest?'

'Yes, yes,' said Sonia. 'We'll have lots of speeches. And the painting will be concealed behind a curtain, and once the speeches are over, someone will pull the cord and reveal it to the world.'

'Which is just the job,' said Mrs Weebly, 'for little Claudia here!'

Sonia's mouth twisted. 'Er, yes. I suppose so. So long as she promises to behave.'

On the afternoon of the party, the house gleamed. Sonia had paid people to clean it from top to bottom and Claude had paid other people to serve the food and do the washing-up. Sonia and Claude carried the enormous canvas from the Studio into the living room, where they propped it on an easel. Claude rigged up a length of curtain in front of it, with a cord dangling down, ready for the Grand Unveiling.

The painting was a portrait of Sonia and Claude, twice as large as life. They were standing beside a tree in a garden, half hidden behind flowering bushes. This was a good thing, because neither of them was wearing any clothes. Sonia was holding out an apple with a big chunk bitten out of it, and Claude had obviously done the biting:

his chubby cheeks, full of apple, looked like a squirrel's. Wrapped around Sonia's arm was a long, purple snake, and the title of the picture was painted above them: ADAM AND EVE IN THE GARDEN OF EDEN.

It was horrible.

Sonia summoned me to the living room and gave me strict instructions.

'It was extremely kind of Deirdre Weebly to think of you,' said Sonia, obviously wishing she hadn't, 'because revealing my painting is a very important job. You will wear your new dress and keep your hair down. I don't want to be embarrassed in front of the mayor.'

She had only agreed to let me pull the cord because Mrs Weebly had suggested it—and also to show the neighbours how *caring* she and Claude were, adopting an orphan with an ugly burn on her face.

An hour before the guests were due to arrive, Sonia and Claude set off in Mildred to collect the drinks and nibbles. Claude was wearing a dinner jacket with a crimson cummerbund and a red bow tie which looked like it was strangling him. Any minute and he'd start to sing, like that opera singer in the TV adverts. Sonia frowned at him and said *she* wouldn't be changing until they returned. She ordered me to *put on your new dress and brush your hair and stay in your room* until it was time to do the unveiling.

I had just done the first of My Three Worst Things, and Sonia and Claude were about to find out what it was. All I'd needed was my bike valve tool.

My plan was to delay them just long enough for me to do My Second Worst Thing.

As soon as I heard Mildred chuntering away down the drive, I tiptoed down the stairs and out of the back door. The Studio was still open. I slipped inside, picked up some tubes of paint and brushes, and hurried into the house...

# THE PARTY

I finished in the nick of time and dashed upstairs. A tow truck rumbled up the drive, with Mildred attached to a rope behind it. Sonia and Claude were sitting in Mildred, along with the drinks and nibbles. Claude was still wearing his cummerbund and bow tie. Sonia was wearing a furious expression.

When he'd paid the driver of the tow truck, Claude hauled out the drinks and nibbles and carried them into the house, while Sonia shouted at him, and I hung over the banisters and listened.

'Not just *one* slow puncture, but *four*! Why didn't you check the tyres before we set out?'

'I checked them just this morning, my luscious lamb chop,' said Claude. 'I can't think who would do such a thing.'

'I can,' said Sonia darkly. 'And I'm going to *have words with her right now.*'

She strode towards the staircase. At that moment, the front doorbell rang.

Sonia gasped.

'The guests are here! And I'm not decent. Let them in while I make myself beautiful.'

'You are always beautiful, bewitching beloved—' said Claude.

'Get a move on, Claude,' snapped Sonia, running up the stairs, 'and *don't* show me up in front of the mayor.'

I ducked into my room. At least Sonia wouldn't have time to tell me off.

The new dress was hanging on the wardrobe door, looking even more like sicked-up porridge in the evening light. I burrowed under my bed, where I had hidden my golden leotard, wrapped in tissue paper. I shook it out and hung it next to Porridge Dress. Its feathery gold embroidery swayed and whispered, almost as if it was alive, and the sequins and pearls and crystals glittered. I was about to do My Third Worst Thing, and if *that* didn't get me sent away to boarding school, I didn't know what would.

I stood outside the door to the living room, waiting for Mayor Abuchi to finish his speech. His rich voice rang out over the rather half-hearted applause from the guests.

'The artist, Sonia Finklebottom—'

'Finkle*bome*,' hissed Sonia.

'—is yet to be recognized,' continued Mayor Abuchi. 'But I am sure that all those assembled here hope that it will only be a matter of time before she takes her place among the great and the good in the world of art. Meanwhile, I ask you all to raise your glasses to her new painting, which she has titled *Adam and Eve in the Garden of Eden*. And I understand that Sonia's daughter Claudia will have the honour of unveiling it.'

I pushed open the door. My heart was beating very fast, but my golden leotard and my bouncing ponytail made me feel strong and brave. I took a deep breath, raised my hands and pushed myself into a handstand. Then I began to walk on my hands towards the painting. All around me, people stared and parted to let me through.

Sonia, who was wearing a long purple shiny dress with matching purple lipstick, gazed at me with her mouth wide open in horror. Claude's face turned the same colour as Sonia's dress. Sonia began to hiss furiously into his ear. I heard the words *common* and *humiliating*, and Claude nodded and patted her hand.

I flipped over on to my feet, and Mayor Abuchi, who had a kind, merry face, escorted me up to the painting.

'Hello, Claudia. What a very fine outfit,' he said. 'Are you ready?'

'Actually,' I said, 'my name is Flynn. And yes, I'm ready.'

'Then,' said Mayor Abuchi, 'with the kind assistance of Miss *Flynn* Finklebottom, I declare this painting open!' And he nodded at me to pull the cord.

I pulled it.

For what seemed like a hundred years, there was utter silence. Then, a whispering and a giggling passed through the guests, like a flame licking along a sheet of paper.

The painting looked amazing. Much more interesting, I thought, than it had looked before. Adam and Eve were still bare. The snake still curled over Eve's wrist. The apple still had a bite out of it. But Claude—or Adam—now had a bushy black beard and a black monobrow. And Sonia—or

Eve—had a huge ginger moustache with curly ends. The title was much more interesting too: ADAM AND STEVE IN THE GARDEN OF EDEN.

Sonia screamed. Pointing at the painting, then at me, she hissed (doing a good impression of Mildred's tyres deflating), 'Sh-sh-sh-she... sh-she...'

Then she dropped to the floor in a dead faint.

Claude flapped a tea towel over her face to bring her round.

I caught Mayor Abuchi's eye. He was trying not to laugh. The guests, however, were in stitches and some of them began clapping.

'Best thing she's ever painted,' muttered one of the guests.

'Not that that's saying much,' added his companion.

Meanwhile, Sonia had opened her eyes. She brushed aside Claude's tea towel.

'Precious pootlekins—you are alive!' cried Claude.

'Barely,' hissed Sonia, holding out her hand so that Claude could pull her upright. '*And don't call me pootlekins.*'

'Of course, pootle—I mean, delicious darling,' said Claude.

Sonia was glaring at me with so much hatred that I half expected my leotard to burst into flames. Just for a moment, I felt guilty about what I'd done. But then Mayor Abuchi winked at me and I remembered that it was all for a good cause.

'That's *it*,' Sonia said. 'The *final straw*.'

The guests were gone, still whispering and giggling. Sonia had poured herself a big glass of wine, and was drinking it very quickly. Claude had loosened his bow tie and his cummerbund. He had carried the painting out to the bins, because Sonia had said she *couldn't bear to lay eyes on it again.*

'Ungrateful child,' said Claude, wiping his forehead.

'Biting the hand that feeds her,' said Sonia.

'A bad apple,' said Claude, 'never falls far from the tree.'

'We are washing our hands of you,' said Sonia. 'From this day forth, you will no longer be a Finklebome.'

'You will go off to boarding school,' said Claude. 'And you will stay there until you are old enough to leave home.'

I dropped my head to hide my smile. My plan had worked.

*The Academy and my twin, here I come!*

# TO BOARDING SCHOOL

**A** few weeks later, on a chilly September morning, I stood on the drive, waiting for the taxi to arrive to take me to boarding school.

Claude had refused to let me anywhere near Mildred after the tyre-letting-down, and Sonia had shut herself in her bedroom since the party and refused to speak to me. Claude told me she was suffering from Nervous Exhaustion. This meant that he had to do all the cooking, and since he didn't know how to cook, we mostly ate baked beans. Sonia sent away the trays he carried up to her room, and instead finished off all the nibbles and drinks from the party. I could hear her hiccoughing from the hall.

It felt strange and scary to be leaving the Gables, even though I knew I was setting off to find my twin. The hardest thing had been saying goodbye to Tree. I clung to Tree's trunk, hugging as hard as I could. A breeze shivered through Tree's branches as if Tree knew that autumn was coming. I felt like a leaf, about to be blown away from everything I knew.

Claude didn't offer to help me downstairs with my bag. Luckily, there wasn't much in it. The only things I wanted to take were the message about my name and my golden leotard. I asked Claude, over baked beans à la Finklebottom, if I needed a uniform for the boarding school.

'A uniform will be provided when you arrive,' he said. 'Which is more than you deserve.'

I liked the sound of this. No more Porridge Dresses and dreary cardigans—I'd be wearing the same as everyone else. So I packed my toothbrush, hairbrush, underwear, pyjamas, slippers, socks and shoes, along with my carefully folded leotard. I left the television, the laptop and the rest of my clothes in my room.

Sonia could donate them to charity. The Andalusian donkeys could watch donkey racing on the television, play games on the laptop and eat my Porridge Dress.

I tried to ask Claude more questions about the boarding school, but he clammed up.

'You can cross that bridge when you come to it,' he said, refusing to meet my eye.

I could hear the taxi coming up the drive. Claude stepped out of the front door behind me. I suppose he wanted to see me safely off the premises. There was no sign of Sonia, but when I looked up at their bedroom window, a curtain twitched and I heard a faint hiccough.

Claude stepped forward.

'Farewell, Claudia,' he said. 'Sonia wishes me to inform you that this hurts us far more than it hurts you. But blood is thicker than water and what doesn't kill you makes you stronger. We can only hope that your new school will help you see the error of your ways.'

47

And with that, he rapped on the driver's window, turned his back and went into the house, slamming the front door. As the taxi slid down the drive, I turned, hoping that Claude and Sonia might at least wave me goodbye, but the house was as shut and silent as if, like them, it had turned its back on me forever.

The drive seemed endless. I sat on my hands and whispered over and over: *'I'm going to find my twin. I'm going to find my twin.'*

We soon left the city behind. There were fields and woods, with villages dotted here and there. Away on a hill, a farmer was cutting grass with a combine harvester. Then, a sign—MIDDLETHWAITE—appeared at the side of the road.

The taxi lurched up a narrow village street, almost knocking over an elderly lady with a pug dog. Then it rattled to a halt outside the Academy. In the shadow of a great pair of metal gates, a long line of children with suitcases queued to get in.

The Academy looked just as it had in the photographs: tall and stately and gleaming white, it was surrounded by high, red-brick walls. Through the upstairs windows I glimpsed girls and boys in uniform. The children in the queue wore uniforms too: navy blazers with crests on them and blue-and-silver striped ties. I couldn't wait to get inside and try mine on.

Next door to the Academy was the other, scruffy school—the Cruet Establishment for Lost and Wayward Children—with its peeling paint and cracked windows.

48

With a flapping of dark wings, a large bird rose from the roof and flew off, croaking. There were no metal gates or brick walls, just an uneven path meandering up to the entrance. On the wall beside the door was an old-fashioned bell with a pull cord. A lone boy, about my age, sat on the crumbling steps, waiting to be let in. His crisp white shirt set off his black skin and ebony curls, and he wore glasses and a worried expression. He was drumming his fingers on the knees of his jeans, surrounded by four overflowing supermarket carrier bags.

'Here we are, miss.' The taxi driver opened the door.

I grabbed my bag, jumped out and joined the queue for the Academy.

The children in the queue stared at my face. One girl nudged another and whispered something, and they giggled.

Chauffeur-driven limousines lined up on the road behind us. One family—a girl, a boy and their mother—were hugging and kissing goodbye. The mother wiped her eyes as she got back in her car and was driven away. I wished I had a mother to hug me.

In front of the high metal gates of the Academy stood a plump woman wearing a navy uniform and a peaked cap which said, SECURITY. A walkie-talkie, attached to her belt, was hissing and crackling. She carried a clipboard in one hand and a large flowery handkerchief in the other. From time to time she blew her nose loudly. As each child's name was ticked off, she muttered into her walkie-talkie and the gates hissed open, just long enough for the child to enter, then clanged shut again.

The girl in front of me in the queue, who was tall and thin with freckles and braces, nudged my arm, making me jump.

'You new?'

I nodded.

'Why aren't you wearing uniform?' Her eyes swept over my face.

I put up my hand to cover my burn.

'They've got it for me inside.' I tried to sound confident.

'Oh, *right*,' said the girl with a smirk. She winked at her friend, and jerked her head at the other school, the ramshackle one next door.

The boy was still sitting on the steps. His mouth opened and closed as if he was talking to himself.

The girl lowered her voice. 'Know what people call that place?'

I shook my head.

'They call it the School for Nobodies.'

'Nobodies?' I said.

'It's where they send the freaks,' said the girl.

'The weirdos,' added her friend. 'The no-hopers.'

'The dangerous kids,' said the first girl, jerking her thumb at the boy on the steps.

'Dangerous?' I said.

The boy looked downtrodden and sorry for himself, but he didn't look as if he would hurt a fly. He pulled a sheet of paper from one of his bags and studied it.

'He looks all right to me,' I said.

The girl pointed at the high brick walls surrounding the Academy.

'What d'you think *those* are for?'

'I don't know,' I said. 'And I don't care.'

Her friend grinned. 'To keep the Nobodies out, that's what.'

I shrugged. All that mattered to me was getting into the Academy as quickly as I could, and finding my twin.

And then I forgot all about the School for Nobodies.

Right at the very front of the queue for the Academy stood a girl. The security guard was bending down to listen to her. She had her back to me, so I couldn't see her face, but her marmalade curls bounced down her back, just the way mine did.

*My twin?!?*

For a moment, my legs wouldn't work. All I could do was to stare at those curls. My heart pounded in my chest. Then I dropped my bag and began to push through the waiting children towards her.

# IT MUST BE A MISTAKE

'**L**et me PAST!'

I elbowed through the queue, and some of the children glared at me. I didn't care. All that mattered was getting to the front before my twin disappeared inside the gates. A tall girl with a hairband was standing in my way, and I gave her a shove. She turned, and I saw that she wore a prefect's badge.

'What do you think you're doing?' she snapped. 'Get to the back of the queue.'

I dodged around her and craned my neck to see the girl with the marmalade hair. The security guard was ticking off her name and speaking into the walkie-talkie. The girl grabbed the handle of her suitcase and moved towards the gates.

'WAIT!' I shouted.

But the gates hissed open and the girl went through them, trundling her suitcase behind her.

I couldn't keep still at all after that. It was like my heart was attached by a string to the girl with the marmalade hair. I jumped up and down on the spot, and twisted and untwisted my fingers, but it didn't make the queue move any faster. The girls ahead of me whispered behind their hands and stared at me. I ignored them and looked instead at the boy sitting on the steps of the School for Nobodies. He was holding a sheet of paper in one hand and was waving the other arm around wildly, his dark curls bouncing. Maybe they were right about him being a weirdo.

At last, the girls ahead of me were signed in and the metal gates hissed closed behind them. The security guard stood before me with her clipboard. She stared down at my burn and I covered it with my hand.

'Dame?' she sniffed.

'Sorry?'

'Whad is your dame?'

I took a deep breath. 'My name is Flynn.'

'Last dame?'

'Finklebottom.'

She ran a chubby finger down the list on her clipboard and frowned. 'No one of that dame here.' And she turned away.

I grabbed at her sleeve.

'Try Claudia then. Claudia Finklebottom.'

The security guard glanced at her list again and shook her head. 'No one of that dame.'

'There must be a mistake—'

She stared at my clothes in a pointed sort of way.

'Duh mistake appears to be yours.'

Then she flicked a superior glance at the boy with the glasses, who had stopped waving his arm about and was staring at me.

'Try next door,' she said, and waddled towards the Academy gates. They hissed open and shut behind her with a clang.

'Wait!' I ran to the gates and rattled them. 'Call Sonia and Claude Finklebottom—they'll explain—'

But there was no answer. The security guard's sneezing faded away.

What should I do? The taxi was long gone. I'd just have to wait here until the security guard realized her mistake and returned.

The boy with the glasses was staring at my face. I felt myself going red. I turned my back on him and sat on my bag, just in case he tried to steal it. A few minutes passed.

'Oi!'

I hunched up my shoulders and ignored him. What had those girls said about the Nobodies kids? *No-hopers. Freaks. Dangerous.*

'Oi, you!'

I jumped. The boy was standing right behind me. His spotless white shirt and black jeans had been ironed into sharp creases and I could see my reflection in his polished shoes. His brown eyes were bright and sharp behind his glasses. He lowered his carrier bags to the ground. A battered violin case stuck out of one bag. Another was stuffed full of sheet music. The third was a jumble of trainers and sweatshirts and socks. In the fourth was a strange triangular metal object with a dial on its front and a wind-up key in its side.

'The queue's over there,' the boy said, pointing at the School for Nobodies.

'Go and stand in it then,' I said. 'I'm going to *this* school.'

'So why wouldn't they let you in?' said the boy.

I shrugged. There was a long silence.

The boy hummed under his breath. Then he pushed his glasses up his nose and spoke again.

'If you're s'posed to be in *that* school...' he jerked his head at the Academy, 'why aren't you wearing a uniform like all the others?'

'It was a mistake,' I muttered. 'They made a mistake.' Any minute now, the security guard would come out again, full of apologies and sneezes, and let me in.

The boy smirked. 'A mistake?' he said. 'Yeah—like it's a mistake I'm going in *there.*' He jerked his head at the School for Nobodies.

At that moment, the Nobodies front door opened. A man stepped over the threshold and, leaning on a stick, limped down the steps.

The boy grabbed his four bags and hurried towards the man, shouting over his shoulder: 'This is the queue, and I'm the first in it!'

I turned my back again. At least he'd soon be gone. After some low conversation, I heard the creak of the School for Nobodies door as it opened then closed.

A shadow fell over me. I turned. The man was standing there, leaning on his stick. He was short and strong-looking, and wore a blue T-shirt and bright red braces with suns and moons on them. The braces were holding up baggy green corduroy trousers. His hair was rusty-red and he had mad curls like corkscrews. His eyes were kind and crinkly, but they were the saddest eyes I'd ever seen.

'Good morning,' the man said. His voice was sort of rusty too. 'My name is Felix Gold. Are you Claudia Finklebottom?'

I shook my head and opened my mouth to tell him my real name, but he said, 'Come with me' and began to limp towards the School for Nobodies.

I stayed where I was.

Eventually, he turned round and limped back.

'Something's wrong?' he said.

'I'm not going in there,' I said. 'There's been a mistake.'

'A mistake?' said the man.

I cast a desperate look at the Academy, and its closed gate.

'Look,' I said, 'I'm meant to be in *that* school. They've got my uniform waiting for me. It's all arranged.'

The man looked at me and said nothing. I had the strangest feeling. As if he wasn't really seeing me. Like I was there, but not.

Then he said, 'I'd come with me, if I was you. You can't sit there forever.'

The last thing I wanted to do was go into That Place. A bank of dark clouds had formed above it, as if to warn me away. But it was getting cold. And there must be a phone inside. I would ring Sonia and Claude—they would sort it all out.

Reluctantly, I picked up my bag and followed the man up the steps and into the School for Nobodies.

# NOBODIES, AND CUSTARD

The front door opened into a long, narrow corridor. I followed Mr Gold's baggy green trousers as he limped ahead of me, past an empty, old-fashioned kitchen with a huge stove and shelves of copper pans and a big scrubbed wooden table. I kept my eyes peeled for the freaks and weirdos. Maybe they were hiding. Maybe they were going to jump out at me. But there was no sign of any other children, not even the boy with the glasses. They must have been locked up in their rooms.

Mr Gold, who had said nothing more to me, was now climbing a flight of stairs—very quickly, in spite of his limp. At the top, he pulled open a door and stood aside to let me in. It was an empty room, apart from two beds and a loudly ticking clock over the door. The beds had sheets and rough blankets instead of duvets. On each one lay a small bundle of clothes.

'The girls' dormitory,' said Mr Gold.

'I want to make a phone call,' I said.

'No calls allowed.' He waved a hand at one of the beds. 'Your uniform's there. Get changed, and I'll be back in fifteen minutes.'

He closed the door and his footsteps, along with the click of his stick, disappeared down the corridor.

*What kind of dormitory is this*, I thought, *with only two beds?*

I tiptoed to the door and opened it. Everything was silent. The rest of the children couldn't have arrived yet.

I turned to the uniform. I certainly wasn't going to put it on—that would be like admitting I belonged here.

I left my bag on the floor and walked over to one of the two windows. Maybe I could see into the Academy. Down below me, a long path meandered past a vegetable plot and a greenhouse. Beyond that was an orchard, with trees bending under the weight of apples and pears. Then the path disappeared into a wood. In the distance, beyond the school grounds, lay a dark, gloomy forest. I shivered. This must be the forest where they'd captured the lion.

I moved to the other window and pressed my nose to the glass. Below, separated from Nobodies by the high brick wall, was a long, low building with a flat roof. It was the back of the Academy! There were skylights in the roof and through them I could see children in navy blazers moving around. I pushed at the window. It slid upwards with a groan, shedding flakes of paint, and I was able to lean out a bit.

I stared down at the children, searching for the girl with the marmalade curls. What if she was making friends already? What if she found a best friend before I got there? I *had* to find a way! I pushed the window higher and a flurry of wings made me jump. A bird must have taken off from the windowsill above me. I peered up, but there was no sign of it. Then I slid out on to the windowsill and sat there, my legs dangling.

My heart sank. Even if I managed to somehow jump down on to the top of the brick wall, there was still no way of getting onto the flat roof without risking breaking my leg, or worse.

'What are you d-doing?' said a voice behind me, and I almost fell out.

I grabbed at the window frame.

A small girl with wispy blonde hair was standing in the doorway. She had a suitcase almost as big as herself. I couldn't think of a good explanation for why I was sitting on the windowsill, so I shrugged, jumped back in and went and sat on one of the beds.

The girl watched me with wide, frightened eyes, as if she was too scared to look away. I was used to people staring at my scar with curiosity, but not staring at *me* with such fear. Maybe she thought I was one of the freaks.

'It's all right,' I said. 'I don't belong here. I'm meant to be at the posh—I mean, the school next door.'

The girl's eyes flickered between me and the open window. She licked her lips.

'Oh,' she said. 'You lucky thing. I wish I could g-go there.' She looked round the room. 'The man said I should come in and g-get into my uniform.'

I pointed at the bundles of clothes.

The girl came in hesitantly, trundling her vast suitcase behind her. She pulled it over to the bed furthest from the door and stood looking at it in a helpless sort of way.

'C-could you help me lift my case, please?'

Between us, we hauled it up on to the bed. The girl unzipped it and pulled out:

1. A large alarm clock.
2. Six books, including *The House at Pooh Corner*, *The Secret Garden* and *Black Beauty*.
3. A family of pink woolly rabbits, a stripy cat, a frog and a penguin.

She lined the soft toys neatly up against the pillow. Then, from the bottom of the case, she pulled out a knitted yellow blanket, very worn and holey, and a fat teddy bear with one eye. She wrapped the blanket round herself and the teddy, stuck her thumb in her mouth and curled up in a ball on the bed. With her blonde hair and the yellow blanket she looked just like a bowl of custard. I couldn't help remembering an old rhyme: *cowardy, cowardy custard!*

Then I heard her snuffling. I went over and sat beside her.

'Look,' I said awkwardly, 'don't cry. It's not that bad.'

'How d-do *you* know?' said the girl. 'It's all right for you. You d-don't have to stay here.'

'Maybe they made a mistake about you too,' I said. She certainly didn't look like a dangerous freak.

'D-d'you think so?' She opened her eyes in a hopeful sort of way. They were very blue and watery.

It was then that I saw the phone, lying at the very bottom of her suitcase.

'Can I borrow your phone?'

She looked at me suspiciously. 'What for?'

'I need to call Claude and Sonia—to tell them to get me out of here.'

'Are C-Claude and Sonia your mum and dad?'

'*No,*' I said. 'They adopted me. I'm an orphan.'

'Oh.' She stared at my scar. 'I'm half an orphan.'

'What?' It was hard to concentrate. My eyes were stuck to the phone.

'I've only got a mum. My d-dad died. And then my mum got ill and had to g-go into the hospital. I d-don't have anyone else to look after me.'

'Sorry,' I muttered.

The clock, an old carved one hanging above the door, ticked on. Mr Gold would be back any moment and my chance would be lost.

'So can I?' I pointed to the phone.

'What if I g-get in trouble for lending it to you?'

'They won't know.'

'But the man's c-coming back soon. He said so. What if he c-catches you?'

I twisted my fingers together to stop myself grabbing the phone.

'He won't. I promise.' I glanced at the clock again. 'Please?'

Reluctantly, Custard handed over the phone. Then she curled up on the bed again.

I tapped in Claude and Sonia's number. It rang for ages. I stared at the door, praying that Mr Gold wouldn't open it.

'The Finklebome residence. Claude speaking.'

'Claude,' I whispered, my words tumbling over one another, 'there's-been-a-terrible-mistake-and-I'm-at-the-wrong-school-and-they-won't-let-me-into-the-Academy-and-you've-got-to-sort-it-out!'

There was a long silence. 'Is that you, Claudia?'

It wasn't the best moment to correct my name.

'Yes. But I've got to be quick because I'm at the wrong school and I'm not allowed to make a call and—'

'The wrong school?'

'The Cruet Establishment for... er... Nobodies.'

'Why, Claudia,' said Claude in a cold voice, 'do you think that's the wrong school?'

And then I finally understood. Claude and Sonia had meant to send me to the School for Nobodies all along.

I swallowed. 'But the girls—the girls from the Academy said...' I cast a quick glance at the custard girl, who was rocking from side to side on the bed, her eyes closed. I lowered my voice to a whisper. 'They said it's dangerous here. They said it's where the freaks are sent.'

'Nonsense, Claudia!' said Claude. 'We sent you there because you need discipline. The school will teach you to behave in a more civilized manner.'

'But I don't want to be here!'

'No use crying over spilt milk,' said Claude. 'Maybe you should have thought of *that* before you disfigured Sonia's masterpiece.' And he put the phone down.

I handed the phone silently back to Custard.

'Are you staying then?' she whispered.

I nodded. I didn't dare speak in case I burst into tears.

'What shall we d-do?' she quavered, pulling her thumb out. 'Whatever shall we d-do?'

I went over to the window and looked down at the Academy. My twin was so close, just a few metres away, but she might as well have been on Mars. And here I was, stuck among the freaks and the Nobodies.

I looked round at Custard, whose eyes were wet with tears. I wanted to creep under her yellow blanket and cry along with her. But one of us had to be strong.

I swallowed, hard.

'Come on,' I said as bravely as I could, heading over to my new bed and my new uniform. 'We'd better get changed.'

# UNREGISTRATION

The uniforms were rough cotton trousers, drab and grey, and sweatshirts to match. Custard's was too big for her. I helped her to roll up the trouser legs and sleeves.

'Leave your old clothes in your suitcases,' said Mr Gold, when he limped in, 'and come with me.'

We followed him downstairs and along another dark corridor. At the end of this, Mr Gold pushed open a door.

We were in a classroom. It was nothing like the classroom at my old school, with its whiteboard and computers and pictures on the walls. This one had old-fashioned wooden desks instead of tables, and on the far wall was a chalkboard.

Standing in front of the chalkboard was a person. She was very short and old—about sixty. She looked plump, but that might have been because of the layers and layers of knitted clothes she was wearing: a lavender jersey, a green spotted cardigan, a stripy red waistcoat and three or four scarves. She was the untidiest person I'd ever seen. Her hair was almost as tall as she was, escaping in every direction from a bun. Every time she moved her head, hairpins fell to the floor.

'Another two for you, Euphenia,' said Mr Gold.

The untidy person looked down her nose at me and Custard.

'Sit!' she said, pointing at two empty desks.

We sat. She had the sort of face you don't argue with.

There were only two other children in the room. Right at the front of the class was the boy with glasses I'd met outside. He was still wearing his shiny shoes, but the crisp white shirt and black jeans had been replaced by the Nobodies uniform of sweatshirt and cotton trousers. He sat bolt upright like a soldier waiting for a command. The other boy was tall and gangly, with a red face and a turned-down mouth.

'Pay attention, if you please!'

The untidy person drew herself up to her full height, which was not much taller than Custard, and rapped on the desk with a ruler. A purple and orange stripy scarf was unwinding itself from her neck and a button pinged off her green spotted cardigan.

'My name,' announced the untidy person, looking at us with sharp eyes, 'is Euphenia... Esmerelda... Boudica... Cruet. You may call me Miss Cruet, or "miss" for short. Welcome to the Cruet Establishment for Lost and Wayward Children.'

The boy with the glasses waved his hand in the air. 'Please, miss—'

Down came the ruler on the desk again.

'Quiet! I will let you know when you are permitted to speak. Now, where was I?' She adjusted her toppling bun and gazed at the ceiling. 'Ah yes. The school. My great-great-grandfather established it, and I took it over from my dear father. Mr Felix Gold joined me five years ago. Its purpose is to take in children whose parents or guardians can no longer manage them, to give these children a new start. From scratch.'

She picked up an enormous tatty book—so big that she almost disappeared behind it—from her desk, and drew out a pen from the folds of her waistcoat.

'We will begin with Unregistration.'

The boy with the glasses was waving his hand again. 'Please, Miss Cruet, what's Un—?'

'Silence!' Miss Cruet looked fierce, and he shut up.

She glanced at her book and waved her pen at me.

'You!' she barked. 'Stand up, if you please.'

I stood up.

'And you are?'

'My name,' I said, proud to be able to say it at last, 'is Fl—'

'Wrong!' interrupted Miss Cruet. 'You have no name.'

My mouth fell open in shock. What did she mean?

Miss Cruet looked slowly round the room. 'And that applies to all of you. At this school, you begin as Nobodies. We shall find out who you are in time. But until then, you have no names. You are *tabula rasa*. Of course, none of you will know what those words mean.'

The boy with the glasses sucked in his breath sharply and waved his hand again. Miss Cruet ignored him and looked at the rest of us. Custard was fiddling with her yellow blanket and sucking her thumb. The gangly boy had pulled the neck of his sweatshirt up over his mouth. I stared at Miss Cruet, feeling dizzy and scared, trying to take in her words. I'd only just found my name. They *couldn't* take it away. Miss Cruet sighed and nodded at the boy with the glasses.

'Well?'

'*Tabula rasa* is Latin, miss. It means a blank slate.'

'A Nobody with a brain,' said Miss Cruet. 'Interesting.'

I couldn't concentrate on her words. My insides were beginning to do That Feeling again, boiling up and fizzing and juddering. How *dare* they try to take away my name? I wouldn't let go of it. I wouldn't. My hand crept up to the tattoo on the back of my neck, and I muttered to myself: 'My name is Flynn. My name is Flynn. My name is FLYNN.'

'Quiet, girl!' snapped Miss Cruet, gathering up a comb and a butterfly clip and stuffing them back into her bun. Then she turned to the others. 'Now, you may each ask me one question, *and one question only*, so think carefully before you ask it.'

The boy with the glasses was, of course, up first.

'Please, miss,' he said, 'what are the rules?'

Miss Cruet smiled. 'How unfortunate, boy. I happen to be on the very point of telling you the rules. You have wasted your question.'

'Can't I have another question then?' he whined.

'No,' said Miss Cruet. 'You only get one. Rules are rules.'

She swivelled to Custard, who was gazing up at her with wide-open eyes, her thumb half out of her mouth.

'You—what is your question?'

There was a pause. Custard seemed to be summoning up the courage to ask it.

'Can I g-go home?' she stuttered.

'No,' said Miss Cruet. She pointed at the tall, sad-looking boy. 'Next!'

'Where are the others?' the boy muttered, his face beetroot red.

'The others?' said Miss Cruet. 'There *are* no others.'

'Funny kind of school,' piped up the boy with glasses, 'with only four kids in it.'

Miss Cruet turned to him. 'Exactly how many Nobodies have you met?'

The boy wrinkled his forehead as he thought. 'None.'

'Precisely. So a School for Nobodies will inevitably be a very small school indeed.' She turned to me. 'You,' she said, 'what is your question?'

I took a deep breath. 'I want my name back.'

'That,' snapped Miss Cruet, 'is not a question. It is a statement. And since you have no question, we shall move on to the school rules.'

My fingers and toes began to twitch. I sat on my hands, but my body just wouldn't stop wriggling.

The boy with the glasses nudged me sharply in the ribs. 'What's up with you? You got ants in your pants or what?'

'*Silence!*' Miss Cruet banged her plump fist on the desk. 'Where was I?'

'The school rules,' said the boy with glasses helpfully. I decided to call him Rule Boy from then on, since he was so keen on them.

Miss Cruet looked sternly at each of us.

'There are three school rules.'

Rule Boy's face fell. 'Only three?'

Miss Cruet scrabbled in one of her pockets and drew out a stick of white chalk.

Then, with much squeaking, she wrote on the board:

1. NO NAMES.
2. NO CONTACT WITH THE SCHOOL NEXT DOOR.
3. ONE POSSESSION ONLY.

She turned to face us.

'We have already covered rule one.' She tapped the blackboard with her pen.

'Rule two: you will have no contact *whatsoever* with the school next door.'

'But *why*, miss?' It was Rule Boy again.

Miss Cruet shot him a withering look. 'Because it is a very different school to this one and would be a bad influence on you.'

She looked very intently at me. 'You—repeat rule two to me.'

I crossed my fingers under the desk, and said: 'No contact with the school next door.'

A bell rang, making us all jump.

'Lunch,' said Miss Cruet.

The tall boy shot to his feet, but Rule Boy had his hand up again.

'But, miss—you haven't told us about rule three!'

'We shall come to rule three later. Meet me at two thirty sharp in the girls' dormitory. Anyone arriving late will be severely punished.'

And she swept out of the room, with the tall boy in hot pursuit and Rule Boy and Custard not far behind him.

The window of the classroom looked out on to a brick wall: the wall surrounding the Academy. My twin would be having *her* lunch right now. Would she choose burgers and chips, or pizza? What was her favourite dessert—ice cream or cream cakes? I knew nothing about her, except that her hair was just like mine. What would she do if she knew I was so close to her? Did she even know I existed?

I sighed. Why, why, *why* was I stuck here at Nobodies?

# RULE THREE

**L**unch was the oddest meal I'd ever eaten. It was served in the kitchen by Miss Cruet, who had a strand of spaghetti hanging over one ear. A big pot of soup—'like a witch's cauldron,' Rule Boy muttered out of the side of his mouth—was bubbling on the stove, making loud snorting and farting noises, while Miss Cruet wielded a sharp knife, cutting sandwiches. She banged the plate down on the scrubbed kitchen table in front of us. We stared at the sandwiches, as Miss Cruet slopped ladles of steaming green soup into bowls.

'What... on earth... is that?' said Rule Boy.

'Eat, and you'll find out!' snapped Miss Cruet, her bun threatening to topple into the cauldron.

The gangly boy gingerly picked up one of the sandwiches between his finger and thumb.

'Yuck!' he said. 'It's got something *fishy* in it.'

He was right. A fish's tail stuck out from between the two slices of bread.

'Mine's got jelly in,' muttered Rule Boy, making a face.

Custard shuddered. 'And mine's g-got...' She screamed and dropped her sandwich, 'A f-frog! It's a slimy f-frog!'

71

'Don't be daft,' I said, picking it up. 'It's lettuce. And, er... broccoli.'

But worse was to come. Miss Cruet slapped down bowls of soup in front of each of us. We peered down at them.

'Is that...?' whispered Rule Boy.

It was. Floating on top of the soup were marshmallows dusted with pink icing.

The gangly boy dipped his spoon and slurped at a marshmallow.

'It's *horrible*,' he moaned, but carried on all the same.

Rule Boy and I picked the fish tails, broccoli and lettuce out of our sandwiches and chewed on the bread and butter.

Custard stuck her thumb in her mouth and pushed her plate away.

'Lost your appetite?' barked Miss Cruet. 'Or are you saving it for supper? I'll be making one of my Specials—baked beans with strawberry sauce.'

We groaned.

The boy with the turned-down mouth ate his way through everything, complaining all the while.

'This soup's too *hot*—it's burning my tongue... it tastes funny too... bet it didn't come out of a tin...'

Rule Boy rolled his eyes, but the boy kept moaning.

'This isn't proper bread—it's *brown*... broccoli's *boring*... Why can't we have crisps and chocolate?'

Rule Boy shook his head. 'Saddo,' he muttered, and I couldn't help thinking he was right. The boy never smiled.

Not that there was anything to smile about. This really was the Worst School in the World.

*

After lunch, we all stood in the girls' dormitory. Miss Cruet seemed to have tidied her bun, though the hairpins and combs were still sticking out of it.

'Rule three,' said Miss Cruet. She glared at Saddo. 'What was it?'

'One possession only,' he muttered.

'Correct. At this school, we go back to basics: no names, no contact with the outside world, one possession only. Choosing your possession will make you decide what's most important to you. It will show us what kind of person you are, so think carefully about what you will keep. The rest of your things will be confiscated.'

'What does c-confiscated mean?' whispered Custard.

'Taken away,' I whispered back.

Her face went pale and her eyes darted to her bed and all her things.

'We may as well begin with you,' said Miss Cruet, looking at Custard. 'Gather round.'

She burrowed in one of her pockets and produced a stopwatch. 'You have one minute *precisely* to make your decision.'

Custard hovered over her things, picking up one, then another. 'B-but these are my comforts,' she whispered. 'I n-need my teddy to cuddle when I'm scared in the night. I n-need my books to read to help me go to sleep—'

'Forty-five seconds left,' said Miss Cruet, looking at the stopwatch.

'I n-need my alarm clock to make sure I wake up in time—'

'Thirty seconds left.'

'But I m-must have my animals.' Custard picked up one of the pink rabbits and put it down, then picked up the stripy cat, then the penguin. 'My m-mum gave me them! She said they'd keep the bogies and ghosts away!'

'Get a move on,' said Rule Boy. 'You've got to choose *one*. It's the rules.'

'Ten seconds,' said Miss Cruet.

I whispered to Custard, 'What's the one thing you absolutely can't do without?'

'Five seconds.'

Custard's hands flew to her blanket. 'My c-cuddly,' she whispered.

And the time was up.

'You,' said Miss Cruet, pointing to me and setting the stopwatch going.

I went to my bag, and slowly pulled out my golden leotard. The sequins and crystals and pearls glittered and sparkled.

'Oooh!' gasped Custard, and Rule Boy whistled.

I turned to Miss Cruet. 'You can stop the clock. This is what I choose.'

'Very well,' said Miss Cruet. 'We will now go into the boys' dormitory.'

We followed her into the room next door. It was just like Custard's and mine, with two beds. One bed had Rule Boy's four overflowing bags on it; the other had a huge suitcase.

'You,' said Miss Cruet to Saddo. She led the way over to the bed with the suitcase on it. 'Open it up.'

Saddo's face was a deep crimson. Slowly, he unzipped his case. It was stuffed with food. Miss Cruet started her stopwatch.

'Choose one item,' she said. 'You have a minute.'

Saddo picked up three giant, family-sized chocolate bars and put them down. He picked up a box of cakes and a packet of biscuits and licked his lips.

'Thirty seconds,' said Miss Cruet.

He pulled out five crisp packets and a huge box of sweetened cereal. His face got redder and redder.

'Fifteen seconds,' said Miss Cruet.

Saddo rummaged in his case. A pair of jeans and two scuffed trainers landed on the bed.

'Ten seconds.'

From the very bottom of his case, Saddo drew out a faded sweatshirt with a huge hood.

'I'll have this,' he muttered, and quickly put it on, pulling the hood right down over his red face.

Miss Cruet led the way to Rule Boy's bed. 'Your turn,' she said, starting the stopwatch.

Rule Boy grinned smugly. 'I don't need any time, miss,' he said. 'I knew straight away what I'd keep. I choose this.' And he drew out the violin case from one of the bags and held it up proudly.

'Very well,' said Miss Cruet, turning to the rest of us. 'You now have exactly ten minutes to pack up all your other things. Girls, please bring your bags into the boys'

75

dormitory. Mr Gold and I will collect them all shortly.'
And she swept out, leaving a trail of hairpins behind her.

Custard and I went into our room. I picked up my
leotard and folded it carefully and placed it under my
pillow. Quickly, my back turned to Custard, I reached
down inside my bag and found the parchment message
with its gold ribbon, and slipped that under my pillow
too.

A snuffling sound came from across the room. Custard
was kissing each of her animals as she put them back into
her suitcase. Her nose was all snotty and she kept wiping
it on her sleeve.

'Don't worry,' I said, taking her hand. 'We'll get our
things back some day.'

'H-how do you know?' whispered Custard.

'I'm sure we will,' I said, hoping I sounded more confident than I felt. 'C'mon. Finish up and we'll take our
cases next door.'

In the boys' dormitory, Saddo was tearing open packets of crisps and chocolate and cramming them into his
mouth as fast as he could. Rule Boy had packed his bags
and was sitting on the bed looking virtuous, his violin
case on his knee.

I looked at Rule Boy's four bags. They had been overflowing when we'd met outside the school—full of sheets
of music, and clothes, and that strange triangular machine.
Now his bags looked half empty.

'Where's all your other stuff?' I said.

Rule Boy avoided my eye. 'What other stuff?'

'You had lots of sheets of music. And that machine with the dial...'

Rule Boy nudged something under the bed with his foot. 'None of your business,' he muttered.

'They're under your bed!' I said.

I got down on my knees and looked. There, piled high, were the sheets of music and the odd-looking machine.

'Don't tell on me!' whined Rule Boy. 'I've *got* to have my music and my metronome. I can't practise without them.'

Saddo stopped cramming his mouth with food. 'That's cheating!' he said.

'You can talk,' said Rule Boy. 'Or rather, you *can't*, with your big mouth full of food.'

'For someone so keen on the rules, you don't seem to mind about breaking them!' I said. 'What if Miss Cruet finds out? You'll be punished—maybe even expelled!'

Rule Boy looked at the floor. 'Don't care,' he muttered. 'Who wants to be in this dump anyway?'

At this moment, Miss Cruet came in, accompanied by Mr Gold.

'Your cases, please,' she barked.

I stared at Rule Boy, and at the things under his bed. He was looking at me in a pleading kind of way. For once, he didn't look smug. Did he think I was going to tell on him? I wasn't a sneak. And anyway, Saddo and I had broken the rules too.

I handed over my bag to Miss Cruet, while he handed his to Mr Gold.

'Thanks,' Rule Boy muttered to me.

When Mr Gold had taken the cases away, Miss Cruet adjusted her bun and glared at us all.

'Here is this afternoon's schedule,' she said. 'Mr Gold will be conducting interviews with each of you in his study.' She pointed at Rule Boy. 'He will see *you* immediately.' Rule Boy made a face. 'The rest of you will see him at half-hourly intervals. Punctuality is of the essence. There will be severe consequences if you are late.'

'Please, miss—what do we do while we're waiting?' said Saddo. 'Can we watch telly?'

Rule Boy was waving his arm. 'Miss, where's the computer room?'

Miss Cruet smiled. 'There are no computers or televisions in the school. You may amuse yourselves in the library. Supper,' she added with a glint in her eye, 'will be at six sharp.'

# THE TALKING STICK

The library was a gloomy room, a long way from the rest of the school. A grandfather clock stood in a corner, its ticking echoing in the silence. There was a massive fireplace with a blackened, empty grate. The wind whistled down the chimney. Bookshelves lined the walls, except for one wall, the bottom half of which was made of panels of dark wood. Above this hung several huge paintings. Luckily, there were no bare people in them. The portraits were of men and women wearing knitted ruffs, knitted ball gowns and knitted riding boots. Their white powdered wigs were high as houses. These must have been Miss Cruet's ancestors.

'This is *boring*,' moaned Saddo, turning his mouth down and kicking at the wooden panels.

Custard curled up in her blanket in an armchair, sucking her thumb.

Next door, just a few metres away from where I was standing, my twin could be playing computer games or diving in the Olympic-sized swimming pool or watching films in the cinema room. I sighed, and looked along the shelves for books about circuses. There weren't any.

A shower of soot dropped into the hearth, scattering over the carpet.

Custard jumped. 'W-what's that?'

'It's only the wind,' I said.

'No, there's... there's something up the chimney! A ghost!'

'Don't be daft,' I said. But I shivered. I had the strangest feeling—as if someone, or something, was watching us. I shrugged the thought away. Sonia always said I had an Overactive Imagination.

Twenty minutes later, Rule Boy came back from his interview with Mr Gold.

'What did he s-say?' said Custard.

'Who? Krusty?' said Rule Boy, pulling out a book from the shelf and opening and shutting it with a bang.

'Why do you call him Krusty?' I said.

'Don't you know *anything*, Antsy?' said Rule Boy. 'He used to be a clown.'

'A c-clown?' said Custard. 'How do you know that?'

'It's obvious,' said Rule Boy. 'There's a big circus poster on his study wall, and he's on it—dressed as a clown, balancing on another clown's shoulders.'

Mr Gold a clown in a circus? I tried to imagine him, with his sad eyes and his limp, as a clown, but I couldn't. Rule Boy must have been making it up.

'How can you tell it's a picture of Mr Gold?' I said. 'Clowns wear wigs and make-up.'

'Because,' said Rule Boy, 'it says "The Gravity-defying Gold Brothers" on the poster.'

Custard took her thumb out of her mouth. 'What shall we d-do now?'

'I know—we'll find out about one other,' said Rule Boy. He picked up a ruler. 'This can be our Talking Stick.'

'It's not a stick,' I said. 'It's a ruler.'

'Duh, Antsy! Like I don't know that? But we can pretend it is.'

'What's a Talking Stick?' said Custard. 'Sticks c-can't talk.'

Rule Boy rolled his eyes at her. 'Talking Sticks were used by the Native Americans when they had meetings. Whoever holds the stick is the only person allowed to talk.'

He walked up and down in front of us, waving the stick about.

'I'll go first,' he said. 'I won't tell you my name, cos that's against the rules, but miss didn't say we couldn't tell each other about ourselves and how we came to be here. I got sent here because my dad went away. He couldn't look after me any more.'

'Where did he go?' I asked.

'Shut up! You're not allowed to talk while I'm holding the stick,' said Rule Boy.

'So, I'm going to be the greatest violinist there has ever been. I'm going to be world famous and make loads of money. I started playing when I was four and I've already done my grade eight. I got a distinction.'

I knew about exams. Sonia had made me take them on the piano. I'd just scraped through grade one.

Rule Boy offered the stick to Saddo. 'You'd better have your turn—you've got to go and see Krusty any minute.'

Saddo blushed and took the stick.

'My sister was looking after me,' he muttered. 'Only she went off to university.'

He tossed the stick back to Rule Boy and set off for his interview with Mr Gold.

'She probably got sick of his moaning,' smirked Rule Boy. 'And eating them out of house and home.' He threw the stick to me. 'Your turn, Antsy.'

'I am an orphan,' I said, standing up. 'I got sent here because I ruined a painting.'

I looked at Custard and Rule Boy. Could I trust them enough to tell them about my twin? It was my biggest secret, but I'd need help to find a way to get over the wall to the Academy, and Rule Boy seemed pretty clever. I made up my mind and took a deep breath.

'I've got a twin. And she's at the school next door so I've got to find a way to get there—'

At that moment, a wild flapping sound came from the chimney, and more soot dropped into the hearth, along with a long, black, oily feather. A terrible smell swirled around the room—a smell so horrible that it made me want to be sick.

Custard shrieked and backed away. 'It's the g-ghost! I knew it! I knew it!'

Rule Boy smirked. 'A ghost, eh? Let's see.'

He marched over to the hearth, got down on his knees and cautiously gazed up the chimney. 'Cor, it stinks up there. Whatever it was, it's gone now.'

I put my arm around Custard. 'There's no such thing as ghosts.'

'My m-mum says there is. G-ghosts and bogies.' Custard's teeth were chattering.

A cold blast of air swept down the chimney and the horrible smell seeped into our nostrils.

Rule Boy ran a hand through his black curls, dislodging flakes of soot, dusted down his knees and stood up.

'Anyhow,' he said, turning to me, 'what makes you think your twin's at the Academy?'

'Never mind,' I said. I didn't want to talk about the messages—they'd never believe me.

I passed the stick to Custard but she shook her head.

'I c-can't.'

'Scaredy-cat!' said Rule Boy.

'I'm n-not scared. I just d-don't want to,' said Custard. She stuck her thumb in her mouth and pulled her yellow blanket tightly round her shoulders.

'It's all right,' I said. 'You don't have to.' If her mum was in hospital and her dad was dead, no wonder she was frightened and shy.

'Well, if you won't talk, we'll have to play another game.' Rule Boy suddenly reached out and grabbed Custard's blanket.

'*Stop it!*' screamed Custard.

But Rule Boy, smirking, dangled the blanket just out of her reach.

'Give it *b-back*!' Custard jumped up and down to reach it.

'Say *please*,' taunted Rule Boy, raising the blanket a little higher.

'It's *m-mine*,' quavered Custard.

'Here, Antsy,' said Rule Boy. 'Let's play piggy-in-the-middle.'

And he suddenly threw the blanket towards me, over Custard's head. It wasn't a very good throw, and I just managed to catch it before it hit the floor.

'C'mon,' said Rule Boy with a snigger. 'Throw it back to me, Antsy.'

Custard's face was white and her eyes were full of tears. I walked over to her and held out the blanket. She grabbed it and wrapped her arms around it.

I turned to Rule Boy. 'Leave her alone, all right?'

Rule Boy snatched the stick from me and twirled it round in his fingers, grinning.

'It was just a bit of fun. Anyhow, what's so special about it? It's only a ratty old blanket.'

'It's *not*!' whispered Custard. 'It's *special*.'

'Huh,' said Rule Boy. 'Who says?'

'It *is* special,' said Custard. 'My m-mum gave it to me. She said it'd keep me safe when I was scared. And it *d-does*.'

'Your mum lied to you,' said Rule Boy. 'How can a stupid blanket keep you safe?'

'Stop being so mean!' I said.

Rule Boy grinned. 'You going to make me, Antsy?' And he reached out and grabbed Custard's blanket from her again. Custard tugged back with all her might, but Rule Boy was stronger. He jerked it away and began to dance about with it.

That Feeling began to bubble in my tummy.

'You think you're so smart,' I said, 'don't you? But you're *not*. You're... you're nothing but a bully and a thief.'

'You'll g-go to prison if you're not c-careful!' shouted Custard.

Rule Boy threw the blanket back at her and glared at me.

'Don't call me that,' he said. 'Don't you EVER call me a thief.'

At that moment, the door opened and Miss Cruet walked in.

'What's going on here?'

Rule Boy pointed at me. 'She called me a thief, miss!'

'Only b-because you stole my c-cuddly!' said Custard.

Miss Cruet looked at each of us, her eyes sharp and cold.

'Stealing and name-calling will not be tolerated at this school. There is a room here where children are sent to consider their behaviour.'

She grabbed Rule Boy by the ear. 'One hour in the Room of Reflection!' she snapped, then turned to me. 'And as soon as he comes out, *you* will go in for an hour.' And with that, she dragged Rule Boy out of the room.

# THE ROOM OF REFLECTION

'**Y**our turn next for the Room of Reflection,' Miss Cruet snapped at me.

Rule Boy, back from his hour in the room, made a disgusting face at me behind Miss Cruet's back.

'But I've got to see Mr—'

'Silence!'

Miss Cruet set off down the corridor. She led me upstairs, past the floor where the dormitories were, and up another flight of stairs, which led to a narrow corridor. We swept past a door marked: MISS E. CRUET—STRICTLY NO ENTRY!!! Then another marked: MR F. GOLD.

What would Mr Gold say when I didn't turn up for my interview with him? I'd be in even *more* trouble.

At the end of the corridor, a flight of spiral stairs wound up, narrow and dark. Round and round we climbed until we came to a final door with a big metal bolt on it. Miss Cruet turned the handle and the door swung open into darkness.

'The Room of Reflection,' announced Miss Cruet. 'Here you will spend one hour alone to reflect upon your actions.'

Then she pushed me inside and bolted the door.

It was pitch black. My heart thumped. Would I have to stay here, alone in the dark, for a whole hour? Cautiously, I ran my hands over the wall behind me until they found a switch. I clicked it on. A single bulb hanging from the ceiling glowed dimly. The attic room was so long and so badly lit that I couldn't see where it ended. It was empty. Not a chair or a carpet or a picture or a window. I took a step inside.

And froze.

Something was moving in the shadows at the far end of the room. I stood stock-still. It too stopped moving. I screwed up my eyes and peered into the shadows, but all I could make out was a shape. Had it seen me? In slow motion I edged backwards towards the door. The Thing was moving again. I grabbed the door handle and rattled it.

'Let me OUT!'

My voice echoed round and round the room, but there were no answering footsteps on the stairs. I spun back to face the Thing. It was still moving about, but it hadn't come any nearer.

What should I do? I couldn't get out of the room. There was nothing for it—I'd have to face the Thing. I swallowed. My throat was dry and I could hardly breathe. Slowly, my legs shaking, I began to move towards it, and it began to move too.

'I'm not afraid!' I whispered. But I was.

Then, as I got closer, I saw that the Thing was wearing a sweatshirt and trousers, just like me. It had curly red hair. I raised my hand in the air, and the Thing did too.

I laughed out loud with relief. How could I have been scared by my own reflection?!

On the far wall—the wall the School for Nobodies shared with the Academy—hung a full-length mirror. I walked up to it. Its wooden frame was carved in the shapes of mermaids and dragons. Its glass was dusty and there were black spots where the surface had worn away. It was so dark in the room that I could hardly see my burn, and I looked like a normal girl. Then I saw something else.

Behind me, in the mirror's reflection, stood a black cabinet.

Had it been there before? I was sure it hadn't. Maybe I was imagining it, like I'd imagined that my own reflection was some kind of monster.

I turned to look, half expecting the cabinet to disappear. It didn't. It stood against the wall, about the same height as me, on long, spindly legs. A key gleamed in its door. I had the strangest feeling: that if I opened it, my life would change forever.

Slowly, I walked towards the cabinet and reached out to turn the key.

A sound came from inside. A shuffling, whispering sound, as if something was breathing very heavily, or shifting about very slowly.

'Open me, Flynn,' said a croaky voice.

I hesitated, my fingers grasping the key.

'Open me,' said the voice again. 'I *dare* you...'

I thought quickly. Who was in there? Would it be safe to open the door? Whoever it was, it knew my real name.

And if it knew my name, maybe it knew other things. I had to find out.

I turned the key, and the door swung open.

The first thing that hit me was the smell. It was just the same as the smell in the library chimney—rotten eggs, dirty drains, poo and a whole lot else. Then, in the darkness at the back of the cabinet, something moved. The Thing was black, and I couldn't make it out, except for a gleaming, yellow pair of eyes. I stepped backwards.

As I did so, the Thing shuffled towards me. It was a bird, but nothing like the soft, grey dove that had helped me free the balloon. It was large, with oily black feathers, a hooked beak and withered claws. It waddled to the edge of the cabinet and stared at me, its head on one side. Then it opened its beak and spoke.

'Well, Flynn,' it croaked, 'you finally got here.' And it slowly closed one of its yellow eyes in a wink.

'How do you know my name?' I whispered.

The Bird gave a rasping chuckle.

'I know all about *you*,' it said. It raised one of its claws and scratched at the side of its head. A black feather floated to the floor.

'What do you mean?' My heart was beating so loudly I could hear it. 'How do you know about me?'

The Bird gave a hoarse chuckle.

'I watch, Flynn,' it whispered. 'I listen. I know. More than you can ever imagine.'

If this creature knew my name, and if it really knew all about me, then maybe it knew what happened to my parents. Maybe it could even tell me how to get to the school next door and find my twin.

'You have questions,' croaked the Bird. 'If you want answers, then you must come closer to me.'

The closer I got, the worse the smell. I pinched my nose between my fingers. When I was near enough to touch it, the Bird opened its beak, revealing a stubby black tongue, and cackled again.

'What is your question?'

My fingers crept up to my burn. 'What happened on the day my parents died?'

The Bird rummaged among its feathers as if searching for fleas. After some time, it said: 'That is a secret.'

'You said you would answer my questions,' I said.

'I *said* that if you want answers, you must come close. They may not be the answers to your questions.'

Then, with a terrible flapping, the Bird jumped out of the cabinet and into the air.

The next thing I knew, it had landed on my shoulder. Its sharp talons dug into my skin. I tried to brush it off, but its claws dug in even deeper.

'Oh no, missy,' it croaked. 'I have things to tell you, and tell you I will.'

The smell was so bad that I turned my head away.

The Bird bent its beak to my ear and began to whisper, so I could barely catch the words.

'If you remain at the School for Nobodies, you will *become* a Nobody. You do not belong here. You are different. You have a special gift.'

'What do you mean?' I couldn't think of anything special about me.

The Bird gave a horrible chuckle. 'Don't you wish you were next door, Flynn? At the Academy? There's a pool, you know, with water slides and a wave machine... a cinema... a gym with trampolines and swings... Imagine yourself there. Imagine the food you will eat... pizzas and hot dogs and Easter eggs all year long... ice cream and chocolate fountains...'

It pressed itself closer to my ear and I tried not to shiver.

'You must escape this place at all costs, and get to the school next door.'

'How?' I said. 'Over the wall?'

At that moment, footsteps came creaking up the stairs.

The Bird stretched its neck and stared right into my eyes.

'Someone is waiting for you there. Someone you long for with all your heart.'

'My twin?' I said, hardly daring to breathe.

The Bird closed its watery eye in a slow wink.

'How?' I whispered. 'How can I get to her?'

I could hear Miss Cruet muttering on the other side of the door as she pulled the bolt back.

'I will give you your answer when we meet again,' croaked the Bird.

Then it flapped its wings, launched itself into the air and flew into the cabinet. At the same moment, the door behind me swung open and Miss Cruet came in. She wrinkled her nose in disgust and sniffed the air.

'*What*,' she said, 'is that appalling smell? When did you last wash?'

'It's not me. It's—'

'Disgusting!' snapped Miss Cruet. 'You will proceed immediately to the shower. And don't forget to scrub your teeth thoroughly. Go!'

And she pushed me out of the door.

# DO YOU BELIEVE ME?

**I** was glad to scrub away the smell of the Bird. But I couldn't wash away its words.

'*You have a special gift... You must escape this place at all costs, and get to the school next door... Someone is waiting for you... someone you long for with all your heart...*'

I was sitting on my bed, pulling on my socks and thinking about all this, when Rule Boy walked in.

'You're in Big Trouble,' he said, looking extremely pleased about it. 'Krusty's looking for you—he's hopping mad. He's probably going to punish you *properly* for calling me a thief. A punishment *much* worse than the stupid Room of Reflection.'

I stopped. Rule Boy had been in the room just before me—had he seen the Bird too?

'What did *you* do in there?'

Rule Boy shrugged. 'Nothing, of course. What can you do in an empty room? I just sang my music to myself.'

'Didn't you see—?' I said, then stopped.

'See what?' Rule Boy looked innocent.

'Forget it,' I said. He must have been pretending he hadn't seen the cabinet or the mirror or the Bird.

Rule Boy turned to go. 'I'd better say goodbye now, and good riddance—cos when Krusty finds you, he'll probably expel you.' And he disappeared out of the door.

'I hope he *does*,' I muttered, returning to my laces. 'I hope he expels me today. Then I can go to the Academy and—'

'And what?' said a voice.

Mr Gold was standing in front of me. His rusty hair was wilder than ever.

'N-nothing,' I said.

'I've been looking for you,' he said. 'Why didn't you come to my study for your interview?'

'I couldn't!' I said. 'Miss Cruet sent me to the Room of Reflection and locked me in. And then I met the Bird—'

'The bird?' said Mr Gold.

'The Bird who lives in the cabinet.'

There was a long silence.

'What are you talking about, child?' he said. 'There is no cabinet in that room, and there is certainly no bird, to my knowledge. The Room of Reflection is a place to think about things on your own, with no distractions. There's nothing in there. Nothing at all.'

'There *is*,' I said. 'There's a black cabinet, and a bird inside it—and there's a mirror too.'

Mr Gold frowned. 'Child, there is no mirror. As I said, the Room of Reflection is empty.'

I began to feel afraid. What was happening? Had I imagined it? Had it all been a dream?

'I'm not making it up—I'm not!' The words burst out of me. I stood up. 'If you don't believe me, come up to the room and I'll show you!'

Mr Gold was looking at me in that odd way he had, almost as if I wasn't there.

'Very well.'

He limped ahead of me, up the stairs to the next floor, past his and Miss Cruet's bedrooms, and up the spiral staircase to the Room of Reflection. Mr Gold pushed open the door and walked in ahead of me. I clicked on the light.

'See!' I panted.

I looked triumphantly at Mr Gold. Now he'd believe I wasn't telling lies.

Mr Gold peered around the room.

'Show me,' he said.

I pushed past him into the room and stopped.

There was nothing there. No cabinet, no Bird, no mirror. The room was completely empty.

I ran to the far end of the room. Maybe the light was too dim to see the mirror. Maybe the cabinet was standing against another wall. Maybe I'd remembered it wrong. I ran right round the room, feeling the walls, peering into corners. Tears filled my eyes.

'There *was* a mirror. It was here, on this wall. And the cabinet was over there. They *were* here, I swear! I didn't make them up.'

Mr Gold leant on his stick and looked at me for a long time. I rubbed my eyes so he wouldn't see the tears.

'Tell me exactly what happened,' he said.

So I told him about seeing my reflection in the mirror, about opening the cabinet and meeting the Bird.

'And what did this bird do?'

'It spoke to me.'

'A talking bird?' He raised an eyebrow. 'What did it say?'

I hesitated. I wasn't going to tell him that it had told me I must escape from Nobodies.

'It... it said that I had a special gift,' I said.

'A gift?'

'It didn't tell me what it was,' I said.

Mr Gold was silent for a moment. Then he said: 'We all have gifts. Things we're especially good at or passionate about.'

'I'm not good at anything,' I said. 'Except cartwheels and handstands. And climbing trees.'

Mr Gold smiled. 'Those are excellent gifts,' he said. His smile went up at one end and down at the other, as if it wasn't sure whether to be happy or sad. 'But back to your story—what happened then?'

'Miss Cruet unbolted the door and the Bird went back into the cabinet,' I said. 'And then she made me go and have a shower...'

I twisted my fingers together and stared at Mr Gold. Under his shaggy eyebrows, his eyes were kind.

'Do you believe me? Do you believe I'm telling the truth?'

I held my breath. I couldn't bear it if he thought I was a liar. Mr Gold stared down at the floorboards and seemed to be thinking very deeply. Then he looked up at me.

'I believe you,' he said quietly.

My heart felt sort of light and happy.

Mr Gold limped to the door.

'We will go to my study and talk,' he said. And he set off down the stairs.

# IN MR GOLD'S STUDY

The study was warm and cosy. Two armchairs were drawn up beside a crackling fire. The only other furniture was a wooden chest of drawers in the corner and a large, completely empty bookcase. The walls were bare apart from the circus poster hanging above the fireplace. My eyes kept going to it, like it was a sort of magnet. Two clowns stood in a powerful spotlight, one balancing on the other's hands. They wore identical golden coats and baggy striped trousers held up by red braces, just like the ones Mr Gold was wearing now. The balancing clown wore a pointy hat and a curly red wig. His mouth had a huge red smile painted on it, and little diamonds round his eyes. Was it Mr Gold? I wanted to go over and look more closely, but Mr Gold pointed with his stick at the empty armchair, so I sat down and stared at him instead.

He leant his stick against the side of the other armchair and lowered himself into it. The firelight shone on his rusty curls and his strange, sad face. I tried to imagine him without his stick, tumbling around the circus ring.

'A penny for your thoughts,' he said, with his lopsided smile.

'Did you really used to be a clown?'

He nodded. 'I was. And an acrobat too.'

'Were those your gifts?'

Mr Gold smiled again. 'Yes,' he said. 'But then I lost them, and I had to find something else.'

'Did you have an accident at the circus?' I asked. 'Is that why you walk with a stick?'

Mr Gold didn't reply. Instead he bent down and picked up a poker and began to poke it around in the fire. The coals shifted and crackled and glowed red. It was comforting, somehow, to be sitting here. I felt calmer and my hands and feet were happy, for once, to be still. Mr Gold put the poker back on the hearth.

'Gifts,' he said, 'are like presents. We don't choose them—they are given to us. And sometimes they are taken away. So it's good to use them as much as you can while you have them.'

I thought about Rule Boy and his violin playing.

'Some people have really good gifts,' I said. 'And some people just have problems.'

'Do you have a problem?' said Mr Gold.

I thought for a moment. Could I trust Mr Gold? He seemed wise and kind, but he was still a teacher. I made up my mind.

'Sonia and Claude said I did,' I said. 'They said there was something wrong with me, because I can't keep still.'

'Perhaps,' said Mr Gold, 'you just like to move.'

No one had ever said that to me before. I thought about it for a bit. 'Maybe,' I said. Then I remembered my burn. 'But that's not the only problem.'

'What else?'

'*This*,' I said, pointing at my cheek.

Mr Gold carried on peering at me in his strange way. 'What is *this*?'

I felt uncomfortable and cross. 'Don't pretend it's not there,' I said. 'That's worse than staring at it.'

Mr Gold shifted in his chair.

'I too have a problem,' he said. He picked up his stick and began twisting it between his hands.

I didn't know what to say to that, so I stayed quiet and waited to see if he'd explain. We sat for a while in silence. Then he began to speak.

'You asked me if I had an accident,' he said. 'I did. And the result was that I hurt my leg, very badly, which meant I couldn't perform as an acrobat any more, or as a clown. But that wasn't all.' He sighed and looked towards the fire. 'I also lost my sight. Not all of it—I can see outlines of things and people. I can see them move. I can see enough to walk around. I can see bright lights, like this fire. But I can't see small details. I can't see whatever it is you are talking about. I'm sorry.'

Then I understood why he never seemed as if he was really looking at me.

'So you can see me move, but you can't see my... face?'

'That is correct.'

I tried to imagine what it would be like not to be able to see people's faces, not to know if they were happy, or sad, or afraid. I tried to imagine what it would be like to be a circus acrobat, and then to have to stop.

'Child, don't pity me,' Mr Gold said, as if he knew what I was thinking. 'I see all I need to. Remember what I just told you? That, when I lost my gifts as an acrobat and a clown, I found another?'

'What was it?' I asked.

'I discovered that I could see what isn't seen with the eyes: I could see what's inside people. And that's much more interesting and exciting.'

'What, like an X-ray? Like having X-ray specs?' I wondered if right now Mr Gold could see my bones.

He laughed. 'No, child. I mean, I can see how people are feeling, which helps me know what they are like. Sometimes people look very different on the inside to the way they look on the outside.'

I wanted to ask what I looked like on the inside, but I wasn't sure I'd like the answer. What if my inside was just as ugly as my face?

Mr Gold was smiling again. And I thought, *I can't be all that horrible if he's smiling at me*. I looked up at the poster.

'I always wanted to go to the circus,' I said. 'But Sonia and Claude wouldn't let me. They don't believe in circuses. They say they're cruel to animals, and that the people who work in circuses are...' I was about to say *common*, but then I thought that might upset Mr Gold.

'There are good circuses and bad circuses—just as there are good and bad people,' said Mr Gold. 'In the bad circuses, people treat the animals cruelly—they whip them and force them to live in cages that are too small for them and they don't keep them clean or feed them properly.

But good circus folk know that animals are like humans. They perform best when they are happy and well cared for. A good circus is like a big family. We all look out for one another. *All for one, and one for all.'*

'Like the Three Musketeers,' I said.

'That's right.'

I thought about how it must feel to belong to a circus, to be part of a big family where everyone looked out for each other. To live in a caravan, always moving from town to town. To look after lions and tigers and horses and dogs. To perform every day in the Big Top. I'd wanted to do this for so long. And now, meeting a real, live acrobat made me want it even more.

Mr Gold was peering at me again in that strange way he had. Maybe he *could* see what I was thinking. He suddenly pointed his stick at the chest of drawers in the corner.

'There's a box of photos in there. Third drawer down. Go and get them for me.'

I stood up and walked over to the chest of drawers. I pulled at the drawer. It was very stiff and stuck. I tugged even harder, and it flew open with a jerk, scattering photos all over the floor.

'Sorry,' I muttered, getting down on my knees to pick them up.

'Not your fault,' said Mr Gold. 'It hasn't been opened for a very long time.'

The firelight glimmered on the photos—stacks of them, and newspaper cuttings too, about the circus. I longed to look at them more closely, but Mr Gold was waiting.

I bundled them all back into the box and carried it over to him.

'See if you can find the big photo of the Grand Parade,' he said.

I sifted through the photos until I found a large, glossy one. I drew in a deep breath. The photograph was so full of colour and movement: horses pranced around a circus ring, and girls in shiny costumes balanced on their backs. A fat ringmaster, wearing a red-and-gold suit and a black top hat, was blowing a whistle. The Big Top was full to bursting with a waving, cheering crowd. Far above their heads, a man in green sequins swung on a trapeze. A young woman with tattoos all over her arms and legs, wearing a golden leotard—just like mine—was walking round the ring, her hand buried in the fur of a great, yellow lion. And there were the clowns again—walking on their hands side by side, their faces painted into huge grins. My eyes felt like they were stuck to the photograph. I couldn't tear them away. And that warm, chocolatey feeling spread through my body like a hug.

At that moment, a bell rang in the distance.

'Supper time.' Mr Gold stood up.

Reluctantly, I handed him the photograph.

Then I had an idea. It was a bold idea, and I wasn't sure if I was brave enough to say it.

'What is it, child?' said Mr Gold. It seemed like he really *did* know what I was thinking.

'Will... will you teach me?' I said, my heart beating very quickly in case he said no. 'To be an acrobat, I mean?'

Mr Gold picked up his stick. 'Child, I can't see, and I can't move very well any more. How could I teach you?'

'You can see me move. And you can tell me what to do. I won't do anything dangerous or stupid, I promise!' A feeling of excitement was buzzing around inside me where That Feeling used to be.

'Learning acrobatics isn't easy,' said Mr Gold. 'You have to practise every day. You have to be strong.'

'I *am* strong!' I said. 'I can do a handstand for twenty seconds, and I can cartwheel for ages and ages. Please, Mr Gold? Please?'

It felt like the most important question I'd ever asked.

Mr Gold stood very still, deep in thought. Then he gave a big sigh, and said, 'Very well. I'll give you a trial lesson.'

I clapped my hands.

'When? This evening?'

'Certainly not.' Mr Gold gave his lopsided smile. 'The first rule of acrobatics is: never exercise on a full stomach. We'll do it in two days' time. Meet me at seven thirty, before breakfast. And talking of eating, you'd better get a move on. Miss Cruet is a stickler for punctuality.'

'She's *scary*,' I said. Somehow, it felt OK to say this to Mr Gold.

Mr Gold smiled. 'Yes,' he said. 'She's pretty scary. But that's just on the outside.' And with that, he got up and limped over to open the door.

I skipped all the way down the corridor.

# IN THE WOOD

**N**ext day at breakfast, Miss Cruet stirred a huge frying pan full of frothy yellow gunge with fat black objects sticking out of it, bubbling and spitting. She wore a knitted dressing gown with three shawls over the top, and bright green woollen slippers with knitted pom-poms on them. Her face was covered with white cream. She tipped out the contents of the frying pan onto our plates: burnt sausages, swimming in curdled custard.

We all stared in dismay.

'I-I'm not hungry,' muttered Rule Boy.

'Nor me,' I said.

'I've got a stomach ache,' said Saddo, whose face had gone green.

'Me t-too,' quavered Custard.

Miss Cruet fixed us with a beady eye.

'What a strange coincidence,' she snapped. 'And what a sickly-looking bunch you are. Fortunately, I have an excellent remedy. This morning's lessons will be cancelled.'

We all cheered.

'Instead you will go outside and explore the grounds.'

Rule Boy glanced at the window. 'But, miss, it's going to rain any minute!'

'A little bit of weather never hurt anyone,' barked Miss Cruet. 'And fresh air and exercise will help you work up an appetite for lunch.'

We all groaned.

Out in the garden, storm clouds hung over our heads, like big bruises in the sky. The air felt heavy and damp. All the thrilling things that had happened yesterday kept jumping about in my head. I felt fidgety with excitement about what the Bird had told me. My twin was waiting for me at the Academy, just on the other side of the wall! I *had* to think of a way to get to her. And then there were the acrobatics lessons with Mr Gold. What with one thing and the other, I couldn't stand still.

'Ants in her pants again,' smirked Rule Boy.

Saddo immediately began moaning. 'It's *boring* out here... It's going to rain any minute and I'm *starving*...'

The four of us wandered up the path, past the vegetable plot and into the orchard. The old trees bent under the weight of apples, pears and plums. These were Tree's brothers and sisters. I ran my fingers over their soft bark and felt a tiny glimmer of happiness in my heart. Saddo grabbed a handful of fallen plums, crammed them in his mouth then spat them on the ground.

'Yuck!' he moaned. 'Sour.'

Rule Boy imitated his expression, turning his mouth down at the corners.

'Misery guts,' he said. 'D'you know what my dad always said to me when I was miserable?'

Saddo ignored him.

'"Turn that frown upside down,"' said Rule Boy, sounding just like Claude. He stuck his fingers in the corners of his mouth and pulled them up into a grin.

'Oh, shut up,' said Saddo, frowning even harder. Then he looked at Rule Boy with narrowed eyes. 'Anyhow, where *is* your dad? You said he went away. Where did he go?'

'Mind your own business.' Rule Boy turned his back on Saddo and set off up the path.

'He won't talk about where his d-dad is,' said Custard.

'If I had a dad, I'd talk about him all the time,' said Saddo.

'So would I,' said Custard.

A peal of laughter floated over the high brick wall from the Academy. I stopped and listened. Surely there must be some way of getting over it? But the red bricks climbed smoothly up, almost to the sky, without so much as a toehold. I promised myself I'd come back on my own, just as soon as I could. I'd shout to the kids on the other side and tell them about my twin. Then, with their help, I'd find a way to climb over and join her.

'Get a move on, Antsy!' said Rule Boy.

We walked until the path split in two. I set off down the left-hand path, the others trailing behind me. After a bit, the path meandered past an old shed. We peered through the cobweb-covered windows. Rule Boy tried the door, which opened with a creak.

'Nothing here,' he said. 'Just boring old tools and stuff.'

Beside the shed stood a huge oak tree, and hanging from a sturdy branch was a swing. I jumped onto it and kicked my legs back and forth.

'Give us a push!' I called to Saddo, who was the tallest. 'Hard as you can!'

'Nah.' Saddo hunched his shoulders up, his mouth turning down. 'Can't be bothered.'

'Come *on*, Antsy,' said Rule Boy. 'We're meant to be exploring.'

I sighed, and slipped down from the swing. I ran my fingers over its rough wooden seat. 'I'll be back soon,' I whispered to it.

We followed the path further. The trees, their thick old trunks covered in moss and ivy, grew closer together and soon became a proper wood. It was squelchy to walk in, what with the muddy earth and boggy places. Suddenly, it opened out into a clearing and we all stopped in our tracks.

A big grassy circle lay before us, perfectly even and flat. And all around it were rows of stone seats, rising up in tiers, just like in a circus.

'W-what is it?' whispered Custard.

'Don't you *know*?' said Rule Boy.

'Oh, just tell us!' I said. Why did he always have to be so superior?

'It's an Amphitheatre,' said Rule Boy.

'A what?' said Saddo.

'They had them in ancient Rome,' said Rule Boy importantly. 'They were sort of theatres. The audiences sat in the seats around the stage, and they'd have chariot races and athletics competitions and stuff.'

'Why is this one here?' I said.

But even Rule Boy couldn't answer that.

'I d-don't like it,' said Custard. 'It's creepy.'

'Chicken,' said Rule Boy.

'I'm not!' said Custard, sucking her thumb.

'Leave her alone,' I said.

Saddo and Rule Boy, with Custard trailing behind them, wandered over to the lowest row of stone seats and sat down.

'Ugh, they're hard,' moaned Saddo.

My body was bubbling with excitement. The grass circle was just like a circus ring, perfect for performing. I ran full pelt right around it. Then I cartwheeled from one side to the other. Last of all, I stood on my hands and walked around, waggling my legs in the air.

Custard clapped, and even Saddo looked impressed. I took a bow. But Rule Boy looked put out.

'Show-off,' he muttered.

I ignored him. 'Come on.' I grabbed Custard's hand. 'Let's explore the wood.'

'What if we g-get lost?' said Custard.

'What if there are w-wild animals in the wood?' Rule Boy mimicked her. 'What if they eat us for s-supper?'

'Take no notice,' I whispered to Custard. 'Let's pretend we're brave explorers.'

We walked in single file through the trees. It was dank and dark here, and my trainers were soon sticky with mud. Rule Boy's polished shoes were speckled with dirt and splashed with water from the puddles. The wood was silent, except for the distant drilling of a woodpecker. The wind made a rustling, murmuring sound, as if the trees were whispering secrets to one another. The trees grew taller and closer together and the path ahead got darker and darker. Every now and then, a flurry of wings sounded from the trees above us. Was something following us?

'I d-don't like it here,' Custard said, pulling her blanket tighter round herself. I could actually hear her teeth chattering and she jumped a mile every time one of us stood on a twig or kicked a stone.

Saddo looked up at the sky. The dark clouds were right overhead now, and the air had gone very still.

'There's a storm coming,' he said. 'We're going to get *soaked*.'

'Never mind soaked,' said Rule Boy, frowning at his ruined shoes. 'We're going to get in Big Trouble for going so far. And it'll be all *your* fault, Antsy.'

'Oh, shut up,' I said.

Suddenly, the path came to an abrupt halt in front of an ancient, crumbling stone wall. Beyond the wall were trees as far as you could see, so tall that they blocked out the sky.

'It's the forest!' I said. 'Where they captured the lion!'

There was a long silence.

'The l-lion?' quavered Custard.

'What lion?' said Rule Boy.

'There was a lion, living in the forest,' I explained. 'But it's all right. They caught it and took it away to a safari park.'

Custard clutched my hand. 'I d-don't like l-lions.'

Suddenly the wood lit up as if someone had switched on a bright light.

'W-what's *that*?' Custard whispered, her eyes wide with fear.

'It's lightning, of course,' said Rule Boy. 'I *told* you we shouldn't have come this far.'

Then a huge rumble of thunder sounded right above us. Custard threw herself at me.

'M-make it stop!' she yelled. 'M-make it stop right now!'

'It's OK,' I said. 'It's only thunder. It won't hurt you.'

'I w-want to go back,' Custard said tearfully.

'Here comes the rain,' said Saddo.

Heavy drops began to fall.

'At least we can shelter under the trees,' I said.

'Are you stupid, Antsy, or what?' snapped Rule Boy. 'You must never, *ever* stand under a tree in a storm. If lightning strikes the tree, you can get electrocuted.'

Custard began to wail and twist her hands. 'What shall we d-do? Whatever shall we d-do?'

The rain was now teeming down through the thrashing leaves. Saddo pulled his hoodie over his face while Custard hid under her blanket.

Another flash of lightning lit up Rule Boy's face, reflecting in his glasses.

'We've got to get out of the wood, quick!' he shouted, setting off at a run, followed by Saddo.

I grabbed Custard's hand as another bellow of thunder made her squeak.

We'd only been running a short while when Saddo shouted, 'Wait for me!'

We turned to find him leaning against a tree trunk, huffing and puffing and clutching his side. 'I've got a stitch!'

We all stopped. The tree trunk that Saddo was leaning on was thick and ancient-looking. Its huge roots twisted across the path.

Then we heard it.

A terrible roar, echoing round the treetops, right above our heads.

# THE RESCUE

'It's a l-lion!' screamed Custard. 'Up in the tree!'

A cold shiver dropped into my tummy. Could there have been more than one lion living in the forest?

Another roar seemed to split the air apart.

I peered up. At first all I could see were the dark, whipping branches. Then a lightning flash lit up a creature, crouching on the highest branch, tossed around by the wind.

'It's not a lion,' I said. 'It's far too small.'

The creature gave another roar. It really did sound exactly like a lion.

Custard stuck both her fingers in her ears and shut her eyes.

'I think it's in trouble,' I said.

'Who cares?' snapped Rule Boy. 'Let's get out of here.'

'Don't leave me!' moaned Saddo, who was still clutching his side.

Then, as a roll of thunder boomed above us, and another flash of lightning lit up the figure, I saw that the creature had long hair, and that a hank of it had got twisted and caught in a high, swaying branch.

'It's trapped,' I said. 'Its hair is caught in the tree—it can't move.'

The creature gave another howl, even louder than the thunder.

I turned to the others. 'Someone must run back—get Mr Gold.' I looked at Custard.

'No!' she said. 'I can't run through the wood on my own—I c-can't!'

Saddo stepped forward. 'I'll go,' he said. 'But I can't run fast or I'll get another stitch.' And he set off down the path at a slow jog, already huffing and puffing.

'Why didn't *you* go?' said Rule Boy. 'You're the fastest runner.'

'Because,' I said, 'I'm going to climb up and try to get it down.'

'Are you crazy, Antsy?' said Rule Boy, looking horrified. 'That's a wild animal. It'll probably attack you. And anyway, climbing's against the rules.'

'Who says?' I rolled up the sleeves of my sweatshirt and searched the tree trunk for footholds.

'You *can't*!' Rule Boy sounded scared. 'I told you. You must never, *ever* climb a tree in a thunderstorm.'

'What do we do then?' I said. 'Leave it up there?'

I found a knothole in the tree trunk and pushed my foot into it. Far above us, the creature howled again.

'Don't g-go up there!' said Custard, streaks of water running down her cheeks. 'Stay here until Mr Gold c-comes.'

Rule Boy was still chuntering on about electricity. 'If a tree gets struck by lightning, the electrical charge will run right through it and pass through any body that's on it or near it...'

I reached up and grabbed a branch, then scrabbled with my other foot until I found a foothold, and another. The bark was slippy with rain. My heart was beating very fast, partly with fear and partly with excitement. It was like I was climbing Tree again, back in Sonia and Claude's garden. My hands and feet knew what to do.

Below me, Rule Boy was still droning on. 'Human bodies are full of water and that means the electricity can go into them... then they *die*...'

I was halfway. Holding on to the trunk for support, I looked up. Rain splattered down onto my face. My sweat-shirt was already plastered to my skin. But the creature was closer now. It was about the same size as me, drenched to the skin and thin as a stick, and it had the longest hair I'd ever seen, whipping around it in the wind. The tree rocked and creaked and the creature opened its mouth wide and gave another huge roar.

'I'm coming!' I yelled.

The creature gave a yelp, before another roll of thunder, right above us, drowned its voice.

It was harder, now, to climb. The branches were thinner and more wiry and the wind was rocking the tree more violently. I looked down and saw Custard and Rule Boy's faces looking up. Rule Boy's mouth was still opening and closing.

I searched for the next foothold, and the next. Now I was just below the creature. It was sitting astride a thin

115

branch which was waving crazily in the wind. It tried to turn its head to look at me, but the strands of its hair were wound too tightly round the branch. Then I realized that it wasn't a creature at all. It was a boy.

I clung to the slimy trunk as tightly as I could and reached up to where a big hank of the boy's hair was wound round and round a branch.

Then I saw the worst thing. The branch that the boy was sitting on was bending and creaking, and a narrow crack was forming in it. Every time the branch dipped in the wind, the crack got a bit bigger. Any minute, it would break right off and he would fall.

With wet, shaky fingers, I grabbed the boy's hair. He began to struggle, his eyes narrowed into slits, baring his white teeth and growling. Was he going to attack me? If he did, we'd both end up falling to the ground.

'It's all right!' I said, trying to make my voice sound calm. 'Stay still.'

The boy stopped struggling and stared at me. A flash of lightning lit up the tangled hair, which helped for a moment. It seemed to take forever, what with the branches swaying and bucking in the wind and the crack in the branch getting bigger and bigger.

The last strand of hair came free. The boy shook his head and gave a great roar.

'QUICK!' I shouted. 'Get off the branch! It's going to break!'

The boy stared at me. He didn't understand what I was saying. I pointed at the branch beneath him and he looked down at it, his eyes widening with fear. I held out my hand and the boy turned and grabbed it. With his other hand, he grasped the trunk and his legs circled it. As he did so, there was a tremendous crack and the branch he'd been sitting on broke in two and plummeted to the ground.

Custard gave a shriek.

Getting down was difficult. The wind seemed to blow even harder and the bark was slippery and wet leaves slapped our faces. I went first, and the boy followed. He was just as good at climbing as me. At last I slithered down the final few metres and landed, panting, on the ground.

Custard threw her arms around me. 'You nearly got k-killed!'

Rule Boy glared at me. 'That was the stupidest thing *ever*!'

As soon as the boy's feet hit the earth he turned to run.

But Rule Boy was too quick for him and grabbed him by the waist. 'Not so fast!'

The boy wriggled and twisted and growled, but he didn't bite. Rule Boy stuck his foot round the boy's ankle and brought him crashing to the ground. Then he pulled the boy's arms behind his back and sat on him.

Custard cowered away from them, whimpering.

'Who are you? What are you doing here?' said Rule Boy.

The boy growled and spat.

'He can't talk!' I said.

'Or he *won't*,' muttered Rule Boy, tightening his grip on the boy's arms.

I stared at the boy. He wasn't dressed like us. He was wearing a sort of tunic which looked like it had been woven from sheep's wool and grass. His arms and legs were strong-looking but very thin. His feet were bare, and his fingers and toes had the longest, dirtiest nails I'd ever seen. His hair hung down over his body in thick, wet, matted sheets. He was shivering all over.

At that moment we heard approaching footsteps. It was Saddo, puffing like a steam engine, his face beetroot-red and wet, with great patches of sweat under his arms. He collapsed, panting, at the foot of the tree, his eyes goggling at the sight of the boy. Right behind him, a hooded figure limped towards us, leaning on a stick. Mud streaked its face and covered its body.

'It's the b-bogeyman!' Custard yelled, grabbing my hand.

'Don't be daft!' I said. 'It's Mr Gold.'

The figure limped up to us, throwing back its hood to reveal Mr Gold's curly hair and pale, worried face.

'What's going on?' he said, peering from one to the other of us in that strange way he had.

Custard and Rule Boy were like drowned rats, and the boy and I were covered in slime and stains, our hair plastered to our heads and our hands blistered from the climbing. But Mr Gold looked even worse. His raincoat was filthy and dripping wet, and his face and hands were streaked with mud.

'Mr Gold tripped over!' puffed Saddo. 'There was a branch on the path and he fell right over it!'

Then I remembered Mr Gold couldn't see properly.

'It's all under control, sir!' Rule Boy settled himself more firmly on the boy's back.

'Who is that?' said Mr Gold, moving closer.

'It's a wild boy, sir. He's very dangerous indeed. Lucky I've caught him.'

'*She* r-rescued him!' said Custard, pointing at me. 'He was t-trapped up a tree.'

Mr Gold crouched down beside the boy. Gently, he reached out and took the boy's hand. The boy snarled, glaring at Mr Gold with narrowed eyes.

'Hush,' Mr Gold said very softly, as if he was gentling a terrified animal. 'It's all right. You are safe.'

'I think he's hungry,' I said.

'Aren't we all?' muttered Saddo.

'You can let him go now,' Mr Gold said to Rule Boy.

Reluctantly, Rule Boy got off the boy's back.

Mr Gold gently took the boy's hand. 'We're going to get you warm and dry and find you something to eat. You look as if you haven't eaten for a while.' He mimed eating to the boy, who cocked his head to one side, listening.

Then he gave a little nod.

Mr Gold stood up, still holding him by the hand.

'Come with me,' he said.

And we all trooped back to school.

# A FERAL BOY

When we walked into the kitchen, Miss Cruet glared at us.

'You are all late!' she barked. 'And filthy! This will not do! It will not do at all!'

Then she spotted the boy, who was staring around the room with his mouth open and his eyes—which were a strange tawny-brown colour—like saucers.

'What is *this*?' she snapped.

Mr Gold stepped forward. 'Euphenia, the children found this boy in the wood.'

'What was he doing in the wood?' Miss Cruet bent down and stared at the boy, who stared right back at her. 'Who are you? Where are your parents? Did you lose them?'

'He doesn't talk,' I said.

Hearing my voice, the boy turned to look at me, gazing at me with wide eyes. Then he raised one filthy hand and pointed to my cheek, where my burn was. I turned my face away.

Mr Gold drew Miss Cruet aside and began to speak with her in a low voice. I heard the words *police* and *social services* and *abandoned*. Miss Cruet kept saying a word I'd never heard before: *feral*. Then Mr Gold went out of the room, and she harrumphed a few times, and turned to us.

'Under normal circumstances, I would send you all straight up to have a shower. But you clearly need a hot meal. Luckily,' she added with a glint in her eye, 'I've prepared one of my Extra Specials.' And she bent down to the oven and drew out an enormous pie.

We all sat down, keeping one eye on the pie, just in case it exploded or something scary jumped out of it. The boy stayed standing up. Maybe he didn't know about chairs. I took his hand, and gently pushed him down into one. Miss Cruet took a large knife and serving spoon, and cut the pie open. Green steam poured out of it.

We all stared as if hypnotized.

'Wh-what's in it?' whispered Custard, as Miss Cruet ladled portions of the pie on to plates and passed them round the table. 'Is it a-alive?'

'It looks like... spaghetti,' muttered Rule Boy.

'With jam,' said Saddo.

'And bananas,' I said.

Then a strange thing happened. The boy began to eat. He didn't use a knife or a fork—he just grabbed the pie with his fingers and began to gnaw at it, making hungry growly sounds. He chomped and chewed, and when he'd finished his own portion, he grabbed Custard's and ate that too.

Then Saddo, who'd been watching the boy with his mouth open, took a bite of his pie.

'Surprisingly,' he muttered, 'it's not too bad.'

Rule Boy pinched his nose between his fingers and began shovelling in mouthfuls of pie.

I took a deep breath and put a forkful in my mouth. Saddo was right. It may have been the oddest pie ever, but it actually tasted OK.

'What's for afters?' said Saddo.

Mr Gold came back into the room. 'I have reported finding the boy to the police,' he said. 'And I have suggested to social services that we keep him here for the time being, until someone comes forward to claim him. I will arrange an extra bed for him in the boys' dormitory.'

Rule Boy made a face.

Custard clutched my hand. 'I w-won't sleep a w-wink with *him* next door,' she whispered.

'Don't be daft,' I whispered back. 'He's just wild and frightened. He won't hurt us.'

Miss Cruet harrumphed again. 'Felix, this is most likely a feral boy—completely uncivilized. He can't be expected to fit in here.'

'Why not?' said Mr Gold. 'The boy is a Nobody, so far as we know, so he should fit in just fine.'

The boy followed the conversation, his head turning back and forth as if he was at a tennis match.

'Please, Miss Cruet,' I said, 'what does *feral* mean?'

Miss Cruet looked a bit taken aback and glanced over at the boy. He was holding a hank of his hair, inspecting it and occasionally biting at it, like a dog searching for fleas.

'Feral means wild, as opposed to domesticated. A feral cat, for example, is one who has lived in the wild and knows only wild ways. So if such a cat is brought into someone's home, it will continue to act like a wild cat until it is tamed.'

'What if it doesn't want to be tamed?' I said.

Miss Cruet ignored this. She turned to Mr Gold.

'Very well, Felix. He may stay, for the time being. But if he causes trouble, it will be entirely your responsibility. I insist, however, that he washes and wears our uniform. And tomorrow is Haircut Day, so we will dispose of *that*.' And she pointed at the boy's long, matted hair, which was dripping all over the kitchen floor.

Next morning, Mr Gold led Custard and me into the bathroom, which had washbasins in it, along with an old-fashioned bath with clawed feet and a shower cubicle.

'But *why* do we have to? Is it the rules?'

Rule Boy was sitting at one of the basins, a towel round his neck, holding his glasses in his hand. Without them, he looked young and sort of innocent. The floor was covered with black curls. Rule Boy's hair, or what was left of it, stood up in spikes. Standing behind him, brandishing a pair of shears, was Miss Cruet.

'Here you go, Euphenia,' said Mr Gold. 'Two more for haircuts.' And he limped out.

Miss Cruet turned and glared at us. She wore her brightest outfit yet—a knitted dress in mustard yellow with red polka dots, two knitted scarfs in blue and green stripes, and a long pink knitted cardigan.

'Right,' she barked at Rule Boy. 'You're done. Go to your dormitory and wait there.'

'But *why*?' said Rule Boy again. '*Why* do we have to get our hair cut?'

Miss Cruet narrowed her eyes. 'Nobodies must give up all those things which mark them as individuals: their names, their clothes, their possessions. Ergo, your hair.'

'What's *ergo*?' I muttered to Rule Boy, as he pulled on his glasses.

He rolled his eyes.

'Latin,' he said. 'Means *therefore*.' He drifted out of the room, running his hand through his shorn black spikes and grumbling to himself.

'Sit!' said Miss Cruet to Custard and me.

She handed each of us a towel—not very clean ones—and stood behind Custard. Custard's blonde hair, though fine and wispy, was almost down to her waist. She stuck her thumb in her mouth and looked at the shears with terror. Without further ado, Miss Cruet cut a big chunk out of her hair, then another.

'P-please,' stammered Custard, 'my m-mum said—'

Miss Cruet ignored her, and in a couple of minutes, Custard's hair was shorn to her shoulders in a ragged bob.

'Back to your dormitory,' ordered Miss Cruet, and Custard slunk out, sucking her thumb.

Then it was my turn. I wasn't frightened. I *wanted* my hair to be cut, so everyone could see my name. I gave Miss Cruet my best smile. She didn't smile back.

'Can you cut it really short?' I said. 'Like a pixie cut?'

Miss Cruet raised the shears and, in rough hacks, began lopping my hair into exactly the same shoulder-length bob as she'd given Custard.

'A fringe would be—' I began hopefully, then I stopped short as the door was flung open.

Mr Gold stood in the doorway, holding the feral boy by the hand. The boy looked a little more like a human now that his face and hands had been washed. He was wearing a sweatshirt, inside out, and trousers and trainers. His matted hair fell to below his knees.

When he saw Miss Cruet, a low growl rumbled from his throat. His strange, tawny eyes flickered around the room, as if looking for escape. Then he saw me and stared at my burn, just the way he had yesterday. I quickly turned my face away.

Mr Gold sat the boy in the chair beside me and said in a low voice to Miss Cruet: 'Be gentle with him, Euphenia.' Then he limped out of the room.

Miss Cruet lifted a hank of the boy's hair. He gave another growl, baring his teeth like a cornered animal, and pulled away from her. As she raised the shears to begin cutting, he opened his mouth and screamed. It was a terrible sound.

I shrank away from him.

Still holding the shears, Miss Cruet grabbed him with her free hand. He kicked and growled and shook his head frantically.

I jumped off my seat, my heart thudding, and edged backwards until my back hit the wall.

The boy was on his feet, drumming them on the floorboards, twisting and snarling and whipping his long hair back and forth, out of reach of Miss Cruet's grasp.

Suddenly, he stopped struggling. His shoulders slumped and he slipped to the floor as if his legs wouldn't hold him up any longer. His strange, tawny eyes locked into mine. They were full of tears, and as we stared at one another, a single drop tracked down his face. Just for a moment, I stopped being scared of him. He was wild and frightened and alone. I thought of Sonia and Claude, and how they'd stopped *me* from being wild. And before I could think any more, my legs carried me towards him. I grabbed the shears from Miss Cruet's hands and threw them to the floor.

'STOP IT!!!' I shouted at her. 'Stop it right now! Leave him alone!!!'

Miss Cruet seized me by the arm and shook me, scattering hairpins over the floor.

'Impertinent child!' she barked, and was clearly going to say a lot more, only she was interrupted by the door opening.

Mr Gold entered. He scanned the room in that strange way he had.

'Let her go, Euphenia,' he said. Then he limped over to where the feral boy was crouching, growling, and knelt down in front of him, gazing into his eyes.

'We wish you no harm,' he said quietly.

Miss Cruet bent to pick up the shears, but Mr Gold stopped her.

'No, Euphenia,' he said. 'Let him be.'

'You know as well as I do, Felix, that while they are at this school, the children's hair must be cut to a standard length.'

Then I thought of something. 'Please, Mr Gold,' I said.

'Yes, child?'

'What about rule three? One possession only.'

'What about it?'

'Couldn't he keep his hair?'

'An interesting idea,' Mr Gold smiled. 'What do you say, Euphenia? Do you think we could apply rule three?'

Miss Cruet huffed and puffed. 'Very well,' she said at last. 'But don't blame me if this situation comes back to bite us—literally.'

Then she turned to me, and snapped: 'Go to your dormitory immediately.'

I shook the towel from my shoulders and moved towards the door. As I reached it, something made me turn. The feral boy was still sitting on the floor, his wet eyes fixed on me as if I was the most fascinating thing he'd ever seen.

And that was the beginning of the trouble.

# SECRET MUSIC

**M**y golden leotard swayed above me, the pearls and sequins and crystals glinting in the sunlight. Its hem brushed my face, back and forth. I reached up to touch it, and my fingers met something soft and warm. I opened my eyes.

And screamed.

A pair of tawny eyes stared down into mine. The feral boy was bending over my bed and stroking my cheek, where my burn was. His hair hung over me like a curtain and it was this that I'd touched. I pulled my hand away and leapt out of bed.

'STOP IT!!!' I yelled. 'Leave me alone! Go back to your own room!'

He backed out of the room and disappeared.

Custard, who had shot out of bed when I screamed, was cowering against the wall, clutching her yellow blanket.

'Why does he k-keep following you?' she said.

'I don't know,' I said shakily. 'I just wish he'd stop.'

Why, why, *why*, I thought, as I pulled on my sweatshirt and trousers, had I rescued the feral boy from the tree, and then saved his hair from being cut? He'd been here less than two days, but already it felt like forever. Everywhere

I turned, there he was like an extra shadow. He'd stuck to me like glue, staring at me with those strange eyes. It gave me the creeps.

'Where are you g-going?' asked Custard.

'Out,' I said.

Today was the day of my first acrobatics lesson with Mr Gold. He'd told me to meet him in the Amphitheatre at seven thirty, before breakfast. It was only six forty-five, but I might just as well get up now, and go down there early. I could practise my handstands and cartwheels before Mr Gold arrived.

I brushed my teeth and tiptoed down the stairs, avoiding the creaky one near the bottom. Miss Cruet was banging around in the kitchen, so I quietly pulled open the bolt on the back door and stepped out into the garden.

The sun was just rising and the air was cold and fresh and full of the tweeting, chirruping and chattering of birdsong. I hurried through the orchard and took the left-hand path through the wood. Soon it would be autumn. Mushrooms and spotted red toadstools grew in the shady places among the tree roots.

I'd passed the shed and was almost at the clearing, when a sound made me stop in my tracks—the very last sound I would expect to hear in the middle of a wood.

It was music.

I tiptoed towards the Amphitheatre. There, standing in front of the stone seats, was Rule Boy. He had a cloth on his shoulder, and on this rested his violin. His fingers darted over the strings, while his other hand used the bow. Propped against the stone seat in front of him was a sheet of music, and beside that stood the odd triangular machine. Its single hand was rocking back and forth, *tick-tock, tick-tock...*

The music, beautiful and sad, made me shiver and tingle all over. Rule Boy was swaying about and his face looked different, dreamy and intense. Then he opened his eyes and saw me.

'Oh, it's *you*,' he said.

If he had been anyone else, I'd have said how well he played and how the music made me feel, but this was Rule Boy, so I didn't. He'd only use it as an excuse to be smug and superior. Instead I pointed at the machine, which was still tick-tocking.

'What's that?'

Rule Boy leant over and flicked a switch on the machine and the hand stopped moving.

'It's a metronome,' he said. '*Most* people would know that.'

I ignored this, and said: 'What's it for?'

'It keeps time,' said Rule Boy. 'I set it to the speed I need for the piece I'm planning to play and it tells me how fast to go.'

'Oh,' I said. I picked up a piece of the sheet music. I knew about music from when I studied for my grade one piano, but that had been simple. This music looked like a hailstorm of notes.

'Want to hear me play something else?' said Rule Boy, picking up another sheet of music.

'OK,' I said.

Rule Boy fiddled with the metronome until it was tick-tocking really fast, then he picked up the violin and began to play again. Once again, he furrowed his brow and looked serious as he concentrated. But this time the tune was bouncy and jolly, and I found my feet tapping. Then I couldn't help it—my whole body began to dance and jump and whirl and bounce around the grass circle.

I didn't want the music to stop, but of course it did, and I stood there, grinning and panting.

Rule Boy began gathering up the music and the metronome.

When I got my breath back, I said: 'How did you sneak all this stuff out of school without Miss Cruet seeing?'

Rule Boy flushed. 'I used my violin case to bring down my music, bit by bit, and hid it in the shed. Last of all, I brought the metronome. You won't tell on me, will you?' For once, he didn't look superior.

'I'm not a sneak,' I said.

'Thanks,' he said gruffly. Then he picked up his stuff and walked out of the Amphitheatre.

When he'd gone, I stood in the centre of the circle of grass. A grey squirrel pattered along a branch, its cheeks full of nuts. Somewhere nearby a bird gave a strange, croaking cry. The trees whispered to one another.

Rule Boy's music still sang through my head. I began to dance again, round and round the circle, throwing in a couple of handstands and a cartwheel for fun. Then, out of breath, I sat down on one of the stone seats and waited for Mr Gold. I didn't have a watch, of course, so I had no idea how long I'd been waiting. Had he forgotten? What if he'd changed his mind? Maybe he'd decided it was too dangerous, because he couldn't see me properly?

The sound of footsteps approached. Mr Gold limped towards the Amphitheatre, wearing green braces and baggy green trousers. Under his arm he carried two plastic mats.

'Mr Gold!' I shouted. 'Here I am!'

'You are in good time,' he said. 'An excellent beginning.'

'What shall we do first?' My body was tingling all over and itching to move again.

Mr Gold laid his stick down on one of the stone seats.

'Patience, child,' he said, with his crooked smile. 'The muscles must be stretched before we work them. Follow what I do. First, swing your arms.'

He began to swing his arms round and round, and I copied.

'Now, stretch up as high as you can. And bend down and touch your toes.'

He tossed me a mat, and we laid them down in the grass circle.

'Watch me.' Mr Gold lay on his back and brought one of his legs straight up in the air. I was surprised at how easily he did it. 'Now, you have a go.'

I tried to copy him. My muscles felt like elastic bands being stretched further than I ever thought they could go.

When we'd stretched every bit of our bodies, Mr Gold stood up.

'Now,' he said, 'show me what you can do.' And he went and sat on a stone seat.

So I showed him some somersaults, some cartwheels and my twenty-second handstand (I actually managed thirty seconds—it must have been all the stretching).

'Good,' he said, and I felt very proud. 'You have excellent balance. You must practise every day, to build up your strength.'

He delved in his pocket and, with a flourish, pulled out three large spotted handkerchiefs.

'Ever had a go at juggling?'

I shook my head.

'The best way to learn to juggle is with handkerchiefs, because they fall slowly.'

Mr Gold threw one of the handkerchiefs into the air, then the next, then the next. He caught each one as it fell. I remembered what he'd told me about being almost blind.

'Can you see them?' I asked.

'I can see the movement. But I could do this blindfold. In fact, I *did* juggle blindfold as part of the act.'

He threw the handkerchiefs over to me, one by one. I caught them and began to copy him. It wasn't as easy as it looked, but I soon got the hang of it.

'Keep the handkerchiefs,' Mr Gold said, 'and practise.'

I stuffed them into my pocket.

'How long did it take you to learn to be an acrobat?' I asked.

Mr Gold sat down.

'Many, many years,' he said. 'I began when I was younger than you, when me and Fred—'

'Who was Fred?'

'Fred was my twin brother,' said Mr Gold.

'You have a *twin*?'

I almost burst out and told him about *my* twin, then I slapped my hand over my mouth, just in time. Mr Gold must never find out about my plan to escape to the Academy. Luckily, he didn't seem to notice. His eyes were sad, as if they were looking into the past.

'Yes, Fred and I were twins,' he said. 'We trained together from when we were toddlers. Our dad was a great acrobat, the best in the world. So was his dad. Our family were all circus people.'

'Wow,' I said. 'So you were born in the circus?'

'I was,' said Mr Gold. 'Circus was the only life I knew.'

'I've read stories about children who run away to the circus. I used to wish *I* could do that when I lived with Sonia and Claude.'

'Well, Fred and I were a bit unusual,' said Mr Gold. 'Because we ran away *from* the circus.'

My mouth fell open. 'What? Why?'

'Remember what I told you about there being good circuses and bad circuses?'

I nodded.

'Sometimes good circuses turn bad.' He twirled his stick in his hands, round and round. 'And that's what happened to ours.'

'Would you... will you tell me about it?' I said.

'Child, it is not a happy story.'

'I don't mind sad stories,' I said.

Mr Gold thought for a moment. Then he gave a small nod.

'Very well,' he said.

And he began.

# GOOD AND BAD CIRCUS

'**O**ur circus was called Harlequin's,' said Mr Gold. 'We lived with our dad in a caravan.'

'I'd like to live in a caravan,' I said. 'I'd like to always be moving from place to place.'

'Yes,' said Mr Gold. 'Moving around would suit *you* very well.'

'But what about lessons? Did you and Fred go to school?'

'Not much. We learnt through using our eyes and our ears and our hands. And in circus, everyone is your teacher. For instance, there were three clowns at Harlequin's—Zippo, Hippo and Dippo. They were always playing tricks on us.'

'What did they teach you?'

'How to make people laugh—and cry.' Mr Gold smiled his crooked smile, up at one corner, down at the other. 'Then there was Zena Zeferilli, the tightrope walker. From her, we learnt balance, and bravery. The ringmaster, Mr Diogenes Dickens, was very stern, and a great character—he used to wax his moustache so it stuck out past his ears.'

'Did he teach you stuff too?'

'He did. He taught Fred and me how to beat the drum for the Grand Parade.'

'What exactly *is* the Grand Parade?'

'It's when all the acts enter the Big Top at the beginning of the show and parade around the ring. The orchestra played "The Circus March". Mr Diogenes Dickens would come out first, dressed in a top hat and tails, beating his drum and blowing his whistle, followed by the clowns and the acrobats, the trapeze artists, the stilt walkers, the jugglers, the horseback riders and all the rest...'

As Mr Gold talked, it was as if I was there. I heard the roar of the crowd, the piercing whistle of Mr Diogenes Dickens and the beat of his drum; I smelt sawdust and sweat; tasted sweet candyfloss and popcorn and hot dogs; reached out to touch the soft mouths of the horses and run my fingers through their coarse manes; heard the heavy thump of their hooves and their whinnying.

'Were there other animals?' I asked.

'There were dogs. And lions.'

'Lions?' I breathed in, thinking of the lion in the forest, and of the feral boy. 'Weren't they dangerous?'

'All wild animals can be dangerous,' said Mr Gold. 'But humans can be dangerous too.'

'Is that why Harlequin's turned bad? Because of a dangerous person?'

He paused. A bird flapped in the treetops above us. I waited, hoping Mr Gold wouldn't stop. Then he nodded.

'Merrick Murgatroyd,' he said. 'From the day he took over Harlequin's, and changed its name to Murgatroyd's, everything began to go wrong.'

'Who was he? What happened?'

'Murgatroyd was a fire-eater. A very clever one. But he was just about as bad as any human could be. All the circus folk avoided him, and not only because of his cruelty. He never washed. He wore the same clothes—a tattered black suit and dusty top hat—day in, day out. His teeth were broken and black, like old tombstones, and his breath made you want to be sick.'

I shivered.

'The first thing Murgatroyd did after taking over our circus was to cut everyone's pay. Circus performers need good food, and we could no longer afford to eat properly. But that was only the beginning.' Mr Gold's face became very serious. 'He forced the performers to do more and more dangerous tricks. And then he did away with the safety nets.'

I gasped. 'But they could have been killed!'

'You must understand that Murgatroyd loved to frighten and torment. It was said that he had once been married to a beautiful woman and that she died, and from that day on, he swore to make others suffer, just the way *he* had suffered. And of course, word spread, and plenty of people paid to see the new, dangerous acts. Only they were the sort of people who, like him, took pleasure in the prospect of an accident or a death.

'Then, when Fred and I were sixteen, Murgatroyd sent our dad away, to a circus in America. Dad was the greatest acrobat in Europe, and the American circus paid Murgatroyd a huge fee for him.'

'Didn't you and Fred go too?'

'Dad begged us to go with him. But we refused.'

'Why?'

'Because of the animals.' Mr Gold looked grave. 'It wasn't only humans that Murgatroyd tormented. He ordered the animals to be locked up, without exercise, and to be let out only to perform. He stopped the handlers from cleaning out the cages. The straw bedding was filthy and the animals were left to starve. Murgatroyd would cook himself a huge, juicy steak and deliberately eat it in front of the lions' cage. He said animals performed better when they were hungry. We couldn't go off to America and leave them to him.'

'But what could you do?'

'Fred and I used to sneak into the animal enclosure at night and smuggle in food and clean straw. There was an old lioness—Mabel—who had a cub called Kula. Kula was like a big kitten—huge soft paws and long whiskers, and her fur smelt warm and sweet. She loved Fred and me, and we'd let her out of her cage so that she could run and play in the ring.

'One night, we found Mabel sick, and lying in her own muck.' Mr Gold's face twisted in anger. 'She was barely able to stand, and Kula was shivering between her paws. We were about to open the cage when we heard a sound behind us. It was Murgatroyd. He had a gun, and was pointing it at Mabel.'

'What happened?' I crossed my fingers on both hands.

'Fred and I raced over and wrestled Murgatroyd to the ground, but it was too late. The gun went off. Mabel collapsed.'

'Did she die?'

Mr Gold nodded. He rubbed at his eyes, as if he was trying to rub away the memory. 'People came running. And Murgatroyd told them that we—Fred and I—had shot Mabel.'

I gasped. 'Surely nobody believed him?'

'They were too scared not to. Murgatroyd had them all under his thumb.'

'What did you do?'

'That night, when the circus was asleep, Fred and I packed all our things. Then we crept to the animals' cages. They had taken Mabel away, and little Kula was crouching, alone in the filthy straw, whimpering. We opened the cage and got her out. She licked our hands and faces with her rough tongue. Then we put her in the back of our rusty old truck and drove away before morning. And that's how we ran away from the circus.'

'Where did you go? What happened then?'

Mr Gold suddenly seemed to remember where we were.

'Child, you need your breakfast. Sometimes my memories are so strong that I get carried away.' He stood up. 'You have done well. Remember to practise every day.'

'But we will have more lessons?' I couldn't breathe until he agreed.

'Are you sure you want to be an acrobat after all I've told you?'

'I'm sure.'

Mr Gold gave his crooked smile. 'Very well. Meet me here tomorrow at the same time.'

I couldn't help jumping up and down with joy.

'And will you tell me what happened next, after you and Fred and Kula ran away?'

A shadow passed over Mr Gold's face. 'Perhaps. Now, off you go to breakfast. Miss Cruet won't be happy if you're late.'

'I'm not afraid of Miss Cruet!' I laughed. 'I'm not afraid of *anything*!'

I cartwheeled across the grass circle and ran through the wood, just as the school bell rang for breakfast.

# THE SHOW

The others were all tucking into breakfast when I arrived, panting, and slid into my chair. The feral boy stopped eating as soon as he saw me and stared at me, a large piece of toast (smeared with chocolate sauce) hanging from his mouth. Miss Cruet, her bun toppling, glared at me too.

'Punctuality,' she said, 'is obviously an alien concept to you. One more late arrival, and you will be sent to the Room of Reflection.'

'Where've you been anyway?' said Rule Boy, slicing boiled egg into his porridge.

Already we were getting used to the strange meals at Nobodies, and we'd even begun to compete to see who could eat the oddest combinations. I pretended I hadn't heard Rule Boy's question. Acrobatics with Mr Gold was my special secret.

Miss Cruet banged a spoon on the table. 'Pay attention!'

Everyone except Saddo stopped eating.

'I have an announcement.'

Custard looked anxious, and stuck her thumb in her mouth.

'In seven weeks,' said Miss Cruet, 'Halloween will be here, and Mr Gold and I have been talking about creating an entertainment.'

'Krusty can do some clowning,' muttered Rule Boy, with a smirk.

'Shut *up*,' I said.

'Silence!' Miss Cruet barked, scattering hairpins into Saddo's muesli.

He picked them out and carried on eating. The feral boy grabbed one and threaded it in his matted hair.

'You will each have the opportunity to perform,' said Miss Cruet. 'Mr Gold and I will arrange a special audience. We will expect to be entertained.'

'What if we don't want to?' mumbled Saddo through a mouthful of muesli and ketchup.

'I can't p-perform,' said Custard, going pale.

'There will be no excuses,' said Miss Cruet. 'Lessons this morning are cancelled, and instead you will discuss the entertainment and come up with ideas.'

When Miss Cruet had swept out, I said: 'Let's go down to the Amphitheatre and talk there.'

'It's cold outside,' moaned Saddo, taking the feral boy's last slice of toast and cramming it into his mouth.

'Well, put your hoodie on,' I said. 'Come on!'

Grumbling and muttering, the others followed me. The feral boy stayed right at my heels, like he always did. If I'd stopped suddenly, he'd have knocked me over. Custard stayed as far away from him as possible.

*

We sat on the cold stone seats of the Amphitheatre. Saddo shivered.

'This was a *stupid* idea,' he said. 'I'm freezing.'

'Oh, shut up, misery guts,' said Rule Boy. 'If you exercised more, you'd stay warm.' He stood up on one of the seats. 'Now, let's decide about this entertainment. I will be the organizer.'

I felt cross. Why did Rule Boy always have to be boss? I picked up a stick from the ground.

'No one should be in charge,' I said. 'We can all take it in turns with the Talking Stick and say our ideas.'

Rule Boy jumped down from the seat and grabbed the stick.

'Me first then. Because I have a great idea. We'll do a musical show and I will perform on my violin. I shall play Tchaikovsky, Shostakovich and Mendelssohn.'

'What's he on about?' said Saddo.

'Shut *up*, whinger,' said Rule Boy. 'I have the stick, so you can't talk. Now, you've each got to decide what you're going to do in the show.' He handed the stick to me.

'I'm going to do acrobatics.' Little shivers of excitement ran up and down my spine. If I had lots of lessons with Mr Gold in the next seven weeks, I'd be really good by Halloween and Mr Gold would be proud.

Rule Boy grabbed the stick. 'Acrobatics isn't musical,' he said.

'Too bad,' I said. 'Because it's what I'm going to do.'

I leapt into the grass circle and performed some cartwheels. Then I did a backflip and ended with a deep bow.

Rule Boy pointed. There was the feral boy, right behind me, bowing too.

'Lion Boy copied everything you did!' Rule Boy grinned.

All the excitement drained out of me and I flopped down on a seat. *Why* did the feral boy have to hang around and copy me? What if he turned out to be a better acrobat than me?

Rule Boy tossed the stick to Saddo.

'I'm no good at anything,' he said, his mouth turning down.

'You can stand around looking miserable then,' said Rule Boy. 'You'll be dead good at that.'

Saddo looked as if he wanted to hit him. He grabbed the stick out of Rule Boy's hands.

'All right,' he said. 'Let's do a Halloween show. It's Halloween night—we can dress up as ghosts and... and vampires and stuff.'

'No!' whimpered Custard. 'I hate Halloween. My m-mum says it's when the veil between the w-worlds is thinnest, so bad things can happen.'

'Wimp,' muttered Rule Boy.

Then I had an idea. I held out my hand for the stick.

'Let's do a circus show,' I said.

'That's a crummy idea,' said Rule Boy.

'It's not!' I said. 'And I'm holding the stick, so listen.' I jumped down into the grass circle.

'It'll be the greatest show on earth,' I said. 'I'll be the acrobat, and I'll do juggling and handstands and cartwheels and somersaults. And *you*...' I pointed at Rule

Boy, 'can be the orchestra, and you can play your Shosta-thingy—'

'Shostakovich,' said Rule Boy.

'Yes, that. And Feral can be the lion.'

The feral boy gave a huge roar, making us all jump. Custard stuck her fingers in her ears and squeaked.

'See?' I said. 'He'll be brilliant.'

Then, to my surprise, the feral boy spoke. Until now he hadn't said a word, apart from his roars and growls.

'Lion,' he said. 'Mama.'

We all stared at him.

Then Rule Boy began to laugh. 'A lion?' he chortled. 'Your mother is a lion? Liar, liar, pants on fire!'

The feral boy suddenly pushed out his chest, threw back his mane of hair and gave a low growl, deep and menacing.

'Mama lion,' he said again.

'A lion for a mother!' Rule Boy was still laughing. 'Where did you live? In Africa? Did you eat raw meat? You're seriously weird...'

The feral boy's face crumpled as if he was about to cry.

'Stop it!' I shouted at Rule Boy. 'Tell him you don't mean it.'

'Oh yes I do,' muttered Rule Boy, smirking.

I turned my back on him. 'Anyhow, we were talking about the circus show.' I looked at Saddo and Custard. 'What about you two—what can you do?'

'I c-can't do anything,' said Custard.

'Not doing it,' mumbled Saddo.

'Maybe... maybe you could be dogs, or jugglers, or something,' I said.

I could see it already—Rule Boy playing 'The Circus March' on his violin, Feral roaring and scaring the audience, and me in my golden leotard performing acts of daring. Maybe Mr Gold could even teach me how to use the swing as a trapeze.

'All right then,' said Rule Boy—and I could see that he liked the idea of being the whole orchestra and showing off.

'Let's all meet here on Saturday at twelve o'clock to rehearse,' I said.

And because I was so excited I cartwheeled round the grass circle until I was out of breath.

That was the beginning of our circus.

# DODGING FERAL

*TAP... TAP... TAP...*

I woke next morning to a strange sound coming from the wall beside my bed. I put my ear to it and listened.

*TAP... TAP... TAP...*

The clock above the door showed it was just after seven. I was meeting Mr Gold in the Amphitheatre for our next lesson at seven thirty.

Custard was still asleep, her blanket up around her ears. I pulled on my sweatshirt, trousers and trainers and tiptoed into the corridor. The door to the boys' dormitory was ajar. I slipped inside.

Saddo, a long hump in bed, was snoring.

Rule Boy lay on his back, his eyes closed. As the tapping paused, he muttered in his sleep. 'Let him out,' he said. 'Please, let him go.'

*TAP... TAP... TAP...*

Then I saw where the tapping was coming from.

Feral sat cross-legged on his bed, tapping on the wall with his knuckles. He tapped three times and paused, listening. Then he tapped again.

'What do you think you're doing?' I said loudly.

'Whaaa?' Rule Boy woke with a start and scrabbled for his glasses.

Feral looked up and grinned. 'Friend.'

I stomped out of the dormitory and slammed the door hard. *Why* wouldn't Feral leave me alone?

I didn't stop to brush my teeth. I ran down the stairs and unbolted the back door as quietly as I could. As I set off down the path, I glanced back at the school. The back door opened. It was Feral. I ducked behind the greenhouse. Feral sniffed the air like a bloodhound and bounded down the steps.

I began to run. As I got to the orchard, where the path split in two, I swung up into the branches of an apple tree and pressed myself against the trunk. Below me, Feral skidded to a halt and looked around. All I could see of him was his mass of hair and his dirty trainers. I held my breath. How could I distract him?

An apple was hanging just above my head. As silently as I could, I reached up and broke it from its twig. Then I threw it as hard as I could down the right-hand path. It landed with a splat, out of sight. Feral gave a yelp, like a dog chasing a stick, and bounded off down the path. As his footsteps faded away, I slithered down the tree and set off along the left-hand path, through the wood towards the Amphitheatre.

When I arrived, Mr Gold was sitting on a stone seat. In spite of the morning chill, he wore a canary-yellow T-shirt and his old green baggy trousers. Today's braces were turquoise with gold stars on them.

'Ready to begin?' he said, smiling his crooked smile at me.

I practised my handstands and my juggling. Then Mr Gold sent me over to the swing and showed me how to hang upside down from it, with my legs twisted around the ropes. It felt magical to see the world swinging upside down. After that, I did twenty cartwheels.

'Excellent work,' said Mr Gold, as I finished, panting. 'Now, take a rest.'

'I don't need a rest!' I said. 'I could go on forever!'

Mr Gold thought for a moment. 'What you need now is someone to train with, just like Fred and me.'

'It's OK,' I said quickly. 'I like doing this on my own.'

The last thing I wanted was Rule Boy bossing me about, or Custard being scared, or Saddo moaning. Or—worst of all—Feral hanging around me, copying everything I did.

'In circus, we depend on other people,' said Mr Gold quietly, peering at me in his odd, distant way. 'We trust them. If you don't find someone to trust, life will be pretty lonely.'

The wood was very quiet. I kicked at a tuft of grass. There was something I wanted to say, but I was a bit scared of saying it. I looked up at Mr Gold.

'I *do* have someone to trust,' I said, my voice shaking. 'I trust *you*.'

Mr Gold smiled. 'Thank you,' he said. 'I am honoured. But think about what I've said.'

'All right.' I crossed my fingers behind my back.

150

I sat down on the mat. 'Will you tell me what happened next—after you and Fred and Kula ran away from Murgatroyd's Circus?'

Mr Gold sat down. 'Fred and I got a job in another circus. A good one, quite close to here, where the animals and the performers were treated well.'

'What happened to Murgatroyd?'

A shadow passed over Mr Gold's face. 'We reported him to the police, and Murgatroyd's Circus was shut down.'

'Yay!' I said. 'Served him right!'

'Indeed,' said Mr Gold. He didn't look very happy though. 'But, in doing that, we broke the most important rule of circus.'

'What rule?'

'Circus folk look after their own. They don't bring outside people in, and they never betray other circus folk. Do you remember *all for one, and one for all*?'

I nodded. 'But you did the right thing.'

'We had to do it—we couldn't let the animals suffer any more.'

'What about Kula?'

'Kula grew into a fine young lioness. And she always let me and Fred pet her and play with her.'

'Did you train her?'

Mr Gold shook his head. 'We weren't trainers,' he said. 'But the trainer at the circus was the best, even though she was only sixteen.'

'I saw her! She was in that photo of the Grand Parade. What was her name?'

'Leonora. From the moment she and Kula met, they were inseparable. Leonora would often sleep in Kula's cage with her, curled up together in the straw.'

I could almost feel Kula's soft fur and hear her low purring. Then my head jerked up—I realized that the sound wasn't in my head. Someone *was* purring.

It was coming from the wood, behind me.

# FERAL SPOILS IT

I swivelled round, but there was no one there.

'There's something in the wood,' I whispered. 'Can you hear it?'

The purring, growling sound continued, like a distant rumble of thunder.

'Who's there?' called Mr Gold.

From behind a tree, Feral emerged on all fours, his hair sweeping the ground.

'Come,' said Mr Gold, and Feral padded into the grass circle and stood right beside me, staring at me with his tawny eyes.

I turned away. Why did he have to follow me here and spoil everything?

'Were you listening to the story?' said Mr Gold.

Feral nodded. 'Lion,' he said.

'I'd better go,' I said. 'It must be breakfast time.'

'Wait a moment.' Mr Gold looked from me to Feral, and back again. 'You two are the same height and build. The boy would be an excellent partner for you.'

'No!' I clenched my fists.

'What's wrong, child?' said Mr Gold.

'Him!' I said. 'He spoils everything—'

I'd been happier than I'd ever been in my life, because of the lessons. And now Feral would be there all the time, staring at my burn and copying me, and Mr Gold would teach *him* to be an acrobat and he'd probably be far better than me and nothing would be special any more.

I turned and ran into the wood. Mr Gold called after me, but I ignored him. Then I heard footsteps, echoing mine. Feral was following me yet again. That Feeling began to fizz and boil inside me. I ran faster and faster, dodging tree trunks and bushes, crashing through brambles. The trees whizzed past me in a blur, and I kept tripping on roots and stones because my tears almost blinded me. I turned for a moment to see if Feral was catching up with me—and didn't see the tree root snaking over the muddy path ahead. I tripped over it and fell headlong into a large patch of nettles.

'O*w, ow, OW!!!*' I sat in the mud, my hands and arms and face stinging like I'd fallen in a bees' nest.

The next thing I knew, a pair of grubby hands had grasped my arms and hauled me to my feet, and a pair of tawny eyes was staring into mine. That Feeling was bubbling through my insides like molten lava. I couldn't look at Feral because I knew that if I did, I might do something really horrible, like hit him. I bent over and pressed my hands to my scratched legs and ankles. The nettle stings were tingling and itching, making my skin burn.

Then, Feral touched me right on the back of my neck, where my name was.

That did it. I lost my temper. A voice I'd never heard before came shouting out of my mouth.

x

154

'LEAVE ME ALONE!!!'

I pushed Feral with all my strength and he fell over backwards in the mud. He rolled over onto all fours and a low growl came out of his throat. Maybe he was going to spring at me and bite me, but I didn't care.

'Just GET AWAY from me! And don't you EVER come near me again!'

For a long moment, Feral gazed at me, his eyes full of hurt. Then he turned and padded away.

My legs shook and tears rolled down my face. I'd never lost my temper and pushed someone, ever. And now everything was spoilt. Mr Gold's words kept going round and round in my head: *'If you don't find someone to trust, life will be pretty lonely.'*

If only my twin was here instead of Feral. We could train together every day, just like Mr Gold and Fred. I'd trust her with my life, and she'd trust me with hers.

As I thought these things, the wood suddenly became very quiet. It was as if everything had stopped breathing and was waiting for something to happen. Slowly, I wiped my tears and looked around. Was someone—or something—watching me?

Then, high in an ancient tree above my head, there was a flapping of wings. I stared up. A shower of golden-yellow leaves fluttered down like confetti. They lay on the muddy ground around my feet, and that warm, chocolatey feeling seeped through me, as if an invisible someone was giving me a big, comforting hug.

And then the next message came.

# NEXT DOOR

**A**s I stared up at the tree, the flapping got louder and faster and more excited, and lots more golden-yellow leaves came spiralling down. Then a bird flew out from the branches. Its pale grey wings carried it down, down, down... floating on the air... until it landed on a bush, right beside me, and it peered up at me with its soft dark eyes, as if it was trying to speak. It looked exactly like the dove I'd seen before—the one which had untangled the balloon in Sonia and Claude's garden, and which had brought me my golden leotard.

'Is it really you again?' I whispered.

The dove put its head on one side, listening.

*Turrrr! Turrrr!*

Then, before I could say anything else, it hopped to the ground and began to peck at the fallen leaves, carefully lifting each one in its bill and placing it beside the next. Every now and then, it raised its head and gazed at me. What was it doing? Again and again, it picked up a leaf and placed it beside the others. And then I blinked, and realized.

The dove was making words, leaf by leaf, on the ground. At last it placed the final leaf and nodded its head at me.

Then it opened its grey wings and flew up, up through the trees and into the sky, and with its sad, haunting cry, it disappeared into the blue.

I rubbed my eyes, and read the finished message:

*Flynn, of this you can be sure:*
*Your twin is living right next door.*

So it really *was* true—the girl with the marmalade curls *was* my twin, and she was waiting for me at the school next door, just as I'd hoped. I wanted to kick myself. I'd already been at Nobodies for four whole days, but I'd got distracted, what with rescuing Feral and the lessons with Mr Gold. I had to get to the Academy. I just *had* to. In the distance, the sound of voices laughing and shouting drifted through the trees. The children at the Academy were out playing.

I hurried down the path until I got to the orchard. There was the high brick wall which divided the two schools. My twin might be just on the other side of the wall, not even knowing I was here. I looked round to make sure the coast was clear. Then I crept up to the wall. Low voices were talking on the other side.

'Hello!' I shouted.

The voices stopped abruptly. There was a long silence. Then someone giggled.

'Hello!' I shouted again. 'I need help.'

A voice said: 'It's one of the Nobodies.'

'A freak!' laughed another.

'I'm not a freak!' I shouted. 'My twin is at your school. Please help me find her—'

A hand gripped my shoulder. I jumped. Surely Feral hadn't followed me again?

I turned to find the hand belonged to Miss Cruet. And, judging by the look on her face, I was in Big Trouble.

'Remind me of the school rules.' Miss Cruet's voice was dangerously quiet. 'Specifically rule two.'

'No contact with the school next door,' I muttered.

'Then why were you shouting over the wall?'

'I... I just thought I would.'

'*You just thought you would.*' Miss Cruet's knitted boot was tapping ominously on the ground. 'Exactly what is it about the school that fascinates you so?'

I thought quickly. 'It's got a pool, and a cinema and a gym. And... pizzas and Easter eggs and chocolate fountains—'

'Hmph!' snorted Miss Cruet, showering the ground with hairpins. 'So you decided to break a school rule simply in order to indulge your greed for junk food?'

I hung my head.

Miss Cruet grabbed my arm. 'One hour in the Room of Reflection. Now!'

Miss Cruet opened the door to the Room of Reflection and pushed me inside. The bolt snapped shut.

My heart beat fast. Any minute now, I'd see the Bird again and it would give me the answer it had promised—it would tell me how to get into the school next door and find my twin. The room was dark, just as it had been last time. I felt up the wall for the light switch and clicked it on. The bulb in the ceiling slowly lit up, casting a dim light on the bare floorboards and the empty walls. There was the big, carved mirror at the far end of the room. I looked around for the cabinet.

It wasn't there.

'Bird!' I shouted. 'I'm back!'

Nothing happened. No cabinet appeared.

'I'm back!' I shouted again. 'You said you'd give me my answer!'

But my voice echoed round the empty room.

I walked slowly round the room, running my fingers over the bare walls. I didn't know what I was looking for—I just wanted to be sure that my eyes weren't playing tricks on me, that the cabinet really wasn't there. When I got back to where I'd started, I turned my back to the wall and slid down until I was sitting on the floor.

Then I heard a voice.

It wasn't the Bird's croak. It wasn't Miss Cruet's snap, and it wasn't Mr Gold's rusty tones. It wasn't Rule Boy's sneering voice or Feral's growl, or Custard's stutter, or Saddo's whine.

It was the sweetest voice I had ever heard in my life—like birdsong and waves and summer breezes and soft bells chiming.

And it was calling my name.

# I FIND HER

'Flynn... Flynn...'

*Where is the voice coming from?* It seemed to be everywhere, all around me, stealing into my ears and winding around my heart. Was I going bonkers? Maybe there really *was* something wrong with me.

'Flynn... Oh, Flynn...'

My name sounded so lovely whispered by the voice.

Now it seemed to be coming from the mirror. With shaking legs, I walked over to it.

'Look, Flynn. Look in the mirror...'

I stared at my reflection. There I was, with my burn and my curls. But, somehow, I looked different. My eyes looked sort of scared but also full of hope.

'Come closer...'

I moved so that my face was right up against the surface of the mirror. My breath misted the black-spotted glass, until my reflection disappeared and all I could see was the mist.

'Look, Flynn. Look...'

I stared. The mist was clearing. In the dim light, I saw the reflection of myself.

Except that it wasn't me.

It was a girl who looked just like me—the same height, the same brown eyes, the same freckled nose. Her hair was marmalade coloured, like mine, but while mine was cut in a rough, shoulder-length bob, the girl's hair hung in shining curls almost to her waist. And instead of a shabby sweatshirt and trousers, she wore the uniform of the school next door: a crisp white shirt, a navy skirt and a blue-and-silver striped tie.

But what I couldn't stop staring at was her face. Her cheeks were smooth and white and perfect. There was no burn mark at all.

My hand flew out to touch her, and it hit the glass of the mirror. I didn't even cry out. All I could do was stare at my twin, trying to take in every inch of her, just in case she vanished. Then she gave a laugh so beautiful that I wanted to catch it in my fingers and keep it forever.

'Oh, Flynn!' she said, and this time her voice was like honey and wildflowers and rainbows. 'At last—at last you're here! I've been so lonely, waiting for you.'

I opened my mouth to speak, but nothing came out.

'Say something, Flynn! I want to hear your voice!'

'Oh!' I gasped, and words began to tumble out. 'I've-been-trying-and-trying-to-find-you. Is-it-really-you? Are-you-real?'

'I'm real,' said the girl, with the sweetest smile.

'What's your name?'

Was her name tattooed on the back of her neck, like mine? I wanted to ask her to lift up her hair and show me, but it felt too scary to do it.

'My name is Silver,' she said, and her smile was like the warmest hug on the coldest day.

*Silver.* I wanted to say it over and over. *Silver. Silver and Flynn.* The more I stared at her, the more all the mysterious things that had happened began to make sense.

'It was *you*, wasn't it?' I said. 'It was you who arranged all the messages?'

'What messages?'

'Don't you remember? The messages the doves brought— telling me about my name, and about you being alive and living next door.'

'Oh, *those* messages! I'm so excited to see you that I forgot! Yes—yes, it was me who sent them.'

My heart felt like it was being pulled through the glass to her. How could I wait a moment longer?

'I want to be with you!' I cried.

'Me too,' said Silver. 'I've been so unhappy without you.' And a single tear rolled down her cheek.

I couldn't bear it. There *must* be a way.

'I've thought and thought how to get to your school,' I said, 'but the wall is too high to climb, and when I shouted over it, the children just called me a freak.'

'Oh, them.' Silver frowned, and it was like clouds rolling in front of the sun. 'They won't help us. They're jealous of us being twins.'

'How then?' I said. 'How can we be together?'

Silver leant towards the glass and began to whisper.

'There is a way,' she said. 'But you have to make me a promise.'

'Anything!' I whispered back.

'You must promise never, *never* to tell your teachers about me. If they know, they'll forbid us to meet and we'll lose one another forever!'

The thought of losing Silver, now that I'd found her, made my heart squeeze as if it would shatter.

'I promise,' I said.

'Shhh,' said Silver. 'Someone's coming.'

Footsteps were creaking up the stairs.

'Quick, Flynn, listen,' whispered Silver. 'Meet me here at full moon, at the stroke of midnight.'

'But how? Miss Cruet sleeps on the floor below here. How can I—'

'I know you can find a way. I trust you.'

She held her hand up to the glass. I placed my own hand there too, so our palms met, exactly the same size, and we gazed at one another, unable to say goodbye.

There was a rattling of the bolt. Miss Cruet was back. Surely I'd only been here a few minutes? Maybe she'd changed her mind about punishing me.

'Full moon,' said Silver, her voice beginning to fade. 'At midnight...'

Then she was gone, and I was alone, staring at my old self in the mirror, with my raggedy hair and my shabby clothes and my burn.

The door swung open. I turned, expecting to see Miss Cruet, but it wasn't her—it was Mr Gold. He limped in, but instead of looking at me, his eyes peered around the room.

'Child,' he said, 'are you all right?'

I couldn't help smiling. 'Yes—yes, I'm fine.'

If only I could tell him that I had a twin, just like he did. That she was more special than anyone in the world—that soon we would be together forever. But I'd made my promise. I covered my mouth with my hands so that the words wouldn't jump out.

'Did something... happen in here?' said Mr Gold. 'I heard voices. Did you see your bird again?'

I shook my head. I was glad he could only see my outline, not my face, because I was sure I was blushing.

Mr Gold peered at me, then he nodded and limped towards the door.

'Come on then. Miss Cruet has kept you some breakfast.'

'I'm not hungry,' I said, which was true. I felt full—full of Silver. Her face and her voice filled my head.

I followed Mr Gold downstairs. Outside his study, he stopped, leaning on his stick.

'You were upset about my suggestion that you work at acrobatics with the boy,' he said.

I nodded, but everything that had happened before meeting Silver seemed a million years ago.

'You need not work with him if you don't wish to,' said Mr Gold. 'But he wants to come to the lessons, and to learn for himself. So how about it? Do you want to continue with your lessons?'

'Oh... yes. Yes, I do.'

I could teach Silver everything that Mr Gold taught me. *Silver and Flynn, the Daredevil Twins.* We would perform together—Silver in a silvery leotard, me in my golden one—as the audience roared and gasped and clapped.

'Shall we meet tomorrow, at seven thirty?' said Mr Gold.

I nodded. 'When is full moon?'

Mr Gold looked surprised. 'Tomorrow night, I believe. Why do you ask?'

'I... just wondered.'

It didn't matter any more about Feral. Nothing mattered except that tomorrow night, at full moon, I would see my twin again.

For the first time in my life, I didn't feel alone.

# THE LION TRAINER

**N**ext morning, I woke early. All night I'd dreamt about Silver. Tonight, at full moon, we would meet again. Excitement whizzed round my body, streaking about in my tummy and zapping like lightning bolts down my arms and legs. I jumped at a familiar sound from the wall next to my bed.

*TAP... TAP... TAP...*

My heart plummeted as I remembered that Feral would be coming to acrobatics lessons from now on.

I got up and pulled on my clothes. Custard shot up in bed, clutching her blanket around her.

'What's that n-noise?'

'It's Feral, tapping on the wall.'

'Why's he d-doing that?'

'He says he's being friendly,' I said crossly.

'Oh,' said Custard, putting her thumb in her mouth. 'W-why are you up so early?'

There didn't seem to be much point in keeping the lessons a secret any more, not now that Feral was going to be there too.

'Mr Gold is teaching me acrobatics, in the Amphitheatre. For the show.'

'C-can I come and watch?'

'If you want.'

Custard hopped out of bed and began to pull her clothes on. At that moment, Feral appeared in the doorway, his eyes stuck to me as usual.

'Is *he* c-coming too?' said Custard.

I nodded. 'We'd better get a move on. The lesson starts at seven thirty.'

Mr Gold was sitting on a stone seat, his stick propped beside him and the two mats laid out on the grass. His braces today had red-and-green stripes.

'Good morning,' he said, peering at Custard. 'Do we have another recruit?'

'I'm not *d-doing* it,' said Custard. 'I just want to watch.'

She settled herself and her blanket on a seat.

Feral ran round in circles, like a dog chasing its tail.

'Wait, boy.' Mr Gold searched in the pocket of his trousers. He pulled out a rubber band. 'If you want to do acrobatics, you must tie up your hair.'

Feral stared at the rubber band, then shook his head violently.

'No mane,' he growled.

'It's for safety,' said Mr Gold. 'Otherwise your hair may get caught, like it did when you got stuck in the tree.'

Feral growled again. 'No,' he said. 'No mane.'

'Then you must sit and watch,' said Mr Gold.

Feral growled some more, but eventually went and sat beside Custard. She edged away from him. I began to feel better. I was going to be the only acrobat in the circus show after all.

Mr Gold put me through my paces. I cartwheeled, and showed him my forty-second handstand and my juggling. Custard clapped. Feral growled.

'Excellent, child,' said Mr Gold, and I could tell he was really pleased.

'Mr Gold's been telling us about how he ran away from the circus with a lion cub called Kula,' I told Custard, 'and about a young lion trainer called Leonora. Please, Mr Gold, tell us more about Leonora?'

Mr Gold looked sad. Maybe he didn't like thinking about the circus when he couldn't work there any more. Maybe I shouldn't have asked him about it. But Custard was excited.

'Tell me the story! I l-love stories!'

Mr Gold gave his lopsided smile. 'What do you want to know?'

'What did Leonora look like?'

'She was small and thin, rather like you,' said Mr Gold. 'And very strong. She had long, curly hair. And she was covered in tattoos.'

'Tattoos?' I said. My fingers crept up to the back of my neck, where my name was.

'What sort of t-tattoos?' asked Custard.

'Lions, of course. And birds,' said Mr Gold. 'Leonora loved birds. She had a pair of turtle doves which she hatched from eggs. She found an abandoned nest and took the eggs and warmed them until they hatched. Everywhere she went, the turtle doves went too, perched on her shoulders or on her head.'

I thought of the dove that had brought me messages. Maybe I could ask it to be *my* friend if it appeared again.

'How did Leonora get to be a lion trainer when she was only sixteen?' I said. 'She must have been so brave.'

'She was the bravest person I knew,' said Mr Gold. 'But she was also the most frightened.'

'Frightened?' said Custard, her eyes wide. 'But she t-trained the lions!'

'She wasn't afraid of lions. And she trusted Kula with her life. During their act, Kula would open her jaws wide—her teeth were very sharp—and Leonora would put her head right inside Kula's mouth.'

'In h-her *mouth*?' Custard shivered and drew her yellow blanket around herself.

'What *was* she frightened of?' I asked.

'People,' said Mr Gold. 'She didn't trust them. She stayed away from the other circus folk. Sometimes, early in the morning, Fred and I would visit Kula and there was Leonora, curled up with her in the straw.'

'Who was F-Fred?' said Custard.

'Fred was Mr Gold's brother,' I told her. 'They were the Gravity-defying Golds.'

I turned to Mr Gold. For some reason, he was looking terribly sad. 'What happened next, at the circus?'

Mr Gold gave a little shake of his shoulders, as if he was shrugging away a bad memory.

'Fred and Leonora got married!'

'But you said Leonora was frightened of people!' I said. 'How come she married Fred?'

'Because she loved him,' said Mr Gold. 'Because he too loved Kula and she grew to trust him.'

'Tell us about the w-wedding!' said Custard. 'Did they g-go to church? What did Leonora wear?'

'They were wed in the Big Top,' said Mr Gold. 'It was a real circus wedding with a Grand Parade. And because we were the Golds, everyone wore yellow or gold. Leonora wore a golden costume, all sequins and pearls and crystals...'

I remembered my own golden leotard, hidden under my pillow in the dormitory. I longed to try it on again. But I wouldn't—not until the night of our circus show.

'Fred and I dressed in golden costumes too, with our faces painted gold. I was Fred's best man, and Kula was the bridesmaid—Leonora made her a collar of yellow flowers and brushed her golden mane until it shone. Even Leonora's turtle doves had golden ribbons tied around their legs. They carried little boxes of rose petals in their bills and scattered them over Fred and Leonora as Fred put a gold ring upon Leonora's finger, and they promised to love one another until—'

Mr Gold stopped.

'Until what?' I said.

But Mr Gold just ran his fingers through his mop of curls and shook his head.

Feral, who had been listening to the story, suddenly jumped to his feet.

'Train,' he said, and looked at us all.

'He's saying he wants a trainer, for the show,' I said. Then I added quickly: 'I can't do it—I'm going to be the acrobat.'

We all looked at Custard. She shrank back.

'Are you afraid, child?' said Mr Gold. I remembered how he could see inside people, to what they were feeling.

Custard nodded. 'I'm really, really scared of l-lions.'

'It's OK to be afraid,' said Mr Gold. 'There isn't a single person in the world who is fearless, though some make a better job at hiding it than others. But deep down inside, we are all afraid of something.'

'Even you?' I said, feeling a bit cheeky. 'What are *you* afraid of?'

Mr Gold picked up his stick and frowned. 'Remember what I told you about Merrick Murgatroyd?'

'The wicked fire-eater who took over the circus and shot Mabel?'

Mr Gold nodded. 'I feared him.'

'But you wrestled the gun away from him and reported him to the police!'

'I did. Because, just in that moment, Kula and Mabel were more important than my fear. But I still have the fear. I still fear Murgatroyd.'

He turned to Custard. 'Fear is nothing to be ashamed of,' he said. 'The bravest people are those who show courage when they are afraid.'

There was a long silence, as he and Custard looked at one another.

Then Custard shivered and said: 'What does a trainer have to d-do?'

'She teaches the lion to perform,' said Mr Gold. 'She uses a long stick—a bit like this one.' And he held out his stick to Custard.

'B-but that's cruel,' said Custard, putting her hands behind her back.

'The stick isn't used to hurt the lion,' said Mr Gold. 'It's used to get its attention. Have you ever dangled a thread of wool in front of a kitten for it to chase? Well, it's a bit like that.'

'Claude and Sonia said lion taming was wrong,' I said. 'They signed petitions against having animals in circuses. Only... only they spent a lot of time trying to tame *me*.'

Mr Gold nodded as if he understood. 'There's a difference,' he said quietly, 'between training and taming. Training helps someone to become stronger—your training in acrobatics is helping you develop your skills and your strengths.'

'What about t-taming?' said Custard.

'Taming is just a way of stopping the wildness.'

'Wild,' said Feral. His tawny eyes gazed from Mr Gold to me and Custard.

The wood around the Amphitheatre rustled and murmured.

'What did Leonora w-wear when she trained Kula?' said Custard.

'She wore a golden cloak,' said Mr Gold.

Custard looked down at her yellow blanket, then she looked at Feral, who was still watching her, his head on one side.

'How d-does a trainer teach a lion?' she whispered.

'She speaks to the lion very kindly and firmly,' said Mr Gold. 'And gives it instructions. She might point her stick and say, "Kula—roll over!" And Kula would lie on her back and roll.'

Custard's face was even paler than usual. Her legs were trembling so it seemed like she would fall over at any moment. Then, with shaking fingers, she wrapped the blanket over her shoulders like a cloak and picked up Mr Gold's stick. She took a deep breath and pointed the stick at Feral.

'Roll over!' she whispered.

Feral didn't seem to hear her.

'Try it a little louder,' said Mr Gold.

Custard took a deep breath.

'ROLL OVER!'

Feral lay on the ground and gave a great roll.

Custard jumped up and down with excitement.

'I did it! I did it!'

Feral leapt to his feet, opened his jaws and gave an ear-splitting roar. Custard screamed and fell over backwards into the ring, stuffing her fingers in her ears.

Then Feral did a strange thing. He got down on all fours and very slowly padded over to Custard, whose eyes were tight shut. A sound came from his throat, gentle and vibrating, like a cat's purr. Then he leant down over Custard and licked her cheek. Custard shot to her feet, wiping her face, her eyes like saucers. Feral went on purring.

She and Feral looked at one another for a long time. Then, she reached out a trembling hand, and stroked Feral's mane of hair. He purred even louder.

'Train,' he said.

And he rubbed his head against Custard, just like a friendly cat. Custard looked half pleased, half horrified at Feral's matted mane.

'Your mane is in a m-mess,' she said. 'If I'm going to be your trainer, I have to l-look after you. I'll wash it for you when we get back.'

Feral took a step backwards, a growl in his throat.

'OK,' agreed Custard hastily. 'No w-washing.'

'Hooray!' I shouted. 'We've got a lion-training act for the show!'

Mr Gold grinned.

'In the best circuses, people look after one another. They trust one another. They never let one another down. Remember the Three Musketeers?' He held up his hand. '*All for one...*'

'*... and one for all!*' we shouted, high-fiving him.

# MIDNIGHT

That night, I lay wide awake in bed, tingling with excitement. It was quite light in the dormitory, in spite of it being so late, and streaks of pale moonlight crept around the curtains and made strange patterns on the walls and over the floor.

The clock ticked towards midnight. My legs itched to get out of bed and run up the stairs to the Room of Reflection, but I made myself wait. '*Full moon,*' Silver had said, '*at the stroke of midnight.*' So midnight it would be.

The clock said twenty to twelve when I heard a sound: the faint creak of a bed from the boys' dormitory next door. Then the lightest of footfalls and the sound of a door gently opening and closing. I groaned inside. If someone else was awake, it would make my mission hard, if not impossible. I held my breath. Footsteps passed the door and disappeared down the corridor. I waited while the clock ticked on another five minutes, then, as quietly as I could, I got up and pulled on my clothes over my pyjamas.

Custard was deep in dreamland. All I could see of her was her yellow wispy hair under her blanket. I tiptoed to the door, opened it and looked up and down the corridor. It was empty.

Silently, I climbed the stairs towards the floor where Miss Cruet and Mr Gold slept, careful to avoid the second-to-the-top one, which creaked. Loud snoring rumbled from Miss Cruet's room. Moonlight flooded from the window opposite her door, shining on a pile of hairpins on the floor. I stepped over them and made for the spiral staircase. Round and round I climbed, groping my way up the stairs in the dark. Halfway up, where the window was, I stopped for a moment to catch my breath, and looked out.

A huge, full moon floated over the garden, making ghosts of the greenhouse and the plants and trees. The light was silver, full of magic. The best kind of night for meeting my twin.

Then I saw something move.

A figure crept down the garden path, almost hidden in the shadow under the wall that divided Nobodies from the Academy. Who was it? I pressed my face to the window and squeezed my eyes, but it was too dark to see, and it was moving quickly. The figure dipped down into a crouching run and disappeared into the wood.

I climbed the final steps until I stood outside the door of the Room of Reflection.

I grasped the handle, turned it, and the door creaked open. I stood very still on the threshold, listening in case the sound had woken anyone, but all was silent apart from Miss Cruet's distant snoring. Quietly, I pushed the door closed behind me. The room was in pitch darkness. My heart cartwheeled in my chest.

I felt for the light switch and clicked it on.

The room was empty, just as I had left it last time. No cabinet, no Bird. But the old mirror was there, hanging on the wall between Nobodies and the Academy, the glass gleaming in its carved surround. My heart thudded. Would Silver be there, in the mirror, waiting for me?

I tiptoed over to it.

Silver wasn't there. There was just my own reflection—my hair tousled, my clothes pulled on any old how, my burn mark a dark patch in the dim light. I pressed my ear to the glass and listened. Maybe Silver was in bed just on the other side of the wall; or maybe, like me, she'd climbed the stairs from her dormitory towards an identical mirror in an identical room. Except that in the Academy, the room wouldn't be bare and empty: the walls would be painted in glowing colours, and there'd be a rich carpet on the floor, a window with soft, billowing curtains and bowls of pansies on the sill.

There was no sound at all.

*What must I do to summon Silver?* I remembered how we'd parted, our palms touching in the mirror's reflection, and I carefully placed my hand on its cold surface, and waited.

Far away in the distance, a church clock chimed midnight. I held my breath. Surely she would come now?

But she didn't.

My mind began to race. Had she forgotten our meeting? Had she fallen asleep by accident?

177

*No. She couldn't have.* This meeting was just as important to her as it was to me. Nothing would stop her from coming. And I'd wait here until morning if I had to.

I leant closer to the mirror, so close that my reflection became a blur. Then I whispered, right into the glass: 'Silver... Silver... I've come, like you told me to.'

My voice sounded empty and alone, like my words were leaking away into the air and there was nobody to hear them.

'Please...' I whispered. 'Please come. I need to see you again. I need to know—'

Then I stopped. The surface of the mirror had begun to mist over; my reflection slowly disappeared. The faintest sound drifted from the other side of the glass, like waves slipping back and forth on the sand. Then I felt it, like a gentle breeze on my face, whispering and pausing, whispering and pausing...

Someone was breathing on the other side of the glass.

I held my own breath, just in case it was all my imagination—just in case it was only me, breathing on the glass and misting it up.

Then the mist began to clear, and I saw a hand, exactly like mine, meeting my own in the mirror.

And there, smiling at me, was Silver.

# SECRETS

'Flynn,' Silver whispered. Her voice was green leaves and roses and birdsong. 'My own sister. You came!'

I swallowed. Tears wanted to leak out of my eyes, and I blinked a few times to stop them. We just stood there, staring at one another, smiling. Silver was in her uniform, just like last time, her shirt freshly ironed, her hair brushed and shining. She didn't look like she was wearing her pyjamas underneath her uniform, like I was. I tugged my sweatshirt down and ran my fingers through my mop of curls.

Silver spoke again. 'You're so... so beautiful!'

Was she laughing at me? I couldn't bear it if she was but she didn't seem to be.

'It's *you* who is beautiful,' I said. 'I have a burnt face.'

'You're beautiful inside,' said Silver.

'Can you see inside me then? Like Mr Gold can?'

'Mr Gold?' A strange expression crept over her face. She moved her hand away from the mirror. 'Have you broken your promise? Have you told *him*—Mr Gold—about me?'

'Of course not!' I said, shocked that she would think it of me. 'I would never do that—never!'

'Oh, Flynn—I'm sorry. I didn't mean to doubt you. I just... want to be sure you trust me more than anybody else.'

'I'll never, never let you down. I'm your twin!'

'I know that, really,' whispered Silver. 'It's just that my bird tells me about the Nobodies, and how they twist people's minds. And when I think about you living with them it makes me scared—scared that if you stay there with the Nobodies, you'll become like them, and you'll forget about me.'

'Oh, Silver!' It felt so lovely to use her name. 'I'll never, *ever* forget you! But... Oh, there are so many things I want to know!'

'Like what?' Silver's smile was back, like the moon from behind a cloud.

'Our parents—who were they, and what happened to them? How did I end up with Sonia and Claude? What happened to you, and how did you come to be at the Academy? And then there's this room—why do things appear and disappear here? Why do I see you in the mirror? What happened to the cabinet? And where's the Bird?'

Silver laughed. 'So many questions! The bird is my guardian.'

'Your guardian?'

'He looks after me. Protects me. Makes sure only the right people see me.'

For a moment, I thought I caught a whiff of the Bird's foul breath, but it was gone as quickly as it had come.

'He said he knew everything about me.'

'Did he?'

In the distance, the church clock struck the quarter hour.

'But we're wasting our precious time together, Flynn. And I've secrets to tell you.'

I waited, holding my breath.

'You want to be with me, don't you? More than anything else?'

'Yes! But how?'

'Listen carefully.'

I covered my lips with my fingers so that they wouldn't burst out with words.

'By keeping your promise, you've passed the first test. There are going to be other, harder tests. Are you brave enough to face them?'

'I am,' I said in a shaky voice. 'I'll face them and pass them, whatever they are.'

'Good.' Silver's voice sank to a whisper. 'Come close to me.'

I moved so that my ear was pressed against the glass. It felt cold against my cheek, and I longed to feel Silver's warm skin there instead.

'Here's the first secret. You can't escape Nobodies by climbing the walls any more than I can climb them to get to you. They're too high and anyway there are alarms and security guards.'

My heart plummeted into my shoes. So it really was impossible to get to the Academy.

Silver was still speaking. 'But there is one secret way.'

'Tell me—quickly!'

'On one night in the year, and one night only, this mirror becomes a doorway to my school.' Silver traced the edges of the mirror with her fingers. 'On that night, you can walk through it to join me here.'

'What night? Tonight? Now?' I tingled with excitement.

'Soon,' whispered Silver. 'But our time is running out, and I want to tell you the next secret. It's a secret about *our* school.'

*Our school.* A thrill went through my body. I couldn't wait.

'The Academy is the best school in the whole world!' said Silver, her brown eyes bright. 'And d'you know why?'

'It's got a swimming pool,' I said. 'And a cinema. And you can eat whatever you like—'

'Yes, yes,' said Silver impatiently. 'But the best thing... the best thing of *all* is this.' She lowered her voice. 'We get to choose what we learn.'

'Oh.' I felt puzzled, and a bit disappointed. Lessons were boring, unless they were acrobatics lessons.

'Don't you see?' Silver laughed, and it sounded in my ear like a waterfall, a fountain, spring rain. 'Instead of maths and science and history, you can choose to learn the one thing that makes your heart sing! What do you want to learn, Flynn? What's your heart's desire?'

I swallowed. 'Circus stuff,' I whispered, remembering Mr Gold's lessons with a flicker of excitement. 'Acrobatics, juggling, the trapeze...'

But Silver's next words drove all thoughts of Mr Gold out of my head. She gave a little skip and a jump.

'I *knew* it! You love just the same things as me! And when you get here, we'll learn them together. I'm studying the circus arts, Flynn! And I have the best teachers there are! Just think—we'll train together. We'll practise all the time. And one day, we'll perform in a great ring, in front of a thousand people. We'll be famous!'

I gasped. Finding my twin had been my dearest wish. And now, not only had this happened, but we were going to become famous acrobats! I opened my mouth to ask a hundred questions, but Silver raised her hand.

'And now, the last and most important secret.' Her face was serious. 'You must never, *ever* break the mirror. If you do, the doorway will be destroyed—and so will I.'

I took a step back, terrified that I'd accidentally break the glass. Losing Silver would be like losing myself, losing my whole world.

'Don't worry!' Silver smiled, beckoning me back towards her. 'The mirror can't be broken by accident, only on purpose.'

The church clock struck.

'I've got to go now. But we'll meet again, very soon.'

'When?' I whispered.

'Come on Saturday, at noon,' came the reply. 'I'll be waiting.'

'I will!' I said. But then I remembered our rehearsal. 'Oh! But that's when we're meeting to practise our circus show!'

'Your circus show?' Silver suddenly sounded scared. 'But I thought you wanted to be with me? This is just what my

183

bird warned me about—that the Nobodies would make you want to stay with them...'

'I don't—it's just that we agreed—'

'I thought I could trust you.' Silver looked sad, and terribly disappointed. 'It looks like I was wrong.' And a single, silver tear trickled down her cheek.

'No!' I cried. 'No, I'll come!'

But even as I spoke, the surface of the glass began to mist over. I tried to rub the mist away with my fingers, but it was hopeless. Silver was slipping away.

'I'll be here!' I shouted, hoping against hope that she could still hear me. 'I'll be here, I promise!'

But Silver had gone, and I was left staring at my own reflection in the dim light of the overhead bulb.

# INTO THE WOOD

**I** stood in front of the mirror, thinking of everything Silver had told me. Was she setting me a test, asking me to meet her at the same time as the rehearsal for our circus show? And when would this special night be—the night when the mirror became a doorway to the school next door? What would it be like to be a famous acrobat and perform to the roar of a thousand voices? Standing here alone in the dark, all these things seemed so far away, in a world I could only dream of. But once I passed the test, I told myself, I'd be one step nearer to making my dream come true.

As I made for the door, a niggle of worry crept into my mind. How would I get out of our rehearsal? Maybe I could tell the others I was ill. *No, I can't.* I hated telling lies.

Halfway down the spiral stairs, I remembered the shadowy figure I'd seen creeping into the wood. I stared down into the garden. It was still and empty. Whoever they were, they had come out of the boys' dormitory. Where were they going in the middle of the night, and why? I knew I ought to be sensible and go straight back to bed.

But I was wide awake, too excited and shivery about my meeting with Silver to close my eyes and sleep.

I crept down the stairs and into the corridor where Miss Cruet slept. The area outside her room, under the window, was pale with moonlight and the pile of hairpins glittered. I stepped over it and listened. Her snores filled the air like swelling waves.

Down to the dormitories I tiptoed. The door to the boys' dormitory was ajar. I tiptoed past it, along the passage and down the dark stairs, to the back door. It was open. Someone had unbolted it when they left the school just before midnight, and that someone was still out there.

I stepped outside and closed the door gently behind me.

The garden lay silent and still in the moonlight. I stared at the shadow under the wall where I'd seen the figure, but there was no sign of anyone. It was cold, and full of silver light—as if every plant, every blade of grass, had been turned to frost. Even my clothes were silver, and I smiled, remembering my twin. The moon was a great white circle, bigger than any sun, hanging almost close enough to touch. The sky was full of a thousand glittering stars.

Then I heard it.

A distant howl, like an animal in pain, far away and out of sight. I scanned the woods, silhouetted black against the moonlit garden. Another howl echoed over the treetops. Now I knew where it was coming from.

My skin prickled. Maybe I was being stupid, following it into the night. What if it wasn't a person at all, but a dangerous animal? I shook myself. This was a night for daring, for adventure. I headed for the wood and slipped inside.

It was much darker there. All I could see were the tree trunks, dappled by moonlight. Strange rustlings and murmurings whispered around me. I jumped at the hollow hoot of an owl. Moving carefully, my eyes scanning the ground for roots and stones, I felt my way from trunk to trunk. The howling had stopped. What if the shadowy figure was on its way back, and we collided in the darkness?

I heard something. It wasn't the howling. It was something much closer, something moving towards me in the darkness. Something breathing, in a thick, heavy way. I flattened myself to the trunk of a tree and held my breath, not daring to move, as it came closer, and closer still. *Shall I make a run for it? Can I outrun whatever it is?* My legs felt frozen to the ground. My heart hammered against my chest and I shivered from head to toe. I wanted to squeeze my eyes tight, like Custard did when she was scared, but I dared not. The breathing grew louder and louder.

And then it stepped into a pool of moonlight: a huge badger, its black-and-white striped body lumbering through the mud, snuffling about for roots and worms. It raised its snout, catching my scent, and hurried off down another path.

For a moment I stood still, the feeling coming back into my legs, wanting to laugh out loud with relief. Only a badger! The night could make anything seem scary and monstrous. And as if the night could hear my thoughts, the howling began again.

It was much closer now, and I knew for certain that it was coming from the Amphitheatre. I crept past the dark mass of the shed and the silhouette of the swing until I reached the edge of the trees.

And then I saw him.

# UNDER THE MOON

Standing stock-still in the centre of the Amphitheatre, his long mane of hair silvered in the light of the moon, was Feral. He wore only his pyjama bottoms and his feet were bare on the grass. His face was turned up to the moon. His mouth opened in a roar, again and again, and the unearthly sound echoed around the stone seats of the Amphitheatre.

'Mama!' he howled in a voice filled with pain and longing. 'Mamaaaaa...'

I stood, as still as he. Never in my life had I seen anyone so unhappy and alone. It felt weird, and sort of wrong, to be spying on him when he was so upset. Slowly, I turned away. I'd creep back to the school as silently as I could, and he'd never know I'd been there.

'Mama... Mamaaaaa...' Feral's voice cracked and broke, as if it couldn't cry out any more.

I turned back. His shoulders were shaking. He fell on to his knees, his thin arms wrapped around his body as if he was trying to stop it from falling apart.

I couldn't go. I couldn't leave him there, alone and miserable in the moonlight.

189

I stepped forward, into the Amphitheatre, until I was standing right beside him. Then I reached down and touched his shoulder.

Feral leapt up, his eyes wide, and gave a yelp of terror, followed by a furious growl. Would he bite me? I made myself stand still, even though my legs longed to run away.

Then he saw it was me. He swiped tears from his cheeks with his hand and looked at me with overflowing eyes.

'Are you all right?' I said. It felt like a daft thing to say, but I couldn't think of anything else.

Feral nodded his head, then shook it. 'Mama,' he said, as if that explained everything.

'Are you missing your mama?' I said.

More tears began to fall. Awkwardly, I took his hand in mine. He stopped crying and stared at it.

'I don't have a mama either,' I said. 'My mum is dead too.'

Feral's eyes blazed. 'Mama *no* dead!' he growled.

'OK, OK. Whatever you say.'

'Mama took away,' he said. 'Mama gone.'

This was the longest sentence I'd ever heard him say.

'That's bad,' I said.

Feral gazed at me. 'You mama gone?'

'Yes,' I said. 'A long time ago.'

'How?' he said.

'I don't know,' I said. 'They said it was a fire.'

'Fire,' said Feral, nodding as if he understood, and I wondered if he did.

We said nothing for a while. I felt a bit awkward holding his hand, but he was clutching mine and seemed to want me to go on holding it.

'Is your mama really a lion?' I asked.

Feral nodded. 'Mama. Lion.'

'You lived with her in the forest?'

He nodded again. In the light of the moon, his tawny eyes were piercing under the silver thatch of his mane of hair. I couldn't help thinking about the lion they'd captured in the forest. Surely she couldn't be Feral's mother—could she?

I began to shiver. Feral didn't seem to notice the cold.

I gave his hand a little tug. 'Let's go back to school, Feral.'

'Feral?' he said, his head on one side.

I shrugged. 'It's just a nickname.'

'Nick Name?'

'A made-up name. I made up names for everyone.'

'Feral?' he said again.

'It means wild,' I said.

'Wild,' he repeated. He held up his hand, his fingernails as long and grubby as ever, and counted off one finger. 'Me. Nick Name Feral.' Then he counted off the second, third and fourth fingers. 'Others?'

I pretended to play a violin. 'Rule Boy.' Then I turned my mouth down. 'Saddo.' Finally, I sucked my thumb. 'Custard.'

'Custard.' Feral ran his fingernails through his hair and grinned. 'Trainer. Brush Feral mane.'

He suddenly reached out and touched my cheek. His hand felt surprisingly warm.

191

'Hurt,' he said. I tried not to push his hand away.

'Burn,' I said. 'I hate it.'

'Burn,' said Feral. 'Feral like burn.'

'Come on,' I muttered, my face tingling with embarrassment. 'We'd better go back.'

Feral nodded, casting a last, longing look at the moon. Then he dropped my hand and set off ahead of me into the wood. It didn't seem half so scary with two of us. Feral seemed to know the way, even in the darkest parts. We didn't speak until we'd crept up the garden path, pushed open the kitchen door and bolted it behind us, and climbed the stairs to the dormitories.

'Well,' I said. 'Goodnight.'

Feral suddenly leant forward and licked my cheek.

'Friend,' he said.

Then he darted into the boys' dormitory. I turned and tiptoed into my room.

Custard was still fast asleep. I pulled off my clothes and got into bed, my eyes heavy.

I was just dropping off when I heard:

*TAP... TAP... TAP...* on the wall next to me.

I half sat up in bed to listen, then very quietly knocked back.

*TAP... TAP... TAP...* came the reply.

The last thing I knew, as I snuggled under my blanket and my eyes closed, was that, for some reason, I was smiling.

# NIGHT VISITORS

In my dream, we were practising for the circus show. Rule Boy played a jaunty tune on his violin, and the strange, triangular metronome tick-tocked. Custard, in her yellow cloak, was putting her head into Feral's open jaws. Then Silver appeared right beside me, and everyone stopped doing what they were doing and gazed at her. *Tick-tock*, went the metronome.

'This is my twin, Silver,' I said proudly.

But then it all went wrong.

'She's not real,' said Rule Boy. 'She doesn't exist.'

'She's *scary*,' said Custard, and backed away.

And Feral growled and growled and growled...

I woke up with a start.

*Tap-tap... Tap-tap... Tap-tap...*

The metronome was still tick-tocking and my heart was beating three times as fast. Was I still dreaming? Or was it the clock, ticking over the door?

No. This tapping was a lot louder. And the clock showed it was half past five in the morning.

It must be Feral, tapping on the wall to say hello. I sat up and put my ear to the wall.

Nothing.

*Tap-tap... Tap-tap... Tap-tap...*

Then I realized that the sound was coming from the window.

I got out of bed, padded over towards it and pulled back the curtain.

Sitting on the windowsill, its grey feathers silvered by the moon, was the dove. It was tapping at the glass with its dark bill.

'You're back!' I whispered. 'What do you want?'

*Tap-tap... Tap-tap... Tap-tap...*

At that moment, there was a flurry of silver wings and another dove, just like the first, flew down to join it.

*Tap-tap... Tap-tap... Tap-tap...*

'What is it?' I whispered again. 'Do you want to come in?'

The two doves bobbed their heads, as if to say *yes*.

Behind me, Custard turned over in bed, muttering to herself. I put my finger to my lips, and grabbed the window. It was old and battered and would probably squeak when I raised it. I'd have to pull *very* gently and lift it just high enough for the doves to get through. Slowly, I pulled... and pulled... and the window opened with a groan.

No sooner was it open than the two doves hopped over the sill. They fluttered up to land on my shoulders, one on each side. They were light as the air and their gentle cries—*turrrr, turrrr!*—purred in each ear, and suddenly my heart and my tummy and my arms and my legs were filled with that warm, chocolatey, huggy feeling, and my eyes were full of tears.

'Did Silver send you?' I whispered. Maybe Silver was sorry for saying she didn't trust me. Maybe she was waiting for me in the Room of Reflection.

At the sound of Silver's name, the doves leapt from my shoulders, giving strange, haunting cries. They flew to the door, which was ajar, and perched on top of it, gazing down at me.

'You want me to follow you?' I whispered.

The doves bobbed their heads again.

I tiptoed over to the door. Custard was still sound asleep, her thumb in her mouth. Silently, I pulled the door open and we slipped out.

I listened. All was silent and still. The doves glided along the empty corridor, their grey wings brushing the ceiling and the walls as they headed for the stairs. I tiptoed down the corridor after them, the soles of my feet cold against the stone floor. Then I climbed the stairs, hoping against hope that Miss Cruet would still be snoring safely in her room. She was an early riser and would often sweep into the dormitory to wake up anyone daft enough to have a lie-in, shouting, 'WAKEY-WAKEY, RISE AND SHINE!!!!' in your ear and scattering hairpins all over your face.

I was almost at the top of the stairs when I accidentally stepped on the second-from-the-top stair and it gave a loud creak. I froze, clutching the banister, my ears like bats' ears, scanning the air for sound. The two doves landed on the top stair above me and waited, still as statues. I stood there for a minute or two, just in case Miss Cruet got out of bed with a torch, ready to confront any burglar foolish enough to break into Nobodies. The only sound was a distant rumbling snore. Carefully, I took the last stairs. All we had to do now was to get safely past Miss Cruet's door and reach the spiral staircase to the Room of Reflection.

Keeping to the wall, the doves floating above my head, I slipped along the corridor. A huge snort from Miss Cruet's room made me stop. I stood, not daring to breathe, for a few seconds. Then the snoring began again, louder now that I was almost outside her door. She sounded like a warthog, and I had to press my lips tight together to stop myself giggling.

In the window opposite Miss Cruet's door, the moon was hidden behind a bank of drifting cloud. It was dark in the corridor. Then I remembered the pile of hairpins somewhere outside Miss Cruet's door. I must be extra careful when I walked there in case I trod on them and hurt my bare feet. With any luck, the clouds would blow away and the moonlight would shine on to the floor, showing me where the hairpins were.

I edged along the wall until I was almost there, and waited. Miss Cruet's snores echoed down the corridor. I seemed to stand there for an eternity, staring at the dark window. I found myself whispering a prayer to my twin.

'Please, Silver, send the clouds away?'

As if she had heard my words, the clouds magically drifted away and the moon appeared, lighting up the floor and the scattered, glittering hairpins with silver.

And it was then that the strangest thing of all happened.

Instead of flying ahead, up the spiral staircase to the Room of Reflection, the two doves began to wheel and hover over the pile of hairpins. They dived down and began to pick up the hairpins in their bills, rearranging them on the floor. As they did so, the clouds drifted over the moon again so that all I could see were their fluttering wings as they swooped and picked and dived.

Then, as suddenly as they had begun, they flew to the window and began to tap gently on it with their bills. Did they want me to let them out? I tiptoed over and opened the window. Their cries—*turrrr, turrrr!*—whispered in my ears as they fluttered out of the window and disappeared into the night sky, two black specks, and were gone.

As I carefully closed the window, the moon crept out from behind the bank of clouds and lit up the floor at my feet.

And then I saw the message.

# THE NEXT MESSAGE

The hairpins glittered in the moonlight, and spelt out the words:

*Have you found your long-lost sister?*
*BEWARE! Beware the cruel Shapeshifter!*

I stared. What did this mean? It was a warning, that much was certain. But a warning against who—or what? I had never seen the word *Shapeshifter* before.

Then I realized that it was very quiet in the corridor. Too quiet.

The snoring had stopped.

As fast as I could, I kicked the hairpins, sending them tumbling in all directions.

There was no time to escape. Miss Cruet's door was creaking open.

Quickly, I stuck both hands out in front of me, shut my eyes tight and began to shuffle along the corridor. My heart was hammering, but I made myself walk slowly, as if I was fast asleep. A hairpin pricked my foot, and it was all I could do not to cry out.

'Stop!!' Miss Cruet's voice was thunderous.

I lowered my arms and blinked my eyes a lot, then gave a great yawn.

'Wh-a-a-a-t? Where am I?' I said, pretending to be surprised to see Miss Cruet.

Actually, I *was* a bit surprised. I'd never seen her in her nightgown before and I'd never seen a knitted nightgown. Miss Cruet looked as if she had about fifty hula-hoops wound around her, all in different colours. The nightgown ended in a huge knitted bow at her neck. Her hair was all over the place.

'And *what*...' growled Miss Cruet, 'are you doing up here?'

I sort of shrugged and looked at her as if I didn't know either.

'Hmmm,' said Miss Cruet, giving me a very suspicious stare.

I tried to look innocent. The stare went on for a long time.

Eventually, she said: 'Sleepwalking, eh? That's a dangerous thing to do, especially in a building with so many *stairs*.' And she looked meaningfully at the spiral staircase.

'I-I'd better get back to bed,' I said.

'Not so fast, young lady!' snapped Miss Cruet, absent-mindedly bending to scoop up some of the hairpins from the floor and jabbing them into her hair. 'We can't have you *sleepwalking* around the school at all hours. Perhaps we will have to lock the dormitories in future.'

'Oh! Please don't,' I said. 'I've never sleepwalked before. It won't happen again.'

'It certainly won't,' said Miss Cruet with a nasty smile. 'I will accompany you to your dormitory now, just to make sure there are no further *incidents*.'

And she set off down the corridor. I had no choice but to follow her.

Back in the girls' dormitory, the clock said six o'clock. There wasn't much point in trying to go back to sleep—Mr Gold's lesson started at seven thirty.

I sat on my bed, my mind racing. What to do? Miss Cruet was suspicious now and there was no way I could sneak up to the Room of Reflection while her beady eye was on me. If I didn't get into the room at noon on Saturday, I would never see Silver again. And Saturday was tomorrow!

Later that morning, I could hardly keep my eyes open. After all, I hadn't slept a wink, what with meeting Silver at midnight, then following Feral to the Amphitheatre—not to mention meeting the doves and reading the message about the Shapeshifter, and being caught by Miss Cruet.

After we'd had breakfast (baked beans with yoghurt, and chunky chips dipped in porridge), Mr Gold led us all down to the Amphitheatre. Miss Cruet's lessons were always in the classroom, but Mr Gold taught us outside. He must have felt more at home there, like when he belonged to the circus. He carried an orange box under his arm. When we got there, he laid the box on one of the stone seats.

'I've been thinking,' he said, 'about your circus show. And I remembered I had these and thought you might find them useful.'

He took the lid off the box. Inside were lots of coloured, greasy sticks and a pile of small mirrors. An oily smell rose up, a smell which made my nose tickle and my heart thump. It smelt of the circus. I didn't know how I knew that, because I'd never been to a circus, but it did.

Feral leant right down into the box, sniffing at the sticks and giving little purring growls.

'W-what are they?' said Custard.

'Greasepaints,' said Mr Gold. 'And they're used in the circus for—'

'Painting the clowns' faces!' interrupted Rule Boy.

'Mr Gold used to be a clown,' I told Saddo.

'Cool,' he said, looking at Mr Gold with new respect.

'There's a rule in circus,' said Mr Gold, and Rule Boy immediately perked up. 'Every clown's face must be unique—just as every human face is. So paint your face *your* way. No copying!'

We began rummaging in the box. Rule Boy pulled out a blue stick. Custard and Feral both grabbed a yellow one.

'I w-want that one,' stammered Custard. 'It's the colour of my c-cuddly.'

'Lion,' growled Feral. 'Yellow.'

'Take it in turns,' said Mr Gold. He turned to Custard. 'You may paint the boy's face first, then you can swap and he can paint yours.'

Right at the bottom of the box, something glinted. I reached down and pulled out a golden stick—the colour of my leotard.

Saddo, who had hung back until we'd all taken our sticks, stared into the box, looking miserable.

'There's hardly any left,' he said.

I took my gold stick and mirror over to a seat, lifted my mirror and began to slather on the gold paint until my whole face was gold. My burn mark disappeared. Without it, I looked like Silver. When Silver and I performed together, she'd paint her face silver and I'd paint my face gold, and we'd shine like the moon and the sun.

'Now,' said Mr Gold, 'it's time for the Grand Parade. Walk round the ring, one at a time, and show us your faces.'

Rule Boy stepped up immediately, humming his Shosta-thingy tune and marching round the ring in time to it. He'd drawn blue musical notes around his eyes and mouth. We all clapped, and he did a fancy bow.

Then it was Custard's turn. Feral had painted her face yellow to match her blanket, and she'd drawn pictures of lions and birds up her arms, like tattoos. She danced round the ring. For once, she didn't look frightened.

'You look just like Leonora,' I said, and she grinned.

Feral bounded round the ring. His face was yellow, and he'd drawn a black nose and long, white whiskers. With his hair hanging down around his face, he looked exactly like a lion. He gave an enormous roar, and Custard squeaked then giggled.

Then it was my turn. I strode into the centre of the ring and bowed. Then I cartwheeled round and round the ring and ended up standing on my hands for a whole minute.

202

'Wow, Antsy,' said Rule Boy. 'You look really different without your b—'

'Shh!' said Custard.

That left only Saddo. He was lurking at the edge of the Amphitheatre, with his hood drawn down over his face and his sweatshirt zipped up. There were streaks of greasepaint all over his front.

'Go on,' said Rule Boy. 'Show us your face.'

Saddo ignored him.

'You scared or what?' said Rule Boy.

Mr Gold said: 'Let the boy decide for himself.'

Saddo stared at Rule Boy for a long time, until Rule Boy dropped his eyes. Then he got to his feet and shuffled to the centre of the ring. With a shaking hand, he pulled back his hood.

He had painted a red smile around his mouth, a smile the colour of a postbox; a smile so enormous that it took over his whole face. We all gasped, then Custard and I began to giggle, Feral gave a loud growly laugh and Rule Boy doubled over.

Saddo's real mouth turned down and this looked so funny compared with his painted-on smile that we all burst out laughing again.

'I knew it,' he said. 'I knew you'd all laugh.' And he hung his head.

Suddenly, it wasn't so funny after all.

Then I had an idea.

'Our circus show's going to be the best thing ever,' I said. 'We've got an orchestra, an acrobat, a lion and his trainer. All we need now is a clown.' I turned to Saddo. 'Will you do it?'

'Be our c-clown?' said Custard.

'Clown,' said Feral.

Rule Boy said nothing. I gave him a kick on the ankle. 'Yeah, go on,' he muttered.

Saddo blinked hard. Then he gave a gruff little nod.

We all cheered, even Rule Boy. Our circus show was complete. And just for a moment, I felt happy all the way through.

'That's the end of the lesson,' said Mr Gold. 'Off you go, back to school. No doubt Miss Cruet will have a snack for you.'

The others hurried off, but I hung back.

'Mr Gold,' I said, 'can I ask you a question?'

'Go ahead.'

Up above us, a bird fluttered in the branches of an ancient tree. I looked up. Was it the dove again? But I could see nothing.

I took a deep breath. 'What's a Shapeshifter?'

And Mr Gold's face went very still.

# SHAPESHIFTER

'**A** Shapeshifter?' said Mr Gold. 'Why do you ask, child?'

'I... um... I read the word,' I said. 'But I don't know what it means.'

'A Shapeshifter,' said Mr Gold, slowly, 'is someone who has the ability to change shape—to transform into different people or animals.'

'Animals?'

I suddenly thought of Feral, with his mane of hair and his long fingernails, like claws. Last night he'd howled at the moon, calling for his mother, a lion. Could Feral be a Shapeshifter? Was the message in the hairpins warning me about *him*? I shivered, and moved nearer to Mr Gold.

'Have you ever seen one?'

Mr Gold was silent for a few moments. He seemed to be wrestling with whether to speak or not. Then he said: 'Yes. I saw a Shapeshifter once.'

'Tell me!'

Mr Gold peered at me in his odd way. 'Where did you read about Shapeshifters?'

'I can't tell you,' I said.

Mr Gold went on looking at me.

'I'm sorry,' I said. 'I really can't. But it's very important to find out.'

After a moment, Mr Gold nodded. 'My story is a tragic one. Are you sure you can bear to hear it?'

I took a deep breath. 'Yes. I'm sure.'

'Very well.' Mr Gold's eyes went distant, the way they always did when he talked about the circus. 'After we joined the new circus, Fred and I—and Leonora and Kula—were very happy for a while. Murgatroyd was safely locked up in prison for cruelty to animals. Then, one day, to our horror, his rickety caravan appeared. He'd got a job in our circus as a fire-eater. No one knew about his past except for us. On the surface, he was friendly, but his eyes were full of hate. He never forgave us for taking Kula and reporting him to the police. And, finally, he got his revenge.'

'What did he do? What happened?'

Mr Gold ran a hand through his mop of red curls.

'It was the night of Halloween. The show was over and the crowds had long gone. The animals were in their quarters and the other performers were resting in their caravans, except for Fred and Leonora. They were practising in the Big Top, with Kula and their children.'

'They had children?'

'Yes. A boy and a girl.' Mr Gold's face looked sort of closed down, as if he didn't want to talk about that, so I pressed my lips together and waited for him to go on.

'I was in my caravan, reading, but I couldn't concentrate. There was a strange feeling in the air, as if something bad was going to happen. I told myself it was because it was

Halloween. It's said that bad magic is strong on such a night. I must have dozed off.' Mr Gold sighed. 'Suddenly, I jerked awake. And a terrible sight met my eyes.'

'What?' I whispered.

'The Big Top was alight. Smoke billowed out of it, and flames licked over the canvas like they were eating it up. Circus folk ran to and fro, yelling. No one could get inside—the flames leapt right across the entrance, and the tent looked like it might collapse at any moment. The clowns passed buckets of water down a line of people. The ringmaster, his costume black with smoke, beat at the flames with a broom to try to put them out. But the smoke choked them all, and the flames only grew fiercer.'

'What did you do?' I wasn't sure I wanted to know, but it was too late now. I had to find out about the Shapeshifter.

'I ran outside and filled a bucket of water from the tap. I poured it over my head and my clothes until I was dripping. I wetted a towel and threw it around my mouth. Then I ran towards the tent. I could hear Kula, roaring inside. The ringmaster grabbed my arm. "Get back, Felix!" he shouted. But I ignored him and pulled myself free. The smoke was thick as soup. It caught in my throat, making me choke. My eyes were streaming. Then I heard the sound of laughter from inside—mad laughter. And I knew who had done this.'

'Murgatroyd?'

Mr Gold nodded. 'I got down on my hands and knees— the smoke was a little less thick there—and crawled over the blackened grass towards the entrance. There seemed to be no way through. A wall of flames billowed from the tent, and I pulled the towel tighter around my face. Then, for a moment, the flames flickered and faded, and I took a deep breath and somersaulted as fast as I could through the entrance and into the tent.

'At first, I could see nothing. The tent was full of acrid smoke and yellow flame. And all I could hear was the shouting of the circus folk outside, and Kula's angry roaring. The leg of my trousers smouldered, and I slapped at it with my hands. Then, the smoke cleared, and standing before me in the middle of the ring was Murgatroyd, his black, tattered clothes singed and smoking, his evil eyes glinting in the flames and a tongue of fire flashing from his mouth. All around him, the ring was burning. And sitting at his feet in the sawdust was Fred and Leonora's little girl. She wasn't scared—she was only three, too young to understand. She looked up at me and smiled, and reached out her arms to me. Then Murgatroyd saw me.

'"Felix Gold. At last," he said. "Now I have you all." And he began to laugh again, crazy, evil laughter. And as he laughed, more flames poured from his mouth, and I knew he had set the fire, that he would stop at nothing until he had destroyed our whole family. And at that moment, as our eyes locked together, he shapeshifted and escaped through the roof of the tent.'

'What did he change into?'

Mr Gold didn't seem to hear me. He sat with his head in his hands.

At last, I whispered: 'What happened then? What about Fred and Leonora and the children? And Kula?'

It was as if my voice brought him back to the present moment.

He raised his head. 'I am sorry. I should not have told you these things. They are not for a child's ears.'

He stood up suddenly and picked up his stick. 'Miss Cruet will be waiting.'

And he limped out of the Amphitheatre.

'But what happened to Fred and Leonora?' I shouted. 'Did they escape the fire? Where are they now?'

Mr Gold stopped suddenly. He looked unhappier than anyone I'd ever seen, even Feral last night.

'They died,' he said.

'But—'

'And that's the end of the story.'

He turned and limped into the wood.

After a moment, I ran after him and we walked together in silence. Thoughts raced through my head and my heart felt squashed with sadness about Mr Gold losing his twin brother and his family, just like I'd lost mine.

As we went up the path to the school, the breakfast bell rang. Mr Gold stopped, and looked down at me.

'Sometimes, life takes people away. So the thing to do is to make the very most of what happens now, in the present time.'

'Is that why they call it the present?' I said. 'Because it's like a special gift?'

Mr Gold smiled then, the crooked smile that made his face look completely different.

'Yes, child,' he said. 'The present is indeed a gift. Use it well.'

'I will,' I said.

Every moment with Silver was precious. I couldn't risk losing her for a second time. Tomorrow was Saturday, and she'd be waiting for me in the Room of Reflection at noon. But the others were expecting me at the rehearsal.

I had to find a way to get to the room. I just *had* to.

# COUNTDOWN
# TO NOON

**N**ext morning, we had home economics. Most of our lessons involved us *doing* stuff rather than talking about it or writing it down. So what home economics actually meant was Miss Cruet ordering us to chop vegetables for lunchtime soup.

'I will stir in the liquorice allsorts and the ginger beer later,' she said as she swept out.

I glanced up at the kitchen clock. It was already half past eleven. In just thirty minutes it would be noon, and Silver would be waiting for me in the Room of Reflection. Excitement fizzed through me, like lemonade when you shake the can. But how could I get there? Our circus show rehearsal was at noon too. Ideas kept bouncing about in my head like pinballs, but however hard I tried, I couldn't think of a plan.

Custard, her blanket fastened around her neck as a cloak, was rabbiting on about the rehearsal. The more she did, the more I fidgeted.

'Ants in your pants again?' said Rule Boy.

The others all turned to look at me.

'What's the matter?' said Custard. 'You've gone a funny c-colour. Don't you feel w-well?'

Why, oh *why* couldn't I tell them I had a tummy ache or a cold? Only I didn't tell lies. I put down my knife and the potato I was chopping.

'I can't come to the rehearsal,' I said.

There was a long silence.

'What do you mean, you can't come?' said Rule Boy. 'You arranged it!'

'Why c-can't you?' said Custard.

'Yeah, why?' said Saddo.

'Why?' echoed Feral.

The fizzing made my head fuzzy. I'd go pop if I didn't tell someone about Silver soon. And after all, Silver hadn't said I couldn't tell the other children. I took a deep breath.

'Because... because I've found my twin!'

'Your t-twin?' said Custard, her eyes wide.

And then the words poured out of my mouth higgledy-piggledy.

'She's-at-the-school-next-door-just-like-I-said-she-was-and-I've-talked-to-her-and-she's-called-Silver-and-we're-going-to-be-together-soon-and-she-wants-me-to-meet-her-at-noon-and-that's-why-I-can't-come-to-the-rehearsal—'

Rule Boy smirked. 'Your twin, eh?' he said. 'It's bad enough that there's one of you, Antsy, let alone two.'

Feral gave a low growl.

'Anyway,' said Rule Boy to the others, in his most superior way, 'she's obviously making it up.'

'I am *not* making it up!' I said. 'I saw her. I talked to her. She was there, in the mirror.'

'What mirror?' said Saddo.

'The mirror in the Room of Reflection,' I said.

'So you saw your twin in a mirror.' Rule Boy started to laugh. He turned to the others. 'Now we *know* she's lying. There *is* no mirror in the Room of Reflection. I should know—I was in there just the other day. The room's empty. She really is crazy.'

'Don't you *dare* call me crazy!' I shouted. 'I did—I saw her. She was *real!*'

'Crazy,' said Rule Boy. 'Mad as a box of frogs.'

I pushed my shaking hands behind my back and gripped my fingers together. All my excitement about telling them about Silver drained out of me. I might have known Rule Boy would make it all go wrong.

And the kitchen clock was ticking. It was quarter to twelve.

'Anyhow,' said Rule Boy, 'even if there *was* a mirror— which there isn't—'

'There *is!*'

'Even if there *was*, it only proves she's making it up,' said Rule Boy. He looked around at the others, like one of those barristers in a courtroom. 'What do you see when you look in a mirror?'

'You see y-yourself,' said Custard.

'Exactly!' said Rule Boy triumphantly. 'Her so-called *twin* is just a figment of her imagination.'

'Maybe she's made up an imaginary friend,' chimed in

Saddo. 'I had one of those, when I was little. He was called Archibald. I thought he was real for years.' His mouth turned down in its customary frown. 'Only he wasn't. He was just a fig of my imagination.'

'*Figment*, dimmo,' said Rule Boy.

I couldn't stand it any more. The fizzing in my body had turned black, into thunderbolts and fury. How dare Rule Boy accuse me of lying when I *never* lied! How dare he call me crazy! He was just jealous, because I had a bigger, better secret than him, with his stupid metronome and sheet music hidden away in an old shed.

'*You're* the one who's dim!' I yelled at Rule Boy's smug face. 'You're so stuck on rules and facts that you can't see anything else. You can't see magic, or mysterious things. You're jealous of me, aren't you? Because I've got a twin and you have *nobody*. You don't even know where your dad is—'

'I do,' said Rule Boy, who had gone pale. 'I know exactly where he is.'

'Where is he then?' I said.

'In prison,' said Rule Boy. And he turned and walked out of the kitchen.

We all looked at one another. I hadn't meant to be horrible about Rule Boy's dad—he'd just been so mean to me that I sort of burst. Then I saw that the kitchen clock said ten to twelve. It was no good—I'd have to dash up the stairs now. I'd say sorry later.

I yanked open the door—and ran slap bang into Miss Cruet, who fell over backwards. We lay in a tangle on the floor.

'S-sorry, Miss Cruet,' I gasped, scrambling to my feet and helping her up. I was just about to run for the stairs when she grabbed my arm.

'Not so fast, young lady!' She adjusted her toppling bun and looked round at us all. 'I heard raised voices. And one of you appears to be missing. Would someone care to tell me what's going on?'

There was a long silence.

'I'm waiting.' Miss Cruet tapped her knitted boot.

Saddo looked at me. 'She said she wasn't coming to our rehearsal, miss. And then there was a big row.'

'About?' snapped Miss Cruet.

No one spoke.

'I will impose a very severe punishment unless someone explains in the next ten seconds. Ten... nine... eight...'

Custard pointed at me. 'Sh-she said she f-found her tw—'

I kicked her ankle. No way must Miss Cruet know about Silver.

'*OW!* She k-kicked me, miss!'

'Sorry,' I muttered to Custard.

Miss Cruet grabbed my arm and pulled me towards the door. 'Room of Reflection. One hour. And after that,' she added ominously, 'we will have words.'

I'd never felt so happy to be punished. I followed Miss Cruet as she plodded slowly up the stairs, every step using up precious seconds.

At last we climbed the spiral staircase. My ears strained to hear the church clock. Was it noon yet? I tried to see Miss Cruet's watch, but it was upside down and back to front. Did it say five to twelve or five past? My heart was thudding unpleasantly. What if Silver was there already, waiting for me in the mirror? What if she turned away forever, just before I got there?

*Hurry up. Please, hurry up.*

Outside the Room of Reflection, Miss Cruet began jiggling the bolt. After what seemed like hours, she opened the door, pushed me inside and bolted it behind me.

My heart pounding, I ran over to the mirror, just as the church clock began to strike twelve.

# TRUTH AND LIES

**M**iss Cruet's footsteps faded down the stairs as I placed my palm against the mirror. The church clock finished striking twelve. My breath misted the surface of the glass. Any minute now, Silver would appear.

Only she didn't.

The mist cleared, and there was only me in the mirror, my palm still pressed to the glass.

'Silver!' I cried. 'I've come! I'm here!'

But there was no reply. Surely I hadn't got the time wrong? Or the day? Maybe Silver was ill—or maybe...

Her last words to me ran, over and over, in my memory: '*I thought I could trust you. It looks like I was wrong...*'

My hand was no longer resting against the glass, but banging on it. I *had* to make her hear me. But then I remembered that if I broke the glass, I'd lose her forever—if I hadn't lost her already—and my hand slid down to my side.

My reflection in the mirror wavered in the tears leaking out of my eyes and running down my cheeks. I blinked them away. My burn looked redder and uglier than ever. Who could blame Silver for changing her mind about me?

Then something moved in the mirror.

'Silver!'

But it wasn't Silver. The cabinet had appeared on the wall behind me, and the movement I'd seen was its door, slowly creaking open. I whipped round to face it. Inside the cabinet, its yellow eyes fixed upon me, perched the Bird.

'So, missy,' it croaked. 'We meet again.' And the foul smell crept about the room.

'Where's Silver?' I said. 'I was meant to meet *her* here, at noon.'

'Think I don't know it?' said the Bird. 'Think there's *anything* about you I don't know?' It shuffled along its perch, and the smell got worse.

'Please, then,' I said, 'tell me what's happened to Silver?'

The Bird chuckled.

'Come a little closer,' it wheedled. 'Else you might not catch what I have to say.'

Reluctantly, I stepped towards it.

'Closer,' it said, its head on one side.

Trying not to breathe in the smell, I moved nearer.

The Bird stared at me with its cruel yellow eyes. Its feathers were dull; one dropped down to the floor, spiralling in the air. It opened its beak and began to speak.

'You want answers,' it croaked. 'About your twin. Is this correct?'

'Yes,' I whispered.

'Speak up! Or I may give you answers to the wrong questions.'

'Yes.' I raised my voice. 'I want to know what's happened to Silver.'

'Silver.' The Bird gave an evil chuckle. 'Such a pretty name. A pretty girl. Much prettier than *you*.'

I knew that, of course, but it still hurt. I waited for the Bird to speak again.

'Silver is safe,' said the Bird. 'She has been delayed.'

'But I will see her—soon?'

'If you pass the next test.'

'What is it?'

'Not so fast, missy!' The Bird poked around in its feathers as if searching for a flea. It stabbed its beak somewhere in its nether regions. Another feather floated down. Then it raised its head and stared at me.

'First, I will give you your answers.'

'But I haven't asked—'

'In the Room of the Mirror,' said the Bird, 'answers may come before questions.'

It suddenly launched itself from its perch, flapped its tattered wings, and landed on my shoulder. Its hoarse breath tickled my ear and I shuddered.

It laughed. 'Doesn't the ugly girl like the ugly Bird?'

I screwed up my toes to stop my feet from running away. The Bird laughed again, as if it knew what I was doing.

'You want to know about the Shapeshifter, don't you?'

I nodded. Silver must have sent the doves, just as I'd guessed. And she must have talked to the Bird, her guardian, about the message.

'Come on, missy.' The Bird's talons dug deep into my shoulder, and I winced. 'You already know the answer. There is only one among the freaks and the Nobodies who could be a Shapeshifter. Who growls and roars? Who claims his mother is a lion? Who cares more for his mane than for any living person?'

My tummy knotted up. I didn't want it to be Feral, even though I knew it must be. The Bird suddenly grabbed my ear in its beak and twisted it.

'Pay attention, missy! I have more answers for you. I warned you, did I not, about the Nobodies?'

I nodded reluctantly.

'I warned you, yet you chose to ignore me.' The Bird lowered its voice to a whisper. 'This is my final warning. Ignore it at your peril. The boy is evil. But not nearly so evil as the man.'

'What man?'

'Felix Gold,' spat the Bird.

Suddenly I wanted to stuff my fingers in my ears, like Custard did, so I wouldn't have to listen to any more.

'He tells you many tales, does he not?'

'He... he tells me about the circus.'

'Tales, missy, are not necessarily truths. Do you understand me?'

'Mr Gold wouldn't lie!'

I felt a sharp pain in my ear as the Bird tweaked it again. 'Doubt my word, do you?'

I raised my chin defiantly. 'Yes. I do doubt it. Mr Gold is good. He wouldn't lie to me!'

'Good as Gold, hey?' The Bird winked its yellow eye. 'Poor, trusting child. Tell me, has he spun you a pretty tale about his love for animals? About how he and his brother saved the poor little lion cub?'

'He *did* save Kula!'

'He *stole* her. He shot her mother and ran away in the dead of night, like the coward he is.'

'Mr Gold is *not* a coward!' I shouted. 'He saved Kula from Merrick Murgatroyd. He—'

'Lies! All lies! Liars have no conscience. The finest exterior can hide the deepest evil.'

'I don't believe it! It's *you* who's lying.'

'So, missy, you're calling *me* a liar?'

The Bird suddenly leapt from my shoulder and began to flap around the room, its wing tips slashing at my face, hissing words at me.

'He's a *liar*... a *thief*... a *coward*...'

I covered my head with my hands. I couldn't think straight with all the hissing and the flapping. The only thing I was sure of was that the Bird was wrong. Mr Gold was none of these things.

'And a *murderer*—'

'NO!' I shouted. 'Mr Gold didn't murder Mabel. It was Murgatroyd!'

'Never mind the old lion,' hissed the Bird. 'Felix Gold has killed far, far worse than she.'

'Who, then? Who did Mr Gold murder?'

The Bird landed on my shoulder once again. It cackled, and I nearly passed out with the smell of its breath. Then it leant to my ear and whispered.

'*He murdered his very own family.*'

My legs almost gave way with shock; my mouth opened and closed like a goldfish's. No words came out. Then, with all my strength, I shoved the Bird off my shoulder.

With much flapping and hissing, it flew back into the cabinet and perched there, glaring at me with its yellow eyes.

At last, my voice came back.

'I don't believe it! Leonora and Fred and their children died in a fire—the fire Murgatroyd set.'

'And who ran away and left them to die? Felix Gold!'

'No! Mr Gold ran into the tent to save them!'

'So he says,' whispered the Bird. 'Why, then, did he alone survive the fire? Why was he the only one who got out alive?'

'I... I don't know.'

'I told you, did I not, that he's a coward?'

I said nothing.

'Felix Gold murdered the way that all cowards do. He murdered by running away. He ran, and left his family to perish.'

'He wouldn't do that! I know he wouldn't.'

'Did he tell you that he tried to save his family?'

'I... No, he didn't.'

I remembered how Mr Gold had stopped. How he'd refused to tell me the rest of the story. A horrible, niggly, shivery feeling was moving about inside me. It made me want to cry. What if I'd been wrong all along about Mr Gold? What if I couldn't trust him after all?

'Do you swear this is true?' I whispered.

'I swear it,' croaked the Bird. 'I swear it on your own twin's life.'

Outside the room, footsteps clumped up the spiral staircase.

The Bird shuffled back into the darkness of the cabinet, and the door began to close.

'Wait!' I shouted. 'When will I see Silver again?'

The Bird winked its yellow eye. 'Not until the night.'

'The night?'

'The night when the mirror becomes a door to the Academy. The night when you will join your twin forever.'

'When will that be?' I cried again, but the cabinet door had creaked shut.

The door to the room swung open. Mr Gold stood at the entrance. He looked just the same as ever, with his sad eyes, his wild curls and his blue braces. I couldn't help remembering what he'd said to me in his study, about how some people looked very different on the inside to the way they looked on the outside. On the outside, Mr Gold was kind and gentle. But what if the Bird was telling the truth? Its scary words jangled around in my head. *Liar. Thief. Coward. Murderer.*

Mr Gold limped over to me. 'Child, you were shouting. Are you all right?'

I scuffed my trainer on the floor. 'I'm OK.'

There was a long silence, but I didn't look up. I hoped that Mr Gold couldn't see what I was feeling, because I felt angry and betrayed and hurt. If he had lied to me, and—much, much worse—if he had been too cowardly to save his twin and Leonora from the fire, I just couldn't bear it.

I glanced over my shoulder at the cabinet but it had disappeared again.

Mr Gold sniffed sharply. He looked puzzled and worried. 'Go downstairs while I shut the room.'

I ran to the door and hurried down the stairs. I didn't want him to see the tears dribbling down my cheeks and into my mouth. I wasn't just crying about not seeing Silver. I was crying because of Mr Gold.

# IT ALL GOES WRONG

I headed towards the kitchen, where the others were having lunch, and stood for a bit outside the door. Tears kept leaking out of the corners of my eyes. No sooner did I wipe them away than fresh ones trickled down. Mr Gold was the only person I'd trusted in my whole life, apart from Silver. But the Bird said he'd lied to me. And, much worse, that he hadn't even tried to save Fred and Leonora and their children from the fire.

Everything had gone wrong. Silver had disappeared. Rule Boy was angry because of what I'd said about his father. The others thought I was a liar. And even Feral, who I'd just begun to be friends with, had turned out to be a Shapeshifter.

I wiped my eyes with the back of my hand, took a deep breath, and opened the kitchen door.

Rule Boy, Custard and Saddo were eating soup round the big scrubbed table. Floating in it were poached eggs and red chilli peppers. No one looked up as I came in. I helped myself to a bowl of soup from the saucepan on the stove. No way was I going to show anyone I was upset.

I sat down at the table next to Custard. She edged away from me. Saddo, his mouth full, flicked a cold glance at me and turned away. Feral was down on all fours on the floor, licking his plate. He always ate like that if Miss Cruet wasn't in the room. Rule Boy stared at me in a disgusted sort of way, like I'd trodden in something smelly, or hadn't washed for a week.

'What?' I said.

'Don't play the innocent,' he snapped. 'You know *exactly* what you did.'

'I'm sorry for what I said about your—'

'Don't you even *mention* my dad!' hissed Rule Boy.

'We c-couldn't do our rehearsal because of you,' said Custard. 'So we're going to do it now. And you're n-not allowed to join in.'

'So much for the Musketeers.' Saddo raised his voice and mimicked mine: '*All for one, and one for all!* You couldn't care less about our show.'

'All you care about is your stupid imaginary twin,' added Rule Boy.

'Twin,' said Feral.

I screwed up my eyes to stop the tears falling again. 'I *do* care about the show. It was just that I—'

The kitchen door opened and Miss Cruet swept in.

'You,' she said, pointing at me. 'To my study. NOW.' And she stood holding the door.

I turned to Rule Boy and the others. 'I'll come down to the rehearsal and tell you what I—'

'TO MY STUDY!' barked Miss Cruet.

I had no choice but to follow her.

*

Every surface of Miss Cruet's study was covered in something, and most of it was knitted. Even the clock had a sort of knitted hood and the mirror had a knitted frame. The chairs were draped in layers of patchwork, the floor was covered in knitted mats, and an enormous pile of multicoloured scarves, waistcoats, hats with pom-poms and gloves tottered on the desk.

But I only noticed these things for a moment, because my eyes were drawn to two people sitting on upright chairs beside Miss Cruet's desk. My mouth dropped open in horror.

The two people were Sonia and Claude.

And on the floor beside the desk was my old bag, full of the things Miss Cruet had taken away on our first day at Nobodies.

'Sit!' said Miss Cruet.

I removed a knitting needle and several balls of fuzzy purple wool from a chair, and sat down. I couldn't think properly. So many horrible things had happened, and they were all mixed up in my head, like clothes spinning in a washing machine.

Sonia's mouth was screwed up tightly, and Claude was patting her on the hand.

Miss Cruet glared at me. Her hair was pulled back in such a tight bun that her eyebrows looked surprised.

'I have summoned Mr and Mrs Finklebottom—'

'Finkle*bome*,' hissed Sonia.

'—for an emergency meeting to discuss your behaviour.'

'Which is *very inconvenient*,' said Claude, 'since Sonia

227

has the makings of a migraine, haven't you, my delicate duckling?'

Sonia put a hand to her forehead and sighed. 'Please...' she murmured, 'don't call me our special names in public.'

Claude patted her hand again. 'Sorry, my captivating cabbage.'

Sonia glared at him.

'Then the sooner we get this over with, the better,' Miss Cruet barked, and Sonia gave a shudder and shut her eyes.

Miss Cruet picked up a ledger from the desk and turned to me.

'You have barely been at this school a week,' she said, 'but already you have amassed a long list of misdemeanours.' She ran her finger down the page.

'Item one: putting yourself and your classmates in danger by leading them into the wood in a thunderstorm and climbing a tree in said storm.

'Item two: flouting the school rule by communicating with the Academy.

'Item three: wandering the school at night under the pretence of sleepwalking.

'Item four: accusing a classmate of being a thief.

'Item five: taunting that same classmate about his father.

'Item six: letting your classmates down by refusing to attend their rehearsal.

'Item seven: kicking another classmate.'

'But I... They—' My mouth felt all mixed up and I couldn't find the words.

'Silence! In addition, you seem incapable of telling the truth: your classmates tell me that you have made up an imaginary sister, and Mr Gold was concerned that you told him that you'd met a talking bird in the Room of Reflection. These are serious matters, and I see little option but to expel you forthwith.'

'E-expel me?' I whispered.

'Oh, now look here—' blustered Claude.

'*Wait!*' Sonia got to her feet and glared down at Miss Cruet. 'We sent Claudia to your school because her behaviour had got out of control. We are *certainly* not having her back until you can guarantee that she has become normal.'

'Normal?' Miss Cruet harrumphed. 'You are mistaken if you think it is our intention to make any of the children in our care *normal*.'

Sonia gawped. 'Whaaaaat?'

Claude grabbed her arm. 'Scrumptious pumpkin, remember your migraine. You know what happens when you become overwrought!'

Then I stood up. I was shaking all over and That Feeling was churning in my tummy like a whirlpool.

'*Shut up!*' I shouted. 'Shut up, all of you!'

They turned to stare at me.

'I *did* break the school rule, and I'm sorry for that. And I only climbed the tree to rescue... the feral boy. And I'm sorry for saying what I said about Rule B—I mean, my classmate's father. As for the other things, I had good reasons for doing them...'

'Which were?' snapped Miss Cruet.

'I can't tell you!' I hung my head. I'd promised Silver I wouldn't tell Miss Cruet or Mr Gold about her. Then I looked up, right into Miss Cruet's eyes. 'But I have *never* been a liar. And I never *will* be either. So don't you ever call me that—*EVER!*'

There was a long silence. I stared at Miss Cruet's knitted boots. The worst thing in the world would be to be expelled and sent back to Sonia and Claude's, just as I was about to join Silver.

Miss Cruet cleared her throat.

'Very well,' she said. 'You may have one last chance.' She turned to Sonia and Claude. 'I will see you at the children's Halloween circus show.'

'*Circus show?!?*' hissed Sonia. 'I hardly think—'

Claude quickly nudged her. 'Of course we'll be there,' he said. 'Anything for little Claudia—*haw-haw-haw!*' He took Sonia's arm. 'Come, pootlekins. You'll feel much better when you're lying quietly in a darkened room.' And he led her out.

As they walked towards the front door, I heard Sonia's voice: 'And I've *told* you not to call me pootlekins...'

I raised my eyes to look at Miss Cruet. Her mouth was pursed up, but there was a kindly look in her eyes. Almost a twinkle. It quickly disappeared.

'You are dismissed,' she snapped. 'But make no mistake—I shall be watching you very closely indeed from now on. One false step, and you will be very, very sorry.'

# ACCUSATIONS

As soon as I got out of Miss Cruet's study, I pelted down the stairs, out of the back door, down the path and through the wood.

As I got close to the Amphitheatre, I heard music: a circus march which made me want to cartwheel and juggle and dance. The sight that met my eyes as I reached the edge of the ring made me stop in my tracks.

Rule Boy sat on a stone seat, his metronome tick-tocking and his sheet music propped in front of him. His face was very serious under the musical notes he'd painted on it. His bow flew across the strings, his feet tapping in time with the metronome.

A low tightrope had been strung across the ring between two trees and Saddo, his face painted in a big red smile, was balancing on it, holding out his arms. Rule Boy made the music wobble, and Saddo began to wobble too, his arms and legs flailing all over the place. Then, from the other side of the ring, Feral appeared, his face painted like a lion, and began bounding around the ring. Saddo saw Feral and gave a huge, comic jump. He ran along his tightrope, faster and faster. Feral growled, chasing Saddo back and forth. I couldn't help smiling at the expression on Saddo's face. Mind you, if he'd known that Feral was a Shapeshifter, he'd have been *really* scared.

Custard strode into the ring, her blanket tied around her shoulders, her arms painted with tattoos.

'Roll over!' she shouted, waving a long stick, and Feral obediently stopped running and rolled on his back with his hands and feet in the air.

'Now SPEAK!'

Feral opened his jaws and gave an ear-splitting roar. Saddo screamed and fell off his tightrope. He was so funny that I laughed out loud and clapped my hands. They all stopped what they were doing and stared at me.

Rule Boy lowered his violin. The metronome carried on tick-tocking.

'What are *you* doing here?' said Rule Boy.

I stepped forward, into the ring. 'That was really good!'

'No thanks to you,' said Rule Boy.

'I want to say sorry for what I said about your dad. And sorry I couldn't come to the rehearsal.'

'Don't bother,' said Saddo. 'We know you don't care about the show.'

'I *do*!' I said. 'I really do. It's just that I had to see my twin—'

Rule Boy bent down and switched off his metronome. 'Oh yes,' he said. 'Your imaginary twin.'

'She's *not* imaginary!' I shouted. 'She's real. And if I didn't meet her at noon today in the Room of Reflection, she was going to disappear forever.'

'She *must* be a fig of your imagination,' said Custard, 'if she d-disappears.'

'You don't understand!' I said. 'She—'

Then I realized that the others had stopped looking at me. They were staring at something behind me. Footsteps approached through the wood. I turned. It was Miss Cruet. For a terrible moment, I thought she had changed her mind and was going to expel me after all.

Ignoring me, she marched straight over to Rule Boy and pointed to his metronome and sheet music.

'What is *this*?'

Rule Boy blinked. 'It's a metronome, miss.'

'I know that, boy!' Miss Cruet barked. 'Why is it here?'

'I need it,' said Rule Boy, 'to rehearse for our show.'

Miss Cruet was frowning so hard her eyebrows were almost in her eyes.

'Rule three!' she barked. 'Remind me of it!'

'One possession only,' muttered Rule Boy.

'And the one possession you chose to keep was...?'

'M-my violin.'

'Then why do you still have *this*?' Miss Cruet jabbed a finger at the metronome. 'And *these*?' She pointed at the sheets of music.

Rule Boy's face was white. 'I can't play without them.'

Miss Cruet held out her hand. 'Give them to me. They are now confiscated.'

Rule Boy picked up the metronome and the pile of music. For a moment, he looked like he was going to run away with them. Then, with shaky hands, he handed them over.

Without another word, Miss Cruet turned and walked out of the Amphitheatre.

Rule Boy sank down to his knees and covered his face with his hands. Custard patted him on the back.

'Don't worry. You're such a g-good violinist you don't need the m-music.'

Rule Boy ignored her.

'That's right,' I said. 'You're brilliant. You can—'

'I CAN'T!!!' Rule Boy's glasses were steamed up. He looked at me with such hatred that I took a step backwards.

'You just don't get it, do you, Antsy? I MUST have a metronome, else I can't play in time. And I MUST have music. I can't play without it. And *you*—you told on me when you promised you wouldn't!'

'W-what?' I gasped. 'I did *not* tell on you!'

'Liar!' Rule Boy shouted. 'You decided to get your own back on me because I laughed at your stupid imaginary twin. So when Miss Cruet called you to her study, you sneaked and told her I'd hidden my things in the shed.'

'I didn't! Miss Cruet—'

Rule Boy turned to the others. 'Thanks to *her*, that's the end of our circus show.' He glared at me. 'You're a sneak and a telltale and a liar, and I HATE you!'

He picked up his violin, shoved it into its case and ran out of the Amphitheatre.

'Come back!' shouted Saddo, but his voice echoed emptily around the ring.

He and Custard looked at me as if they didn't know me at all.

234

'I didn't do it,' I said. 'I swear.' But I could tell from the way they were looking at me that they didn't believe me.

'Let's go b-back to school,' said Custard, and she and Saddo walked out of the Amphitheatre without another word.

Which only left Feral.

'Go on,' I said to him. 'Run after your *friends*.'

But he stayed where he was, staring at me with his tawny eyes. The more I looked back at him, the more the Bird's words came croaking through my mind. *'There is only one among the freaks and the Nobodies who could be a Shapeshifter...'* Deep in my tummy, That Feeling was starting again. Mr Gold had lied to me, and Feral was a Shapeshifter, yet it was *me* that everyone was calling a liar.

'You,' said Feral. 'Friend.'

'I don't want a Shapeshifter for a friend! Go away!'

Feral growled. Then he gave a massive roar—so loud that it echoed, over and over, round the empty stone seats—and he bounded out of the Amphitheatre.

Then I really was alone.

# I SEARCH FOR
# THE TRUTH

**T**hat weekend was the loneliest I'd ever known, even worse than when I lived with Sonia and Claude. At least then I had Tree to talk to. Rule Boy looked right through me as if I didn't exist. He'd shoved his violin under his bed and left it there. The others turned their backs whenever they saw me. And Feral growled, deep in his throat, and glared at me with narrowed, tawny eyes. At night, I lay wide awake in my bed next to Custard (who even *slept* with her back to me), too frightened to go to sleep in case Feral shapeshifted into a real savage lion and came to get me.

My thoughts went round and round like a dog chasing its tail. Our circus show was ruined now that Rule Boy wouldn't play his music—and anyway, no one wanted me there. And I still didn't know when I'd see Silver again, or which night the mirror would turn into a doorway to her school. I curled into a tight ball to stop my arms and legs from twitching and squirming.

But there were more things to worry about. The Bird's words about Mr Gold kept croaking into my mind.

*Liar...*

*Thief...*

*Coward...*

*He murdered his very own family...*

What if the Bird was right? What if Mr Gold *had* lied to me with his stories about saving Kula and how he'd run into the Big Top on the night Murgatroyd set the fire? *Was* he a coward? *Did* he leave his family to die? I didn't want to believe it. I *wouldn't* believe it. But Mr Gold had shut up in the middle of telling me about the fire in the Big Top, and then refused to answer my questions, so he must have something to hide. And the Bird had sworn on Silver's life that Mr Gold had run away.

I tossed and turned. My eyes wouldn't close. My legs kept wriggling. I *had* to find out the truth. But how?

Then I sat up in bed with a start. Of course—the box of photos and newspaper cuttings in the chest of drawers in Mr Gold's study! Maybe—just maybe—there was something in the box that would prove Mr Gold was innocent. But did I dare sneak down there and look? Miss Cruet had threatened to expel me if she caught me breaking the rules again.

I had to.

It was too dark to see the time, but it must have been well after midnight. I pulled on my clothes and tiptoed past Custard's bed, through the door and into the corridor. I stood absolutely still for a moment, listening. No sound came from the boys' dormitory. I crept down the stairs to Mr Gold's study. Would it be open?

My heart beating fast, I turned the handle and the door creaked open into darkness. I tried to remember where the lamp had been—yes, on top of the chest of drawers. I inched my way across the room, my hands out in front of me.

*Crunch.*

My knees hit something low, and an object rolled and then crashed to the floor. I stood stock-still. If Mr Gold or Miss Cruet woke, they'd be bound to come down here, and then I'd be done for. I waited, counting to twenty and rubbing my knee. Then, in slow motion, I shuffled over to the corner of the room, until my fingers found the outline of the chest of drawers and the shape of the lamp on top. I clicked on the lamp.

The room looked strange and empty without the fire and Mr Gold. But the circus poster was still there above the fireplace. Then I saw that what I'd tripped over was a low table. A pot plant had fallen on to the rug, scattering it with soil. I scooped up as much as I could, stuffed it back into the pot and put the pot back on the table. As I did so, I couldn't help looking up at the circus poster one more time. There was Mr Gold, balancing on Fred's shoulders. And there in the distance, a tattooed girl in a golden leotard, riding on the back of a lion, two little grey birds on her shoulder. I crept closer, and that warm, chocolatey feeling hugged me again. My eyes longed to stare and stare, but I mustn't waste time.

I hurried back to the chest of drawers. Which drawer

had the box of photos been in? I pulled open the top drawer and looked inside. It was full of things—magnifying glasses and pens and light bulbs. I tried the second drawer. There was a box, but it wasn't the box of photos—it was the orange box of face paints we'd used to paint our clown faces. The greasepaints' circus-y smell stole into my nostrils.

The third drawer stuck, and I remembered how it had jerked open last time I'd tried it. I began to jiggle it. It was very stiff, but at last it came open with a loud squeal.

I froze. If Miss Cruet or Mr Gold woke up, they'd find me and expel me. My ears wanted to run up the stairs and listen outside their doors. I counted to twenty again. All was silent. I peered inside the drawer. There was the box, full of photos. Carefully, I lifted it out and went over to the armchair.

I began to sort through the photos. There were pictures of Mr Gold and Fred performing, and others of Leonora and Kula. I longed to look at each one, but I had to hurry. My fingers found pictures of the ringmaster and the trapeze artists, the big photograph of the Grand Parade, photos of dogs and horses. A nasty voice in my head kept saying: *What are you doing? There's nothing here. Give up and go back to bed.* I tried not to listen to it. Then my fingers found something right at the bottom of the pile. It was a newspaper cutting. I pulled it out and began to read it by the dim light of the lamp.

## TRAGEDY AS CIRCUS TENT BURNS TO GROUND

Three circus performers and a child, together with a lion, are believed to have been killed after a circus tent caught fire in mysterious circumstances near the village of Middlethwaite.

Fire engines were called at seven o'clock on the evening of 31st October, following reports of smoke and flames billowing from the tent.

Merrick Murgatroyd, a fire-eater, acrobat Fred Gold and his wife Leonora, a lion trainer, together with one of their two children and a lioness, are all thought to have perished in the fire.

My hands shook. So the Bird had been telling the truth. Mr Gold *had* left his family to die. I brushed away a tear which was rolling down my cheek.

Then I saw that the cutting was folded in two, and that there was more. I unfolded it and read on. There was another, smaller headline:

## HERO SAVES CHILD FROM BLAZING TENT

Felix Gold, brother of Fred Gold and also an acrobat, ran into the fire and dragged out the other child, a three-year-old girl.

'He was a hero,' said clown Everard Golightly. 'He ran right into the flames and, shielding the child with his body, he somehow managed to get her out. But a steel tent support crashed down on him and he collapsed, unconscious.'

Mr Gold is now in hospital in a coma. Doctors say he is in a critical condition with a broken back, fractured legs and loss of vision.

I sat, reading the words over and over. Mr Gold wasn't a coward or a murderer—he was a hero. And if the Bird had lied about Mr Gold, then maybe he'd lied about Feral being a Shapeshifter too.

And then I heard a sound. It was coming from Miss Cruet's study next door. Holding my breath, I slipped the newspaper cutting back into the box, tiptoed over to the chest of drawers and put the box inside. I pushed the drawer shut as quietly as I could and reached up to switch off the lamp.

Then the door opened behind me and someone grabbed me and pulled me to the ground, and a voice hissed: *'GOT YOU!'*

# NIGHT MUSIC

**I** fought and wriggled, but the other person was just as strong as me and had their hands over my mouth. I bit as hard as I could.

'*OW!!!*' the person yelled, and let go.

I scrambled to my feet and switched on the light. There, lying on the ground and clutching his hand, was Rule Boy. His glasses had been knocked off in the struggle. His violin case lay near the door.

I picked up his glasses and held them out to him. He snatched them and put them on.

'I might've *known* it would be you,' he said. 'What are you doing, sneaking around in Krusty's study? Looking for your imaginary twin?' He got to his feet. 'Know what I'm going to do? I'm going to report you to Krusty—just like you told on *me* to Miss Cruet. Then you'll get expelled, and good riddance.'

'Oh yes?' I said. 'And just what were *you* up to in Miss Cruet's study?'

Rule Boy flushed. 'Who says I was in Miss Cruet's study?'

'I heard you! And you've broken the rules just as much as I have, so there!'

I suddenly remembered that it was the middle of the night, and we were in Mr Gold's room, and talking loudly.

'Shhh! Someone'll hear us. And then we'll *both* be expelled.'

'Huh,' said Rule Boy. But he lowered his voice.

'Let's get out of here,' I whispered. 'And then we'll sort this out once and for all. We could go to the library—no one will hear us there.'

Rule Boy gave a reluctant nod and picked up his violin case.

We crept through the corridors, our ears straining for any sound. When we got to the library, I pushed open the door, shut it firmly behind us, and switched on a lamp. We sat opposite one another, Rule Boy still holding his violin case.

'Let's talk,' I said.

'What's the point of talking,' snapped Rule Boy, 'if all you ever do is lie?'

That Feeling began to churn in my tummy. This was so unfair.

'I don't lie. But all right—let's each make a promise, like they do in a court of law.'

Rule Boy's head jerked up. 'What d'you know about that?'

'I've seen it on TV. The person raises their hand and says: "I solemnly swear that the evidence I shall give shall be the truth, the whole truth and nothing but the truth."'

'People say that and they still lie,' said Rule Boy. 'It's called perjury.'

'Then let's swear. I swear on... on my mother's life that I didn't sneak on you.'

'I thought your mother was dead.'

'She is. I just don't know whose life to swear on,' I said. Then I remembered Silver. 'I swear on my twin's life.'

'Your imaginary twin?' said Rule Boy, with a smirk.

I jumped to my feet. 'You're never going to believe anything I say, so let's just forget it!' I went to the door and jerked it open.

'All right, all right,' snapped Rule Boy. 'I'll listen. Come back here.'

I stayed where I was. 'Do *you* swear to tell the truth too?'

'I swear...' Rule Boy raised his hand, 'on my father's life.'

I shut the door and sat down.

'Go on then,' he said. 'Ask me a question.'

'Why were you in Miss Cruet's room? And why have you got your violin with you?'

'I was looking for my metronome and my music. I was going to get them back and practise. Only I couldn't find them.' He put the violin case carefully down at his feet. 'Now it's my turn to ask a question. What were *you* doing in Krusty's study?'

'Someone told me something bad about Mr Gold. Something really bad. And I was trying to find proof that it isn't true, that he's innocent.'

Rule Boy leant forward. 'And did you find it? The proof?'

'Yes. The person was lying. Mr Gold is innocent.'

'Like my dad.' Rule Boy stared at me. Suddenly, he pulled off his glasses and started to rub them with his sleeve. 'He's innocent, but they sent him to prison just the same.'

'Why did they send him to prison?'

Rule Boy stared at his feet. 'They said he'd broken the law. He didn't! My dad would never do that.'

I thought about how I'd been scared that Mr Gold was a murderer, and how horrible that had made me feel. No wonder Rule Boy was upset.

'What happened?'

'My dad's a musician. He was first violin in a famous orchestra. He taught me how to play.' Rule Boy opened the violin case and pulled out his violin. 'He saved up for ages so he could buy me this—it cost a thousand pounds.'

My eyes opened wide. 'A thousand pounds!'

'Around then someone started stealing from the orchestra and nobody knew who it was. The money was kept in a big safe in the office. One night, after he'd been practising late, my dad heard a noise coming from the office. He crept in and saw a man taking money from the safe. It was the conductor of the orchestra.'

'What did your dad do?'

'He did just what *I* did when I found you in Krusty's study. He sneaked up behind the conductor and grabbed him. The conductor started screaming and shouting and saying it was my dad who was the thief and that he'd been using some of the money he stole to buy my violin! And because the conductor was so important and famous, everyone believed him. And my dad had to go to court, and even though he swore he was innocent, they sent him to prison.'

Rule Boy's voice went all trembly. I put my arm round him.

'So... so I've got to practise. I've got to become the best violinist in the world—then, when my dad gets out of prison, he'll never have to worry about money and we'll be happy again. Only I *can't* practise now, because Miss Cruet's confiscated my metronome and my music.'

He sat with his shoulders slumped, looking like he'd given up.

I picked up the bow and held it out to him.

'Try it,' I said. 'If you don't, you'll never know whether you can or you can't.'

Rule Boy grabbed the bow and threw it back in the case. 'I told you, I *can't*! I need my music to show me the notes I have to play. And I need my metronome to tell me how fast to go. Those are the rules.'

'What if you trust *yourself* to know those things?' I said. 'What if you don't need rules?'

Rule Boy was clenching and unclenching his fists as if he wanted to hit someone. Then, he blinked very hard, pushed his glasses up his nose and picked up the bow. With shaking hands, he rested the violin on his shoulder.

I held my breath.

He drew the bow harshly across the strings. It made a horrible sound, like a yowling cat, or fingernails scraping over glass.

'See?' he said. 'I *told* you!'

'Close your eyes,' I said. 'Pretend the violin is your very best friend.'

'I don't have any friends.'

I didn't say anything, because I didn't want to lie, and anyhow, Rule Boy didn't *want* me to be his friend. But he wasn't looking at me. He was staring at his violin. I thought about everything he'd told me.

'Pretend you're playing for your dad.'

Rule Boy closed his eyes, took a big breath and drew the bow across the strings.

A slow, melancholy note sounded around the room. He paused, listening to the sound as if he couldn't quite believe it. Then he played another, and another. He stood up, bent his chin over the violin and began to play.

I'd always thought his music was brilliant, but this was different. It was like the notes poured into my ears like a waterfall and filled up my head with their deep sounds. Then he stopped playing the sad notes and began playing swirling, joyful sounds, faster-and-faster-and-faster until I could hardly see his fingers moving on the strings.

I couldn't help it—I had to get up and move. I danced and cartwheeled and somersaulted round the room until I was dizzy. Then Rule Boy stopped playing and I stood panting and grinning at him. His cheeks were wet with tears, but his eyes were shining like I'd never seen them shine before.

'I can do it!' he said. 'I can do it!'

'And now you can practise—and you can be the orchestra in our show!' I took a deep breath. 'I want to say something else too.'

'What?'

'I *do* mind about the show. And... and I do care about you. I want to be your friend. Will you let me be part of the show again?'

There was a long silence. Then Rule Boy nodded.

'All right,' he said gruffly. 'I'd like that. Just so long as you promise you'll never let us down again.'

'I promise,' I said.

We grinned at one another, and Rule Boy held up his hand. '*All for one...*'

'*... and one for all!*'

# PREPARATIONS

Everything got better after that night. Rule Boy must have told everyone about what happened, because next day they began to talk to me again. The best thing of all was that I said sorry to Feral for thinking he was a Shapeshifter, and he licked my nose and said 'Friend'. And when Mr Gold smiled his sad, crooked smile, and told me how well I was doing as an acrobat, and when Feral tapped on the wall between us to wake me up, it was as if the Bird, and everything it had said, had happened in a dream—or a nightmare.

Only I couldn't help remembering the Bird's words about the special night when the mirror would become a doorway to the Academy: the night I was to join Silver. Had it been lying about that too?

As the weeks went by, and September became October, I tried again and again to creep up the stairs to the Room of Reflection. But every night, Miss Cruet seemed to be suffering from insomnia, or indigestion. Just as I got to the top of the stairs, she would come zooming out of her door to the bathroom, carrying a glass of fizzing water, or a hairbrush, or a radio or a book—and I had to duck down and scurry back to the dormitory. I told myself that as soon as the show was over, I'd find a way of getting up to the room.

All the same, uncomfortable thoughts ran through my mind. Was Silver still waiting for me to come? Had she given up on me?

Surely she hadn't. Not if she felt the same way about me as I felt about her. She'd wait for me forever. She *would*.

It was almost Halloween, and we were counting down the days to the show. Everyone was busy making their costumes. Feral was going to wear a yellow rug with a long, woolly fringe which Miss Cruet had produced from a cupboard. Custard cut up a bed sheet to make herself a glamorous dress. Rule Boy made a bow tie out of crêpe paper and a black top hat out of cardboard. Saddo borrowed a pair of Mr Gold's red braces, with yellow ducks on them, and Custard helped him make a pair of outsize trousers from the rest of her sheet, which we were all taking in turns to paint with massive red diamonds.

'What are *you* going to wear, Antsy?' said Rule Boy.

It was good to be friends, even though he still insisted on calling me Antsy. I couldn't help thinking how I'd miss them all—Feral, Rule Boy, Saddo and Custard—once I'd joined Silver in the school next door.

'That's a secret,' I said. 'You'll find out on the night.'

I still slept with my golden leotard under my pillow. I longed to try it on again, but I was determined to wait until the big night. The others had probably forgotten about it—it felt like a million years since we first arrived at Nobodies and chose our one possession to keep.

The day of the show arrived at last. That afternoon, we had a final rehearsal, and it went brilliantly, even though it was icy cold, and a bit creepy in the Amphitheatre without the lanterns that we were going to light for the show itself. The wind rustled dead leaves about, and an owl hooted right in the middle of the day, which Rule Boy said they never usually do. Custard muttered about it being Halloween, and what her mum had told her about it being the day when evil is at its strongest. Saddo shivered and told her to shut up. I sort of wished Mr Gold was there, because he made things feel safe, but we'd given him strict instructions to stay away from rehearsals. We wanted him to see the show for the first time that night, like Miss Cruet and whoever else came.

'The only thing is,' Rule Boy had said, 'there'll be more of us in the show than there'll be in the audience.'

Mr Gold smiled his crooked smile. 'Wait and see,' he'd said.

My heart sank a bit. Miss Cruet had invited Sonia and Claude to the show. I couldn't bear it if they made a fuss about circuses being *cruel* and *common*. Maybe Sonia would develop a migraine so they couldn't come. Then I had a brilliant thought. What if Miss Cruet and Mr Gold had invited pupils from the school next door? What if Silver came to see me perform in my golden leotard?! I was so excited at this thought that I couldn't sit still, and wriggled so much through Miss Cruet's lesson that she stopped calling me *girl* and called me *worm* instead, and the others all laughed like hyenas. I didn't care. I was itching for six o'clock, when we'd go up to the dormitories to put on our make-up and costumes for the show, which was to start at seven.

'Wow!' I said, as Custard came out of the bathroom, where we were taking it in turns to do our make-up.

She'd sprinkled glitter in her wispy hair and painted black around her eyes so that they looked enormous. Her arms and hands were drawn with tattoos of lions and birds. Her long dress drifted down to her ankles. She'd borrowed Mr Gold's stick, and tied brightly coloured ribbons all over it.

'Do you s'pose I look like Leonora?' she asked.

For a moment I felt sad, remembering that Leonora and Fred were dead, killed in the fire. I shook the thought away.

'Even better, I reckon,' I said, and Custard gave a huge grin. 'Come on—let's go and see how the boys are getting on.'

In the boys' dormitory, chaos reigned. Feral, his face painted as a lion's and the old yellow rug around his shoulders, was romping around the room on all fours, his mane sweeping the floor, roaring with excitement. When he saw me, he rushed up and licked my face like a hyperactive puppy. Rule Boy, in his top hat and bow tie, had drawn twirly blue musical notes on his face with greasepaint and was tuning up his violin, making a series of caterwauling noises to rival Feral's roaring. And Saddo, his huge red smile painted on, was galumphing around in his outsize, diamond-patterned trousers held up by Mr Gold's red braces. He still insisted on wearing his hoodie on top of everything though. Then I noticed his feet.

'Where did you get those?' I asked. His shoes were enormous, as big as flippers, and knitted in all the colours of the rainbow.

'Miss Cruet made them for me,' he said. 'Cool, aren't they?'

Rule Boy stopped his tuning and looked at me. 'You'd better get ready. We're starting in an hour.'

Custard gave a shiver.

'I think I'm getting s-stage fright,' she quavered.

'Remember what Mr Gold said?' I reminded her. 'It's not really fright—it's just excitement in disguise. And anyway, you're brave now, so you'll be fine.'

She nodded. 'We must go down to the Amphitheatre,' she said, 'and get it ready for the audience.'

'We've got all the lanterns to light,' said Saddo, heading for the door.

'Hurry *up*, Antsy!' said Rule Boy. 'Get your costume on.'

'I'll catch you up,' I said.

As soon as they'd gone, I pulled out my leotard from under my pillow and hurried into the bathroom. Using a sponge, I carefully painted my arms and legs with gold greasepaint. I sponged the paint over my neck and face until my burn disappeared. Then I wriggled into my leotard.

I stared at my reflection in the mirror, hardly believing what I saw. I was a beautiful stranger, a golden statue.

Except that *this* statue moved. At last, I looked the way I'd always dreamt of looking, and Silver would be proud of me. In the mirror, I read the back-to-front message embroidered on my leotard:

> *You aren't alone—it's not too late!*
> *Your Twin's ALIVE, in Middlethwaite.*

The message, and all the other messages, had told me the truth. Silver was alive and living right next door. And I wasn't alone any more. Not only did I have a twin—I had Rule Boy and Custard and Saddo and Feral, and Mr Gold. I began to cartwheel round the bathroom. Then I stood on my hands and waved my golden legs around. The leotard flashed and glittered in the light.

'This is me, FLYNN!' I shouted.

For the first time in my whole life, I felt like myself, all the way through.

My name seemed to echo round the room.

'*Flynn!... Flynn!... Flynn!*'

I laughed. It was lovely to hear my name being called, again and again, in the empty house.

Only, it didn't stop. Again and again and again it called: '*Flynn!... Flynn!... Flynn!*'

I began to feel frightened. I crept to the bathroom door and listened. And then I realized. This was no echo.

It was another voice, calling my name. And it was coming from the Room of Reflection.

# THE DOORWAY

The voice was my twin's, I was sure. Was Silver in trouble?

With shaking legs, I raced out of the bathroom and along the corridor. Miss Cruet's bedroom door was firmly shut and, apart from the usual scattering of hairpins, there was no sign of her. She would be sitting in the Amphitheatre with Mr Gold, waiting for the show to begin. It was like I had an anxious clock inside me, counting down the minutes until the show. They were all waiting for me—Feral and Mr Gold and the others. I'd promised never to let them down again. But I couldn't be in two places at once. And I *had* to make sure Silver was safe. I took the spiral stairs to the Room of Reflection two at a time.

The voice called again: '*Flynn... FLYNN!*'

At the door to the Room of Reflection, I twisted the handle and it swung open into darkness. I groped up the wall and clicked on the light.

The room was empty. On the far wall hung the mirror, its surface dim and dusty. I glanced over to where the cabinet had been. It had vanished, as if it had never existed.

I ran over to the mirror and stared into the glass. My golden face stared back at me. My hand shook as I placed it on the mirror and closed my eyes. Had I imagined the sound of Silver's voice? Had it been a fig of my imagination? I couldn't bear it if Silver didn't come—if she didn't exist. All my dreams would turn to dust.

Then I heard it. The sound of gentle breathing.

My eyes snapped open. The surface of the mirror was misting over. Through it, I could just make out the figure of a girl, shimmering like a mirage. And as the mist slowly cleared, there was Silver, her palm touching mine in the glass.

'You *are* real!' I whispered. I longed to feel her warm skin against my hand rather than the cold surface of the mirror, but she was there, and that was all that mattered.

Silver smiled, her eyes brighter than the stars.

'Oh, Flynn—of course I'm real!' she said. 'And now, at last, we're going to be together.'

'How?' I gasped.

'This is the night,' said Silver.

My heart began to beat very fast.

'The night when the mirror becomes a doorway to your school?'

Silver nodded. 'Yes. We must both be ready. Place your hand on the glass. It will happen when the clock strikes seven.'

I swallowed and pushed my palm against hers on the cold, hard glass as, far in the distance, the church clock began to strike.

One... two...

Just for a moment, I thought of Feral and the others, waiting for me down in the Amphitheatre, angry because I'd broken my promise never to let them down.

Three... four...

I thought about Mr Gold, and our acrobatics lessons, and how disappointed in me he would be.

Five... six...

And then I gazed at my beautiful twin, who was smiling at me, her bright eyes full of love and longing. She was worth it. She *was*.

Seven...

I waited, hardly daring to breathe.

But nothing happened. The mirror stayed the same.

'It won't let me through.'

Silver was staring at me as if, like Mr Gold, she wanted to see right through my skin and into my soul.

'Is there *any* bit of you—even the tiniest part—that is unwilling to be with me?'

'No!' I said. 'I *want* to be with you. With all my heart.'

But something niggled in my chest. Why wouldn't the mirror let me through? Was it because I'd thought about Feral and the others, and Mr Gold? My face burned, and I was grateful for the greasepaint.

Silver leant close towards me.

'Flynn.' Her voice was soft and slow, like the waves of the sea, lapping on the sand. 'It's time. Close your eyes. Wipe away everything from your mind—everything and everyone, except for me.'

My eyelids were heavy. As I closed them, the carved wooden frame of the mirror shimmered into the shape of a doorway. And as it did so, the glass under my palm seemed to melt into liquid, and then to dissolve into air, and suddenly soft, real flesh pressed against mine.

And at that moment, the door behind me flew open and slammed against the wall with a tremendous crash. My eyes started open and I whirled around.

A figure stood in the doorway. It was Feral, dressed in his yellow rug.

'Come,' he said, his tawny eyes staring into mine. 'You late. Late for show.'

'I can't!' I cried. 'I have to be with my twin. Look—she's waiting for me!'

I turned back to Silver.

And then my heart toppled into my shoes. The doorway had disappeared. The mirror was just a mirror again, its surface dusty.

Silver was gone.

# THE CHOICE

**I** reached out, my hand shaking, and touched the surface of the mirror. It was hard and cold again.

'Silver?' I whispered. 'Silver—please, come back. It's only Feral.'

There was no reply.

My legs seemed to have lost all their strength. I shuffled down to sit on the floor by the mirror. I'd wait for Silver. Even if it took the rest of my life, I'd wait for her.

Feral padded over and sat down beside me, his tangled mane falling around him on the floor. He'd thrown off his rug but his face was still painted as a lion.

'Why did you come?' I asked him. 'How did you know I was here?'

'Feral look in all rooms,' he said. 'Right to top.'

'Go back,' I said. 'You've got to do the show.'

'Feral stay.'

I nodded. I knew if I said anything, I'd begin to cry.

'Friend.' Feral licked my cheek, just where my burn was, his breath warm and sweet. Then I *did* cry. I couldn't help it. And words began to pour out too. About how I'd heard Silver calling and thought she was in trouble, and how I'd never meant to miss the show, and how the mirror had turned into a doorway, and how she had disappeared...

Feral listened, his head on one side. How much he understood, I couldn't tell, and it didn't really matter. I had the feeling that he understood the important things, just the way Mr Gold did.

'She *was* here,' I ended. 'Do you believe me?'

'Twin,' said Feral. 'Here.'

'Yes!' I grabbed his hand. 'She was here, in the mirror.'

I stared up at the glass. If only I could conjure Silver back, and prove to Feral that she existed. But the reflection showed just him and me, side by side, his face painted yellow, mine gold.

Feral got up and pulled me to my feet. 'Come. Circus show.'

'I can't!' I said. 'I have to wait for her.' How could I make him understand? 'Silver is my most important person in the world. She's my family.'

'Mama,' said Feral. 'Family.'

'She's the only family I've got,' I said. 'That's why I have to be with her.'

Feral gave a big sigh. Then he shook his mane back. 'Find,' he said. 'Find twin.'

'But I don't know how!'

'How before?'

'I put my hand on the mirror, like this,' I said, placing my palm on the glass. 'And I closed my eyes.'

'Close,' said Feral, and I did.

I felt his hand slip into mine. It felt warm and comforting.

We stood there for a long time. It was so quiet I could hear every breath we took. We breathed together, in and out, in and out... And after a while, it mattered just a little bit less that Silver wasn't there.

Then Feral growled—a low growl, deep in his throat. His hand, grasping mine, suddenly clenched. His long nails dug into my palm and I opened my eyes.

There, in the glass, was Silver, standing between our two reflections.

Feral growled again.

'It's all right,' I whispered. 'This is *her*. My twin!'

Silver was staring at Feral.

'What is *this*?' she asked.

'He's Feral,' I said. 'He's my friend.'

Feral went on growling.

'He doesn't sound friendly!' said Silver, with a smile, but somehow it felt like she wasn't really smiling. Then she looked at me, deep into my eyes. 'I was saying, Flynn, before we were interrupted, that it's time.'

'Time to join you?' I whispered, placing my hand on the glass.

Silver shook her head. 'Time for your final test.'

'But I'm here! I'm ready! What else must I do?'

'Who is most important to you in all the world?'

'You are!' I cried.

'Am I, Flynn? Am I really? Then prove it.'

'How? How do I prove it?'

'Choose,' said Silver. She pointed at Feral. 'Choose between me and... *him*.'

'I-I don't understand—'

'Tell him to go.'

I turned to Feral, who was still holding my hand. His tawny eyes seemed to stare right into my heart. I gently pulled my hand from his.

'Feral, I have to be with Silver. Do you understand?'

Feral shook his head stubbornly. 'Friend,' he said.

'Yes—yes, you are my friend,' I said. 'But Silver is my family.'

'You Feral family,' said Feral. And a single tear ran from the corner of his eye down over his cheek.

'Make him go—now!' said Silver. She sounded frightened.

I opened my mouth, but no words came out. Feral grabbed my hand again.

'Feral stay,' he said.

I turned from him to Silver. My legs were shaking.

'Can Feral come too? Can he come through the mirror with me?'

A strange expression crept over Silver's face. I blinked. Just for a second, she didn't look so beautiful. Then she smiled again.

'Yes,' she said. 'He can.'

My heart leapt with joy, and I squeezed Feral's hand. Another low growl shook his body.

'It's all right,' I whispered to him. 'She says you can come too!'

Silver reached into her pocket and pulled out a pair of silver scissors, exquisitely made and studded with diamonds and pearls. She held them up to the glass.

'Take these.'

Just as before, the glass seemed to melt and our hands touched as I took the scissors.

'If *he* wants to come through the mirror with you, then you must both pass the final test.'

'Anything!' I said.

Feral said nothing.

'A proper friend,' said Silver, smiling at Feral, 'will sacrifice *anything*—anything in the world—to be with you. Isn't that right... Feral?'

Feral looked at Silver and growled.

'Let's see if he's really your friend,' whispered Silver, 'when you cut off his hair.'

# FERAL'S SACRIFICE

**W**hen Silver said these words, Feral dropped my hand. He opened his mouth and a terrible sound came out of it—like the sound he'd made in the forest when he was trapped in the tree, or when he'd cried for his lost mother, or when Miss Cruet had tried to cut his hair. A sound of hurt and pain and fear.

Silver lowered her voice and whispered to him, 'I understand, Feral. Your mama is gone, and all you have left is your mane. You *can't* lose that as well, can you? Say goodbye to Flynn now, and go back to your show.'

'Go back, Feral. Please,' I whispered. 'You *are* my friend, and I will always remember you.'

Feral looked straight at me with his tawny eyes. They were bright with terror, and with something else.

'Feral stay,' he said. 'You cut mane.'

'W-what?' I gasped. 'You mean you'd give up your mane... just to be with me?'

Feral nodded. He didn't seem able to say anything else. I swallowed. Feral had fought to keep his mane since we arrived at Nobodies. It was his most precious possession.

I turned to Silver.

'Silver—oh, Silver! Feral's proved how much he wants to come. You *must* let us join you now!'

'*Must?*' said Silver in a voice I'd never heard her use before. 'Words alone mean nothing! Only actions prove them true. Use the scissors on his mane, and watch your *friend* run away.'

I looked from Silver to Feral, who stood, his head hanging.

'I can't do it. I can't!' I dropped the silver scissors to the floor.

'You *can*,' said Silver, her voice as cold as ice. 'But you *won't*.' Her face was sad, sadder than I'd ever seen it. 'You choose *him* over me.' She turned away. 'My heart will break if I lose you. But lose you I must. Goodbye.'

'No!' I shouted. 'Why must I choose?'

The faintest traces of mist began to appear on the mirror, or maybe my tears were making it go blurry. I'd failed the final test. I was losing my twin—the only family I had—forever.

Then, something cold and hard was pushed into my hand. The scissors.

'Cut,' said Feral.

'But—'

'Cut. Now.' And he turned his back to me so that all I could see was his long mane, hanging to his knees.

And I knew this was my last and only chance—to be with Silver, and to take Feral with me.

The scissors sliced through Feral's mane as if it was a cobweb. At the first cut, a shiver ran right through his body and he gave a little yelp.

I stopped.

'*Cut*,' he whispered.

Soon, long strands of matted hair covered our feet and lay in a circle around us on the floor. At every snip of the scissors, Feral jumped. I had to keep stopping to wipe away my tears, but each time I did, Feral said '*Cut*' again, and I tried to concentrate on how we would soon join Silver at the school next door, and how much Feral would love the circus lessons.

After what seemed like a hundred years, Feral's mane was cut to his waist. I turned to Silver, who was watching us with a strange expression in her eyes. Shouldn't she be glad that we were passing the test? But she didn't look glad at all. The niggling feeling twisted in my chest again.

'I've done it,' I said.

Silver smiled. It wasn't a pleasant smile.

'Higher,' she said.

'But look—I've cut all this.' I pointed at the strands of Feral's mane strewn over the floor. 'We've proved—'

'Higher,' repeated Silver. 'You've proved nothing yet.'

'Feral?' I whispered.

A low growl vibrated from Feral's chest.

'Cut,' he said again.

I took hold of another hank of his mane, and sliced it right up to his shoulders. The scissor blades were blunted from all the cutting. Feral shivered, from the top of his head to his toes, and I stopped and rubbed his shoulder. He dropped his head.

'Finish,' he said.

At last, it was done. Feral stood before me, his hair the same length as mine, cut to the shoulders. He no longer looked like a lion. He looked like a boy with shaggy hair and whiskers painted on his face.

I sniffed, and wiped my eyes. My fingers were blistered from the scissors. I turned to Silver, who was standing like a statue in the mirror.

'Can we come through now?' I whispered.

Silver's face was white as a ghost. Her lips were pinched together.

'What is it, Silver? Are you—'

'*Higher*,' she hissed.

'But I've—'

'Do it.'

I moved round to face Feral. Tears had left tracks through the yellow paint on his face, and his whiskers were a blackened mess. I raised the scissors and cut higher, until his hair was up above his ears.

'I'm sorry,' I said, my own tears falling again. 'So sorry.'

Then Feral reached out and touched my cheek with his hand, where my burn was.

'Friend,' he said, and gave a strange, watery smile. Without his mane, he reminded me of someone, but who?

'Done?' he asked.

'There's just one last bit. Right at the back of your head.'

The scissor blades were so blunt now that they would hardly work, and the blisters on my fingers were raw and weeping. I took the hair on the back of Feral's neck, and very carefully cut a straight line through it, just below his ears.

Then I gasped.

Because right at the top of Feral's neck were a single word and a date, written in blue ink:

*FINN*

*11 JUNE*

And then I understood.

*Feral—not Silver—is my twin.*

# MY TWIN

Time stood still. And then memories began to tumble through me, memories of the messages.

The message on my leotard, telling me my twin was alive. It had never actually said my twin was a girl, or that she looked like me—I'd jumped into thinking that because I'd wanted a sister.

The message in the leaves, telling me my twin was next door. He wasn't at the *school* next door—he was sleeping in the next-door dormitory!

The last message, made out of Miss Cruet's hairpins, telling me to beware of the Shapeshifter. It hadn't been warning me about Feral.

*It had been warning me about Silver.*

Slowly, I looked up at the mirror, into her eyes.

Silver stared at me, her face pale and cold as the moon.

Feral gave a shiver and a growl and his hand reached for mine. I grabbed it. It was warm and comforting.

'That boy is dangerous,' Silver whispered. 'Send him away.'

'That boy,' I said, 'has a name. He's Finn.'

Silver's face went even whiter.

'Lies,' she said. 'The boy has no name.'

I turned Feral around so that his neck was facing Silver. There was a terrible silence.

'You didn't know, did you?' I said. 'You didn't know that we both had our names tattooed on the backs of our necks?' I turned away from Silver and lifted my hair. 'Look—here's mine.'

I turned back to face her.

'You thought Feral—Finn—would run away and leave me rather than having his mane cut. But you were wrong! He loves me, you see.'

'Loves you!' hissed Silver. 'He's deceiving you. I told you—he's nothing but a lying little Shapeshifter.'

I stared at her. Suddenly, she was no longer beautiful. She was as cold and hard as the mirror.

'No,' I whispered. 'It was you all along. *You're* the REAL Shapeshifter.'

The silence stretched out like an elastic band. Then Silver reached out her hand to the mirror.

'Give me the scissors,' she said.

I let go of Feral's hand, picked up the scissors and walked right up to the mirror, so that Silver and I were face to face. The glass around her hand began to melt.

Behind me, Feral's growls echoed around the room.

'Give them to me,' whispered Silver, '*now.*'

I raised my arm, and with every bit of strength I had, I brought the scissors stabbing down to break the glass. But Silver was faster. Just before the scissors hit the mirror, her hand reached through and gripped my wrist. The scissors dropped from my fingers.

Feral gave a gigantic roar and leapt towards us, grabbing my other hand and pulling with all his might. But Silver was stronger. I stared at the hand gripping my wrist, and it was no longer the pale, slim and beautiful hand I'd loved, but a skinny talon with blackened, broken nails. And a terrible smell seemed to wrap around me like a filthy cloak.

Dog's breath, coffins, drains.

Pus, sweat, sick.

Feral gave a snarl, his fingernails squeezing my arm, his eyes fixed on Silver.

I raised my eyes to look at her. An icy coldness filled my tummy and the hairs on my arms stood up.

Silver's perfect face was crumpling and shrinking. Her shoulders stooped and her chest caved in. Her mouth opened, baring tombstone teeth, and a familiar, raucous laugh echoed round the room. There, instead of my beautiful twin in her smart uniform, stood an old man with a hooked beak of a nose and cruel yellow eyes, wearing a stained, black suit with tattered sleeves and a dusty top hat. His breath stank of dead fish and smoke.

'Well, well, missy,' he croaked. 'We meet at last.'

I took a step backwards, but the man twisted my wrist.

And as I did so, the door behind us burst open and a voice shouted: 'What's going on here?'

It was Mr Gold.

# THE TRUTH

**M**r Gold peered towards us, and I knew he could only make out our outlines in the dim light.

The old man laughed again and I almost passed out from the stench of his breath.

'Felix Gold,' he hissed. 'At last.'

At the sound of the other man's voice, Mr Gold stiffened and clenched his stick. All the colour fled from his face.

'Murgatroyd,' he said.

I gasped, and Feral's hand tightened on mine. Merrick Murgatroyd, the evil fire-eater who had shot Mabel the lion. Who had set the fire in the Big Top that killed Fred and Leonora and their child. Suddenly, my throat was dry as sandpaper.

'Mr Gold!' I shouted. 'Make him let me go!'

'Child?' Mr Gold's face changed and he limped towards us.

'Not another step, Gold!' Merrick Murgatroyd snarled. 'Or she will suffer and die, like your beloved brother and his wife.'

There was a terrible silence. Then Mr Gold spoke in a low voice to Feral.

'Boy, let go of her hand, and come to me.'

A chill ran through my body. Was Mr Gold going to take Feral and leave me to die? He'd said he was afraid of Murgatroyd.

'Feral stay,' said Feral, grasping my hand even harder.

'Let her go, boy,' repeated Mr Gold, so sharply that Feral let go of my hand and backed towards Mr Gold, low growls echoing in his throat.

My wrist was numb from Murgatroyd's grip and my heart was hammering. I opened my mouth, but no sound came out.

'Is missy afraid?' Murgatroyd's voice was full of triumph. 'She has every reason to be.' He bent down and whispered in my ear, 'Tonight is Halloween, when my power is at its strongest—just as it was at this very hour on the night of the fire, seven years ago.'

'What... what do you—'

'Let her go, Murgatroyd,' said Mr Gold. 'She has done you no wrong.'

'Done me no wrong?' hissed Murgatroyd. 'By the very fact that she has *lived* she has done me wrong. She should have died that night.'

'What do you mean?' said Mr Gold. He sounded as confused as I felt.

Murgatroyd's eyes narrowed into slits, and his fingers tightened on my wrist.

'Felix Gold. Such a clever man,' he sneered, 'but too stupid to work out the truth. Or perhaps I should say, too *blind*.' And he gave a horrible cackle—a sound I'd heard before. I tried to pull away from Murgatroyd's grip, but he wrenched me roughly towards him.

'Let me GO!' I yelled.

My wrist was burning from his fingers and the reek of his foul breath made me want to be sick.

'Oh no, missy,' he whispered to me. 'You escaped me seven years ago, you and your *lion brother*, but I've got you now.'

He jerked me round to face Mr Gold.

'Take a last look—oh, but of course, you can't *see*,' he laughed.

Mr Gold gripped his stick as if he wanted to use it to kill Murgatroyd. Out of the corner of my eye, I saw Feral slip out of the room.

'Felix Gold,' hissed Murgatroyd, 'the blind man. Too blind—and stupid—to see what's been under his nose all along. Allow me to introduce your *niece*, Flynn Gold.'

Time stood still.

I gaped at Mr Gold. He had turned even whiter than before. For a moment, he swayed.

'More trickery, Murgatroyd?' he said. 'More lies?'

Murgatroyd cackled again. 'For once, Gold, I give you the unvarnished truth.'

Mr Gold stood still as a statue, his eyes screwed up as if that might help him to see me better.

'Flynn? Is it really you?'

'I am Flynn,' I said, 'but I don't understand what's—'

'Oh, child, I never thought to see you again!' Tears were pouring down Mr Gold's cheeks.

'How *touching*,' murmured Murgatroyd. 'A family reunion. What a pity this will be the first and only time.'

My mind raced. What was Murgatroyd talking about?

But Mr Gold was limping towards me, his eyes full of light and love.

'One more move,' hissed Murgatroyd, tightening his grip on my wrist, 'and I'll pull her through the mirror. Then you'll never see your darling niece again.'

Mr Gold froze.

'I don't understand,' I whispered, turning to Mr Gold. 'What does he mean?'

His voice seemed to come from a long way away.

'Flynn, you are Fred and Leonora's child. I am your uncle. The night of the fire, seven years ago, you were just three years old.'

My head spun. My knees began to shake so I could hardly stand. Mr Gold—my uncle? Leonora and Fred—my real parents? For a moment, everything went black and I thought I was going to faint.

Then I heard Mr Gold's voice: 'Flynn! Flynn, are you all right?'

'Y-yes. I think so.' My body hardly seemed to belong to me. 'But I still don't understand—'

'Explain it to her, Gold,' sneered Murgatroyd.

'Remember what I told you,' said Mr Gold, 'about the night of the fire? How I crawled into the Big Top and found him—Murgatroyd—in the flaming ring, standing over Fred and Leonora's little daughter? Well, that child was *you*, Flynn.'

'Me?'

I suddenly remembered the newspaper cutting in Mr Gold's study. So the baby girl who Mr Gold had saved from the burning tent was *me*! I stared from Mr Gold to Murgatroyd and back again, trying again to take in the meaning of it all. I was Fred and Leonora's daughter. Mr Gold was my uncle. If it wasn't for him, I'd have died in the fire that Murgatroyd set.

'You saved my life!' I whispered to Mr Gold.

A strange, warm feeling was bubbling in my heart. I didn't care that Murgatroyd had me by my wrist. Nothing mattered except that I had a family of my own. An uncle and a brother.

I turned to Murgatroyd. 'But why do you hate us so?'

Murgatroyd glared at Mr Gold. 'I hated *him*. For getting my circus closed down, for sending me to jail.'

'But it wasn't only that, was it, Murgatroyd?' said Mr Gold. 'You hated me because I was *happy*. Because I was surrounded by a loving family, and you had nothing... and no one.'

Murgatroyd's face twisted.

'So you decided to get your revenge. You decided to murder my family, so that I would suffer. You wanted me to lose what was most precious to me, just as *you* did when your wife died.'

Murgatroyd bared his tombstone teeth in a cruel grin. 'I watched and waited. And on Halloween night, after the show was over, I found them all together in the Big Top: your show-off brother, hanging upside down from

276

the trapeze; Leonora, training her pathetic lion; and the children, playing in the ring. One fiery breath from me, and the sawdust was ablaze. They would all have perished. But, once again, you had to interfere. I knew the game was up when you burst in and picked up the girl. So I did what I do best.' His yellow eye closed in a wink.

'You shapeshifted and escaped through a tear in the roof,' said Mr Gold.

'You shapeshifted into Silver?' I couldn't see how Murgatroyd shapeshifting into the form of Silver would have helped him to escape through the roof of the fiery tent.

Murgatroyd gave a high, piercing laugh.

'Think, missy,' he croaked.

And then everything fell into place. The tattered black wings; the croaking voice and the yellow eyes; the terrible smell.

'It was you,' I said. 'You were the Bird. The Bird in the cabinet.'

Mr Gold ignored my words. He was gazing at me as if willing me to hear him. 'I picked you up and ran with you to the entrance, but it was a wall of fire. Just for an instant, the smoke cleared, and I saw a tiny gap in the tent and crawled through it. Then a great piece of steel fell on me and I remember nothing more...'

'And that's how her pretty face burned,' cackled Murgatroyd.

My hand went up to my burn. No wonder Sonia and Claude had refused to tell me about my family and what had happened to them. No wonder they'd hated circuses.

Murgatroyd wrenched me towards him, pulling me closer and closer to the mirror. I dug in my heels and pulled back with all my strength. Then suddenly, he stopped, and a savage grin spread across his face, his yellow eyes alight with cruelty.

'But wait—what am I thinking?' he whispered. 'Why should I trap you in the mirror, when I can finish what I set out to do, seven long years ago?'

He looked at Feral's shorn hair, lying on the floor all around me.

'Human hair—dry as sawdust, and so flammable. I need only to breathe on it and you will be trapped in a circle of flames. You will not escape *this* fire.'

And he took in a deep, rasping breath.

'*No!*' Mr Gold shouted. 'Let her go. Take me instead.'

'You *still* don't understand, do you, Gold? I have no wish to kill *you*. Where would the fun be in that? It is much, much more satisfying to separate you forever from all those you love. To make you suffer for eternity, as I have suffered.'

'And you have succeeded,' said Mr Gold quietly. 'You took away my family: my brother and his wife and my nephew.'

Murgatroyd began to laugh, wheezing his foul breath around me. But I hardly noticed. My thoughts were whirling. If Mr Gold was my uncle, and Feral was my twin...

'Mr Gold!' I shouted. 'You haven't lost your nephew! Finn is alive!'

# FIRE

**M**r Gold went very still. 'What do you mean, Flynn?'

But Murgatroyd interrupted.

'Wretched girl!' he snarled, pulling my wrist so hard it felt like my arm would be torn from its socket. 'If it was not for you, Gold would have lived the rest of his life alone and grieving. And if it was not for the lion, your twin brother would have died in the fire, along with his parents.'

'The lion?' I said. 'Kula?'

'Yes, Kula,' spat Murgatroyd. 'The stupid creature who adored you all. Who risked her own life for her precious Golds.'

'What about her?'

Murgatroyd threw a furious glance at the door through which Feral had disappeared.

'The lion did not die in the fire. And neither did your nephew, Finn.'

Mr Gold's face was white.

Murgatroyd went on speaking. 'The lion took the boy and escaped into the night. I hoped she'd devoured him. But instead the animal *cared* for him.'

'You mean... the boy is alive?' whispered Mr Gold.

'Alive, yes,' snarled Murgatroyd. 'And more of a little savage than a human. What else could you expect, brought up in the forest by a lion?'

Mr Gold shook his head as if trying to understand.

'You are lying,' he said finally. 'This can't be true.'

'It *is* true!' I shouted, the words tumbling out of my mouth. 'It really is! It's Feral—Feral is Finn. He's my twin!'

Mr Gold stared at me. He spun round and stared at the empty doorway. There was a long silence, then he began to speak, as if he was trying to piece everything together.

'They told me Finn had died in the fire... and I didn't know... How could I have known?'

'And you would *never* have found out,' hissed Murgatroyd, 'had missy here not discovered she had a twin, and ended up at your pathetic School for Freaks.'

It was all beginning to make sense. I turned to Murgatroyd.

'So *that's* why you pretended to be the Bird. And I bet you were spying on me at Nobodies all the time—'

Murgatroyd winked his yellow eye. 'A bird can eavesdrop anywhere. Up a chimney in a library. Hidden among the branches in a wood. I'd been keeping watch on Gold for seven years, making sure that he suffered and grieved for his lost family. Then *you* arrived at Nobodies, looking for your twin, and I feared that you—or he—might discover the truth. So I hatched my little plan...'

'You made me think my twin was definitely at the school next door,' I whispered. 'And you made me want to escape there—just to get me away from Mr Gold. Only, then I found Feral in the forest—'

Murgatroyd spat. 'I hadn't counted on you rescuing him. After that, it was *vital* to stop you finding out who he and Gold really were.'

'You told me Feral was the Shapeshifter, and that Mr Gold was a coward and a murderer—'

Mr Gold gasped.

'And then you shapeshifted into Silver, and told me that if I came through the mirror into the school next door, we'd be together forever.'

'Correct,' snarled Murgatroyd, crushing my wrist so that I cried out in pain. 'I knew that tonight, Halloween night, is the only night of the year when bad magic is so strong that I could pull you through the mirror and separate you from your uncle and twin forever. What I didn't bargain for was the boy becoming attached to you. So attached that he was prepared to sacrifice his precious hair to be with you.' He glared down at Feral's hair, lying in a circle around my feet. 'But tonight is Halloween, just as it was seven years ago—and this time, Gold, there will be no rescue. Tonight, you will watch your beloved niece *die...*'

He took a deep, hoarse breath, his thin chest filling with air and his eyes squeezing shut with the effort. As he did so, Mr Gold leapt to my side. Throwing his arms around me, he tried to drag me away from Murgatroyd's grasp, but Murgatroyd held my wrist like a vice.

Then Murgatroyd breathed out.

A torrent of flames streamed, red and yellow, from his open mouth, scorching my face. They caught at the strands of Feral's hair lying around my feet, and suddenly—and it could only have been the bad magic of Halloween that made it happen so fast and so furiously—we were surrounded by a blazing wall of fire. The fire was everywhere, licking at our clothes. There was no way out, or through. Murgatroyd's crazy laughter echoed through the room. Mr Gold tightened his arms around me, shielding me from the savage flames with his body. And I thought, *If I must die, this is how I want it to be. Safe in my uncle's arms.*

Somewhere, in the distance, I heard a familiar sound, almost drowned in the roar of the flames and the high screams of Murgatroyd's laughter. The sound came nearer and nearer. Then I realized what it was.

It was Rule Boy's violin. And it was playing 'The Circus March'.

# ALL FOR ONE,
# AND ONE FOR ALL

'*H*ELP!!!' I screamed.

The music stopped abruptly. Then everything seemed to happen at once. Murgatroyd let go of my wrist and drew his hand back inside the mirror. A huge roar split the air. And a chorus of voices shouted.

'*ALL FOR ONE, AND ONE FOR ALL!!!*'

Through the wall of flame, I glimpsed Rule Boy, Feral and Saddo. Rule Boy wore his top hat and carried his violin and bow. Saddo wore his clown's outfit, with his hoodie on top. Feral's woolly rug hung down, brushing the floor. And then I saw Custard, bringing up the rear, clutching her yellow blanket. But what was that, sitting on her shoulders?

I screwed up my eyes against the smoke. Four grey wings were fluttering and I heard two familiar, soft cries:

*Turrrr! Turrrr!*

'Feral told us you were in trouble, Antsy!' Rule Boy yelled.

'We've come to save you!' shouted Saddo.

'And we're n-not scared!' squeaked Custard.

Feral gave another gigantic roar and threw himself towards us, but Custard grabbed him and pulled him back.

'*No!*' Mr Gold yelled. 'Stay *away* from the fire!'

'Your little playmates can't help you now, missy,' Murgatroyd hissed from inside the mirror. 'Like me, they can only watch you *burn*.'

I stared up into his face, twisted with cruelty. He was safe behind the glass. The fire couldn't hurt him.

Then, out of nowhere, I remembered Silver's words.

'*You must never, ever break the mirror. If you do, the doorway will be destroyed—and so will I.*'

I raised my free hand and brought my fist down, as hard as I could, on the glass.

Nothing happened. The glass was too strong.

'We must break the mirror!' I screamed.

Mr Gold stared at me for a moment, sweat pouring down his face, then he turned and began beating at the glass with his fists. But the glass stayed unbroken, and Murgatroyd, safe behind it, cackled. The heat was unbearable now. A tongue of flame caught Mr Gold's baggy trousers and I smacked at them, my palm blistering, trying to put it out. Mr Gold ignored it. Now his sleeves were smouldering, but he kept on battering the glass, while Murgatroyd's cackles of glee tore the air. The flames licked at our faces, as if hungry to eat us.

A voice called from beyond the flames.

'Antsy! CATCH!!!!'

I watched as, as if in slow motion, Rule Boy's violin sailed into the air, its polished wood caught for a moment in the light of the flames. It seemed to hover in the air before falling down, down, down...

... into my waiting arms.

For a moment, I just stood there, staring at it. Then I grabbed its long neck with both hands, raised it high above my head and I smashed it down against the mirror with all my strength.

The mirror shattered. Shards of glass flew in all directions. A terrible cry echoed through the room, followed by the sound of beating wings. The circle of flames surrounding us died away as suddenly as it had started. Then all was silent, and I stood looking at the mirror, or what was left of it: nothing but an empty, carved frame and a blackened, wooden back. I gave a sob, and turned to hug Mr Gold.

I gasped at what I saw: his clothes were aflame. Tongues of fire were eating at his trousers, his shirt, his red braces, even his hair. He stood, still as a statue, staring at the flames as if hypnotized. *He must be in shock.*

'Mr Gold!' I screamed. 'You're on fire! WAKE UP!'

But Mr Gold didn't move. It was as if he was locked in a trance.

'HELP ME!' I screamed.

Then Rule Boy was at my side, frantically beating at Mr Gold's clothes. But it was impossible. No sooner did we douse one flame than another licked its way up his body.

Three figures came running.

Feral tore his woollen rug from his shoulders and wrapped it around Mr Gold's baggy trousers.

Saddo pulled off his hoodie and covered Mr Gold's burning shirt.

And Custard hesitated, then tore her yellow blanket from her shoulders and stood on tiptoe, waving it at Mr Gold's burning curly hair.

'I'm n-not tall enough,' she shrieked. 'Help me!'

*Turrrr! Turrrr!*

The two little doves circled Custard, fluttering their grey wings. Then they swooped down to Custard's blanket. Each dove snatched a corner of it in its bill and soared up, up to hover above Mr Gold's head. Then, as one, they dropped the blanket over Mr Gold's rusty, burning curls. For a split second, he stared at the doves as if he couldn't believe his eyes. Then he grabbed the blanket and pressed it to his head and a singeing, smoky smell rose from his hair.

For a long moment, I stared at Feral, Custard, Saddo and Rule Boy. Their face paint was smeared and their eyes were pouring with tears from the bitter smoke. But they were grinning at me.

'You all gave up your most important possessions,' I whispered, as the doves came to settle on me, one on each shoulder. 'You saved me—and you saved Mr Gold.'

Rule Boy grinned and wiped his glasses. 'Just like the Three Musketeers,' he said.

Mr Gold held out his arms to Feral and me and the others, and we hugged and hugged and hugged, while the two little doves fluttered and hovered around us.

'*What*,' barked a voice, 'are you thinking of, Felix?'

We all turned. Miss Cruet stood in the doorway, her hands on her hips, hairpins clattering to the floor. She was dressed in a knitted evening gown with multicoloured stripes, and wore a fluorescent green shawl around her shoulders. A pair of binoculars hung from her neck, and she was clutching an embroidered fan in one hand and a hot-water bottle in the other.

'I have been waiting in the Amphitheatre for the last *forty-five minutes*, and no sign of the show. And here you all are...' she peered at the area around our feet, 'with the floor covered in glass... hugging.' She gave a sharp sniff. 'And if I am not mistaken, someone has been *smoking*. This will not do, Felix. It will not do at all.'

And we all burst out laughing and crying at the same time.

'Apologies for keeping you waiting, Euphenia,' said Mr Gold, winking at me.

'Not only me,' snapped Miss Cruet, 'but the children's families.'

'My sister?' said Saddo.

'Indeed,' said Miss Cruet. 'She's come down from university especially.'

'My mum?' said Custard.

'Yes. She'll soon be well enough to look after you again.'

'My dad?' said Rule Boy, his face full of hope.

'Correct,' said Miss Cruet. 'He's been given special permission to come tonight. They are all waiting for you.'

Mr Gold took my hand, and Feral's.

'Your uncle will be there too,' he said, and that warm, chocolatey feeling filled my heart.

'But what about my violin?' said Rule Boy, looking at the pile of shattered wood and strings on the floor. 'There'll be no music.'

'And my cuddly?' said Custard. Her blanket was nothing but a charred square of wool.

Saddo tried to pull his hoodie over his eyes, then remembered he didn't have it any more.

'Mane.' Feral ran his fingers through what was left of his hair, and gave a tiny growl. 'Gone.'

'You have learnt a very important lesson,' said Mr Gold quietly. 'Remember rule three?'

'One possession only!' said Rule Boy. 'Only now they're all gone.'

'You each gave up your most precious possession in order to save Flynn and me,' said Mr Gold.

'And Feral gave up his mane because he loved me,' I said.

'And you, Flynn, risked everything to find out the truth.' Mr Gold peered round at each of us, one by one. 'I may not be able to see your faces, but I know one thing.'

'What's that?' said Saddo.

'There isn't a single Nobody standing before me. Each of you has proved, by your sacrifice and your bravery, that you are a Somebody. A Somebody to be proud of. And from now on, you will choose what you want to be called. You have each earned your name.'

Everyone looked proud. But Miss Cruet was tapping her knitted boot.

'Felix,' she said, 'they're all waiting for the show.'

'H-how can we do it, now all our things are burnt?' said Custard.

Mr Gold smiled. 'There's an old circus saying,' he said. 'No matter what happens, *the show must go on.*'

And he led us down the stairs, closely followed by a muttering Miss Cruet.

# AFTERWARDS

***B****OOM! BOOM! BOOM!*

Rule Boy led us round and round the ring, as the audience applauded. A huge frying pan—the one Miss Cruet used to make her Specials—hung from his neck as he beat it with a wooden spoon. Two saucepan lids, strapped to the insides of his knees, clashed together like cymbals. With his free hand, he held a comb covered with tissue paper to his lips and blew. The Amphitheatre echoed with the sound of the notes.

Saddo lumbered along the tightrope in his outsize trousers and shoes with a beaming smile. He carried a tray full of glasses of water and plates of sandwiches and kept almost tripping up and spilling them, much to the horror of Claude, who was sitting near the front in his cummerbund and bow tie. Feral was scaring Sonia with his ear-splitting roars, while Custard, who'd wrapped a towel around her neck for a cloak, kept him in check with Mr Gold's stick.

And me? I leapt into the audience and grabbed Miss Cruet's binoculars, fan and hot-water bottle and juggled them, sending them high up into the air. Then I cartwheeled round and round the ring in my gold leotard until I had no breath left.

As we all took a bow, Rule Boy's dad got to his feet and shouted, 'BRAVO!!!!' Saddo's sister and Custard's mum cheered. Even Sonia clapped daintily, and Claude's belly jiggled with laughter—*haw-haw-haw!*

As for Mr Gold, his whole face lit up, and he stomped and whistled and punched the air, his eyes no longer sad but filled with pride and love.

And the two little doves swooped and dived between Feral and me, brushing our faces with their soft wings. Then they gave their gentle cry—*turrrr, turrrr!*—and spiralled up, up into the night sky, their grey wings caught by the moonlight. I watched them until they disappeared.

That night, Miss Cruet excelled herself. Her Extra-Super-Special Halloween cake—dripping with sticky black icing and spaghetti spiders' webs and cream-cheese ghosts and fizzing sparklers—towered a metre high, and we all had a gigantic slice, along with her Halloween soup, which was green and wriggly with jelly Loch Ness monsters floating in it.

Feral and I showed the others our tattoos and I told everyone about how Feral had been my twin all along and how his name was really Finn. And Feral told us about his 'mama', Kula: how they'd lived together in the forest until the day she was captured. And Mr Gold told the story of the fire, and Murgatroyd, and how he discovered he was our uncle.

'Mr Gold—' I said.

'I think it's time to call me Felix, don't you, Flynn? Or Uncle Felix... if you want to, that is.'

'I *do* want to,' I said, and Feral nodded furiously.

'Uncle Felix,' I said, and my heart felt all warm and cosy as I said the words, 'there's just one thing I don't understand.'

'What's that, Flynn?'

'Why did you let Sonia and Claude adopt me? Why didn't you take me to live with *you*, after you rescued me from the fire?'

Mr Gold shook his head. 'I was in the hospital, unconscious, for months. When I woke up, my leg was shattered and I could barely see. The first thing I asked about was you. They told me you'd been adopted by a rich couple who would give you a wonderful life. As for me, I was a wreck, with no money, no job and little sight. What could I offer you? I believed you would be better off with them.'

'I *hated* living with Sonia and Claude,' I said, and Mr Gold's face changed.

'If I had known you were unhappy, nothing—*nothing*— would have stopped me from finding you and getting you back.'

I knew, by the look in his eyes, that he was telling the truth. He wiped his eyes.

'When I was able to walk again, and see a little, I decided to become a teacher... I wanted to help children who were alone and unloved... who were Nobodies. I wanted to help them find their true gifts and to learn to believe in themselves. But for seven years, there was not a single day—a single *hour*—that I didn't think of you.'

He took my hand. 'Is there anything else you don't understand?'

'Yes,' I said hesitantly.

'Tell me,' said Mr Gold.

'The doves,' I said, 'and their messages. The message in the balloon, telling me how to find my name. The message on my leotard, saying my twin was alive. The message in the leaves, telling me my twin was living next door. And the message in Miss Cruet's hairpins, warning me about the Shapeshifter. Who really sent them? It wasn't Murgatroyd, though he pretended it was.'

Mr Gold put down his mug.

'I don't know,' he said thoughtfully. 'But there are only two people who would have wanted you to know these things, who would have wanted to keep you safe...'

'Leonora and Fred? My mum and dad?' It still felt really strange to call them that.

Mr Gold nodded.

'Your mother and father wore golden costumes—just like the one you're wearing now. And remember how I told you that Leonora hatched two turtle doves, and how they loved her so? Perhaps, just perhaps...' He stopped, and shook his head. 'Some things will always be mysteries. But I do know one thing—'

'What's that?' asked Rule Boy.

'People may die, or be lost, or sent away,' said Mr Gold, 'but love doesn't die. It can't—not while it lies safe in our hearts.'

'Love,' said Feral. 'Family.'

I put my arm around him and he licked my nose.

# 11TH JUNE

It was going to be the best birthday *ever*.

I woke early, to the sound of tapping on the wall.

*HAP-PY BIRTH-DAY TO YOU!*

I tapped it back.

Lying on the bottom of my bed were five envelopes.

Custard sat up and rubbed her eyes, yawning. She had a different name now, Ariale, but she still looked just the same, with her yellow wispy hair and her wide eyes.

'Happy birthday, Flynn!' She pulled out yet another envelope from under her pillow and padded over to me.

I tore it open. Inside was a card with a picture of Wonder Woman on it.

'It reminded me of you,' said Ariale. She didn't stutter any more.

'Thanks,' I said. 'It reminds me of *you* too.'

And we grinned and hugged one another.

The second card was from Miss Cruet, in loopy purple ink:

Happy birthday, Flynn.
And congratulations on earning your name.
With best wishes,
Euphenia Esmerelda Boudica Cruet (Miss)

Saddo (whose name was actually Isaac) had made a card with a picture of a beaming clown on it.

Rule Boy's card said:

*Happy Birthday, Antsy! (Sorry — Flynn!!!)*
*from Amadeus xxx*

Finn's card had a paw print and lots of crosses, and said:

## HAPY BIRDAY TWIN

Uncle Felix's card was a picture of a circus ring, with an acrobat standing on her hands, wearing a gold leotard just like mine. He had cut out her head and stuck on a photo of me. Inside he had written:

*To my dearest niece, Flynn Gold,*
*Enjoy the enclosed!*
*With all my love,*
*Uncle Felix xxxxxxx*
*PS 'Felix' means 'happy' — and I am, now that*
*I've found you and your brother again.*

There were two smaller envelopes within the card. I opened the first envelope, and gasped.

'What-is-it? What-is-it?' said Ariale.

'It's for me and Finn to go to circus school all through the summer holidays!' I said, and cartwheeled round the room.

The sound of music filled the air, and in walked Amadeus, a violin under his chin, playing 'Happy birthday' while Isaac and Finn (carrying a handful of envelopes of his own) bounced along behind him, singing the words.

'You've got a new violin!' I said. 'Where did you get it?'

'Isn't it brilliant?' he replied. 'It's a present from my dad. And there's something even better.'

'What?' I said.

'My dad's been proved innocent! The conductor of the orchestra admitted that it was *him* who stole the money. My dad's coming home.'

I gave him an enormous hug.

'Come on, Flynn!' said Ariale. 'You've still got another envelope to open!'

I opened the last envelope. Inside were six tickets.

'We're all going to the circus tonight!' I said.

Ariale and I grabbed each other and danced round and round.

'What did you get, Finn?' I asked him.

He handed over three tickets.

'A trip to the safari park—today!' I said. 'Just you and me and Uncle Felix!'

'So far away park?' said Finn, looking puzzled.

'It's a big sort of wildlife park you drive through,' explained Isaac. 'Where there are wild animals.'

'Animals,' said Finn, nodding. 'Lion.' And his face lit up in a huge smile.

*

It was a long drive to the safari park—by taxi, of course, as Uncle Felix couldn't drive. Luckily the plump taxi driver, whose name was Maurice, was friendly. I sat in the front, next to him, telling him about circus school and how Uncle Felix had taught me to be an acrobat and a juggler. Uncle Felix and Finn were in the back. Finn had fallen asleep. He looked really different with short hair—and now that he allowed Ariale to wash it for him, it sprang from his head in rusty curls, just like Uncle Felix's and mine. We'd had to coax him into the taxi, as he'd never been in one before, but once inside he'd been fascinated by the numbers on the meter, and had got Maurice to wind the windows up and down, and to let him open the doors and slam them, over and over.

When we got to the safari park, there was nothing to see at first. It looked like any old park, with grass and trees and a few other cars winding their way through it. Far in the distance, a group of zebras grazed. Then we rounded a corner and Maurice brought the taxi to a halt.

'Over there—see?' he said. 'By those rocks...'

I looked. There, on the grass, lay a lioness. I could tell she was a female lion, because she didn't have a long mane. I'd never seen a real lioness before, but I'd always imagined them as graceful and strong and power-ful. This one's fur looked moth-eaten and mangy, and her tail barely flickered to keep away the flies. Her ear twitched at the sound of the taxi and she yawned. Then she lifted her head and stared at us for a moment with sad, blank eyes.

I turned to Uncle Felix. 'There's a lioness,' I said in a low voice, because I didn't want to scare her away. 'Wake up, Finn!'

Uncle Felix gave Finn's shoulder a gentle shake, and he opened his eyes.

'Look,' I whispered.

Finn sat up quickly and gazed out of the window. I felt a bit worried that the lioness looked so old and sad. What if we'd driven all this way only for Finn to be upset and disappointed?

But Finn had his nose pressed to the window, staring at the lioness as if his body had turned to stone. From his throat came a sound I'd never heard him make before. Then, before any of us could stop him, he'd unlocked the door, flung it open and leapt out into the road.

''Ere!' shouted Maurice. 'You mustn't—'

'Finn!' I screamed. 'What are you doing? Get back in the car—it's dangerous!'

But for once, he ignored me.

I turned to Uncle Felix, who was sitting quite still, peering towards the lioness, a strange look on his face. Maybe he hadn't realized Finn had got out of the taxi.

'Uncle Felix!' I yelled. 'Finn's got out. *Do* something!'

To my surprise, Uncle Felix was smiling—really smiling—a broad beam which almost cut his face in two. 'It's OK, Flynn,' he said quietly. 'Let him be.'

Finn dropped on to all fours and moved slowly towards the lioness, never taking his eyes from her. When he was a few metres away, he stopped.

He and the lioness faced one another. I could barely breathe. The lioness was three times as big as him. *Please*, I thought, *don't let me lose him as soon as I've found him.*

Then Finn got up on his knees in the dust.

'Mama!' he cried out.

The lioness lifted her muzzle as if to smell his voice. She raised herself unsteadily on all four paws and limped to him. He stayed stock-still as she lowered her face to his and licked his nose.

Her whole body vibrated with a mighty, echoing roar, and Finn roared back, over and over again, and suddenly there was no way of telling them apart. They were a rolling, licking, growling, crying, pawing, yelping, stroking, roaring bundle.

I looked at Uncle Felix. He too had tears in his eyes.

'Kula?' I said, but I already knew the answer.

He nodded, and we held hands, and I knew that from now on, everything would be different. Soon, Finn and I would be at circus school. It would be exciting. But could it be even half as exciting as the School for Nobodies?

'I thought life hated me,' I said. 'It took away my mum and dad and made me live with Sonia and Claude. But it's given me back my twin brother, and my uncle, and Kula and all my friends. It's given me a real family.'

Uncle Felix smiled his crooked smile.

'Maybe,' he said, 'life loves you after all.'

# ACKNOWLEDGEMENTS

Writing a book is a strange, solitary thing to do—months of sitting alone in front of a screen with only your imagination for company—which makes me so very grateful to all the people who helped this book come into the world.

Thanks to my brilliant agent Silvia Molteni for loving and believing in *School for Nobodies* from the very start and taking it—and me—on. For your wise advice and brilliant notes, and above all for your tireless enthusiasm on its behalf.

Thanks to the amazing Sarah Odedina, editor-at-large, and all at Pushkin Press for bringing *School for Nobodies* to birth; to Madeleine Stevens for her eagle-eyed edit; and to Thy Bui, whose illustrations made me cry, literally, with joy. It has been a privilege to work with you all.

I've been lucky enough to have a band of cheerleaders and teachers, without whom not a single word would have been written. Huge thanks to Louise Dean at The Novelry, whose Classics course planted the seed for *School for Nobodies* and who spoke a lot of sense when I hit my customary doldrums. To Alison Powell of Write Club, and all the writers who read the early chapters and offered wise feedback. To Jane Pollard, whose course kick-started my writing in a new direction back in 2006. To all the members of Book Frisbees—the best writing group in the world—for cheering me on and keeping my head above water when the waves hit. And to my dear friends—you know who you are—who listened, laughed and cared.

Flynn was lucky enough to find her pot of Gold—loyal friends and a loving family. May you all be similarly blessed.

PUSHKIN CHILDREN'S BOOKS

We created Pushkin Children's Books to share tales from different languages and cultures with younger readers, and to open the door to the wide, colourful worlds these stories offer.

From picture books and adventure stories to fairy tales and classics, and from fifty-year-old bestsellers to current huge successes abroad, the books on the Pushkin Children's list reflect the very best stories from around the world, for our most discerning readers of all: children.